C000093775

THE STORY OF
THE CLOTH

Ken Paterson

Jean & Jetta

ACKNOWLEDGMENTS

Many thanks to Christine Abel for her reading of the first draft of the manuscript; to Miranda Miller (The Literary Consultancy) for the first manuscript assessment; to the Hilary Johnson Authors' Advisory Service for the second manuscript assessment; to Rebecca Baker for her copy-editing; and to eBook Partnership for the cover design.

1

Alex thought about a lot of things on his long walks home from the office: Shangri-La, for example, from Frank Capra's *Lost Horizon*, and how his life might pan out there once he'd chosen to stay on; Gemma at work, and whether he really risked asking her out; Céline, and why she had dumped him. And sometimes – more frequently than he would like to admit – what he should say to the fairy who would surely materialise in his path one day, offering to grant him a wish. Occasionally, he even made a decision. In the case of the fairy, for instance, he reckoned that, although in theory you could probably ask for anything, you really ought to put some kind of restraint on yourself, or else you'd go crazy. And, of course, you had to get the wording right.

So when it actually happened – when a young, white-robed woman, pale within her silvery aura, appeared in front of him in Regent's Park near dusk one day in June – he stood quite still and resolute, despite the tear of sweat that rolled down his forehead and into his eye.

"Relax and listen," she said in a soft transatlantic tone. "I have the power to grant you any wish you choose. I don't want to put you under any pressure, but you've got ten seconds to think and then twenty seconds to speak. After that, I touch you on the shoulder with my wand and off I go again." She accompanied this last part with a raised fist and puff-of-smoke gesture of flicking out her fingers. But Alex was ready.

"I want to be able to return instantly," he replied, "to any spot in the world I've previously visited just by thinking of it and saying 'Let's travel' aloud, and then tapping my left knee three times. And I can take one person with me if I'm holding their hand, and come back in the same way. Above all, let the wish happen as I intend it to."

Anyone, thought Alex, who'd travelled down the same mental side roads as he had would appreciate the contractual nature of his wish. With the spoken instruction and the knee touching, he was on the double-authorisation track: what he didn't want was some idle daydream sending him to the bit of Nile he'd once travelled down in a cruise ship, only to find that the boat had long since departed, and there he would be, treading water gamely, waiting for a pair of crocodile eyes to break the surface. And the last part, about it happening the way he intended it, was to make sure he didn't get any of that *Monkey's Paw* nonsense where he was whisked safely away to the Mexican pyramids, but re-entered London as a corpse or with his limbs hanging off.

Anyhow, the fairy showed no signs of making a value judgement. "Have you finished?" was all she said, tiptoeing towards him.

Alex couldn't resist. "Unless you could throw in an aphrodisiac that would make women faint with desire for me," he added. Instead of a reply, he felt the wand lightly descend on his shoulder. After that, he didn't really feel anything at all.

When he came to, somewhere towards dawn, the dew seeping cold into his shirt and a few bright stars above him, Alex had absolutely no idea where he was. His first thought was Tuscany, where he'd drunk half a bottle of grappa at the age of eleven and collapsed in a wood till nightfall. Propping himself up on his elbows, he made a brief inspection of his body, checking first that his feet were upright and the standard length from his head. It was only when he turned onto his side that he recalled the electrical charge from the wand, tearing its way through his chest like a small bolt of lightning, setting his lungs on fire and, unless his mind was playing tricks on him, flinging his limbs about in an abbreviated tribal dance.

He got onto his knees amongst the waist-height shrubbery he must have crawled into, looking over the top at what he guessed were the streetlights of Camden. Then he leant forward to let the retching begin.

I'm still alive was his first thought as the evening sun swung low through the bedroom window. Burying his head in the pillow, he spent the next ten minutes trying to arrange snatches of memory into a sequence that might explain how he'd got back. Mostly he recalled the people he had passed: guys in T-shirts going home from clubs half-wrecked but bright-eyed, or blokes in caps and jackets whose jobs brought them out onto the streets unhappily early. Perhaps he'd attracted their attention in turn by looking both shattered *and* miserable. Anyway, he had certainly walked all the way home, guided by magnetic north or the pole star and therefore turning left at key points rather than right or climbing a hill instead of crossing a road, until he had made his way through two or three London boroughs to his own front door.

As for the primary incident, the folds of white muslin and the transatlantic tones, he deliberately kept the lid on that. It seemed obvious he had had some kind of hallucinatory blackout brought on by working too hard and then drinking outside the pub with his workmates, but he would be able to explore the implications of all that later. For the moment he focused on recovery - on shopping, cooking, and watching a film on telly.

So it wasn't until eleven that he finally made his way through the kitchen, picking up a Coke on the way, adding ice from the cobalt-blue fridge-freezer his landlord had recently installed, and opening the door onto the dark garden to let the memory in. Maybe he was still in shock, but it seemed important to lay out all the possibilities in a scientific way. After a few sips of his drink, he decided he was ready.

The first and overwhelmingly likely option was a drunken fall, during which he had had an unusually vivid dream. The second, more disturbing, was a waking hallucination followed by some kind of seizure. In the third scenario, the fairy was a complete impostor, a strange park person whose personal goals you wouldn't care to examine, and his blackout was coincidental. Fourthly, he reckoned, after a gulp from his glass, the rules of the universe do in fact offer more latitude than we allow and a real fairy appeared in front of him and granted him a wish, causing him to stumble in shock. And fifthly, the fourth option, except she got the granting bit wrong in some way - was a novice, perhaps, or only pretended to grant him a wish, while maliciously electrocuting him.

He went to bed.

"God, you look awful," said Bill.

This was Sunday, the next day.

"Well, I feel bit wrecked," said Alex.

"You look terrible. Really sort of puffy."

"I *am* a bit under the weather at the moment."

"Yes, you must be. Your skin is manky, like it's been marinated in seawater, or you've been found in the river."

Alex felt a throb at his temple. "You've made your point, Bill. In fact, you've hewn it from the rock, chiselled and sculpted it, and put it on public display."

They were in Chinatown on Gerrard Street in the first rain for weeks, passing the Royal Dragon with its sweet, hot breath of plum sauce, and the Chinese supermarket with its strange-looking vegetables outside, pale swollen marrows and mushrooms like tumours.

Bill was a friend from schooldays – handsome, blustery – and they were going to see an old arthouse movie, pre-1980 being their preferred option for all films. Both of them were committed to the genre, too, returning to it time after time despite, or rather because of, some epically boring sequences, including one at the Curzon Bloomsbury that had featured a distant silhouette of Bedouins with their camels inching their way across the width of the screen, no music or any other form of action for at least three minutes.

"So what have you been doing?" asked Bill.

Alex wasn't sure whether he meant in general or to cause his creased grey skin. "Very little," he replied, not being ready to share his incident in the park.

They walked on and got a beer at the cinema.

"Bill?" asked Alex, when they were nearing the end of their conversation. "Have you ever thought what you would choose if you were granted any wish?"

"Yes."

No hesitation. So everyone actually *does* go about getting ready for their fairy encounter, thought Alex. But Bill looked serious. "I would always be able to score a goal," he said, "within ten minutes of going on in any football match." He drank some more beer, still serious. "England, for example, would know they could always rely on me to put one in, but I wouldn't need to be particularly fit. I could even take up smoking. I'd only stay on for the ten minutes, and the opposition, of course, would put five men on me. That would be part of the fun. I'd still score somehow. Always."

They shared a moment of awe. Then Bill returned the question out of politeness. The film was about to start.

"I'd ask for another three wishes," replied Alex, getting up. Bill grimaced – appropriately, as his companion had to admit.

An ordinary five days followed in Alex's life. For ordinary, of course, read excessive. Too much of working too hard, of watching TV, of googling and Facebook, of red wine, of envy and regret, of rage, of depression and absurd elation, of lying, of drawing up a list and carrying only one thing out, of imagining escape. Too much *pointless* thinking.

When Alex was a child, his adoptive father would get home at four on a Sunday, after visiting his parishioners. If it was a rainy day or winter, Alex and a friend would be messing about with a toy train set or a racing track, and his father, a tall man with a short back and sides, and a grey fringe that flopped over his forehead, would come in with a tea tray, acknowledge them with a smile, and sit down at the table. Picking up a white loaf, he'd butter the cut end and slice off a piece an inch thick, spooning on jam and spreading a thin layer, his slicing arm making shadows on the wall. But what Alex remembered most was the deliberateness of his movements and his simple need for food. The *only* thing he was up to in his head, it seemed, was having his tea.

Alex, at least, had postponed any further examination of the incident in the park. Now, as a murmur of anticipation rippled its way through the queue outside the surgery, he turned to watch Dr Patel getting out of his old, well-kept (by his son) Bentley. Unbuttoning his topcoat while grinding a half-smoked cheroot into the pavement, the GP strode towards the door.

One hour and forty-five minutes later, Alex was sitting opposite him. Though he had planned his overall strategy, Alex was immediately wrong-footed by the generosity of the doctor's opening gambit: "And how are you doing in overall terms, Mr Harrison?"

Alex ran a hand through his hair. "I'm fine, I think. I'm trying to cut back on the drinking."

"Really? What are you aiming for?"

"A single glass of wine in the evening. When I'm at home. Or a Coke instead."

"Before or after the beer?" said the doctor with a smile. "Anyhow, what are you here for today?"

Alex cleared his throat.

"Bit of a cough, is it?"

"No."

"Or the guts playing up?"

"No."

"Oh, I see." He smiled and shook his head. "The dick is it, then? You young chaps. Let's have a look, shall we?"

For a moment, Alex might have stood up. "No, it's nothing like that. But I think I had a blackout on my way home through the park."

The doctor looked serious. "And *had* you been on the liquor?"

"Not really. No more than a couple of pints."

The medic narrowed his eyes. "Well then, are you sure your booze wasn't laced by a chum? I heard of that the other day."

"I don't think so. I had a kind of hallucination, though."

"Go on."

"I saw a woman. She appeared in front of me, but she didn't seem quite right. She looked odd. Then I woke up on the ground a bit later, feeling pretty sick."

Dr Patel stroked his chin. While he clearly wasn't about to enter into a lengthy discussion on the subject, he wasn't dismissing it either. After getting up and taking Alex through one or two balance-and-grit-your-teeth checks, he reached for his computer mouse.

"We'll send you for a hospital test. Report to reception, please, old man," said the GP, adding, when Alex got to the door, "Cut down on the beer, Mr Harrison, or change your friends. That's my advice."

Back at his flat after a brief swim and some listless cycling at the gym, Alex got himself a glass of white wine and sat in the window chair. The garden itself was half in sunlight and half in shade. Idly, he started to think about some of the places abroad he had visited. More particularly, he started scanning his mind for precise locations that were likely to be deserted. He tried visualising himself in several of these, sitting comfortably on grass or sand.

In the end he settled on a small patch of beach on the Arabian sea near a port in Oman. He had had the good luck to stay in the hotel close by as the work experience member of a team bidding to design a spa resort, and had gone for early walks along this stretch of shore, hot even before breakfast. All you might see was a man on a camel a mile or so away, fuzzy like Omar Sharif in *Lawrence of Arabia*, or a colony of small birds with long legs, darting around and attempting to spear baby crabs on their beaks. The sea, surprisingly, was grey and boomed and crashed as if it were a Cornish tide.

He could have thought of somewhere less exotic, perhaps. He could even have pictured himself on the bed in the room next door, though somehow it seemed unsporting. So he picked up his phone, and googled the time difference. Plus four hours. This meant he would need to be ready at three in the morning. After cooking some dinner, he dozed off for a while, had a shower, and watched a movie on Netflix.

Alex knew he was about to rule out an option he shouldn't even have entertained. The blackout must have unhinged him. In the country of the mind, he had allowed the terrorist campaign against reason to pull off a victory. But what if there *were* curves in the logic of the universe, and every billionth person encountered one, say, every hundred years? And what if we dressed these abstract curves in commonplace images such as fairies?

Alex put on his backpack, picked up his passport, checked he had thirty quid in his wallet, and looked at the time, which was coming up to three. So he sat, breathed in, and holding the image of the beach in his mind, said, "Let's travel." And he tapped his left knee three times.

Afterwards, for a moment or two, he surveyed the flat, as if the walls themselves might dissolve into sand and the view of the garden turn to grey sea. Then, trying to bury a feeling of shame, he got up, his rucksack still on his back, and made his way through the kitchen, picking up a carton of milk on the way and opening the door to the garden for a draught of night air. Somewhere in the bushes at the end of the lawn, there was a rustling sound. A fox, perhaps, or his neighbour's fat tabby. Alex took a long pull of milk. Soon he would go to bed, unpacking his bag and finishing off the *Modesty Blaise* novel Bill had lent him.

The moment he had returned the carton to the fridge, however, a great pressure pushed its way into the room from the garden behind him like a wave, forcing his face and chest into the blue metallic door. And before he could turn, his wrists had been seized, and the pressure began to ebb, pulling him backwards across the kitchen floor, a sticky, sucking sound of shingle in his ears.

"Help!" he shouted, though most of the air had left his lungs.

When he reached the garden, the door slamming shut behind him, Alex was thrust face down onto the grass, a knee, or what felt like one, on his backpack, and muscular hands at his wrists once more, this time stretching his arms upwards and outwards to the sky until he thought the tendons would snap. As his mouth filled with saliva, Alex closed his eyes against the pain.

When he opened them again, extreme cold was the first thing he registered, an oncoming wind that wanted to flay the skin off his face; and afterwards a roaring, hurtling motion, as if he had been flung onto a mattress in the back of a speeding, open-top truck. But all he could actually see was blackness, pinpointed with golden light.

Finally the wind dropped, and he was tumbling downwards through the night sky, as though the truck had tipped its load over a monstrous cliff. And after a while, that too stopped, and Alex seemed to be floating now, face upwards on a dark liquid, thicker and warmer than seawater. As he lay there, flickering images began to appear above him, projected onto the dark sky, scenes from his past life, episodes when he had been the cause of pain or minor wanton cruelty. Some of the images he already knew to be significant. Others gained significance by being there now. And with each one, it felt as if a brick had been placed on his chest.

Just when it seemed as if his ribs might crack under the pressure, the weight was taken away and there was a moment of oblivion, followed by a sensation he recognized but hadn't experienced since childhood – of waking in the holidays with the sun pushing at closed curtains and not feeling bad, not feeling guilty, about anything.

A warm wind was blowing, and, realizing his eyes were glued with sleep, Alex picked and rubbed at the corners to let in the first grey glimmer of morning light. Putting his right hand out onto what he thought might be his bed, he felt sand instead and beyond it heard the sound of birds and breaking waves.

2

Alex knows him now as Burhan but then, on the beach, he appeared in front of him a stranger with his beard and gold-rimmed glasses, his brown V-neck jumper (thin at the elbows), his barrel belly and plump fingers, saying in English with a slight Arabic accent, "Hello, my friend. Have you spent the night on the beach? Were you washed up from the briny? Were you spat out by a whale?"

"No," said Alex, his arms still stiff and painful, "But I think I must have fallen asleep for a moment."

Burhan put his plastic bag on the sand and sat beside him on a rock. "Where are you staying? At the Holiday Inn?"

Alex improvised: "Actually, I've just flown in from Muscat for a couple of days. I was planning to find somewhere in town."

"You look rather done in. Are you all right?"

"A bit tired, that's all."

"Well, that's fine. After a journey. Would it do you good to walk?"

For a while they made their way along the beach in silence, Burhan padding along by Alex's side, left shoulder forward and then right, like a sumo wrestler on a day off, his face at rest settling into a grin. Alex meanwhile felt strange and mad, having travelled several thousand miles across the world on a mattress.

Finally Burhan said, "In a moment we'll turn inland, shall we, into the town? Have you been to the town yet?"

"Not this trip."

"Ah. An old hand, back for another visit." Alex nodded. "You would have seen the fish market last time," continued Burhan, "and you would have bought a small plastic container of frankincense, which you burned a few times for your friends when you got home. The remainder is now in a drawer with similarly redundant exotica."

Alex had recovered enough to feel slightly irritated by this remark, and Burhan seemed immediately to know. In the sea of human interaction, Alex later decided, Burhan was always lowering a sail or inching the tiller to port or starboard.

"I'll show you something different, anyway, if I may," concluded his companion.

They followed a track that led from the beach through a plantation of coconut trees. Soon they were on the outskirts of the town. Burhan took Alex along a series of back streets with shuttered sand-coloured buildings on either side. Alex caught sight in passing of a small shaded courtyard with tiled walls, a dry fountain, and a plant with spear-like leaves. They came to a junction in the road. Burhan pointed to the left, "My house is down that way. I have a wife and five children. It keeps me out of trouble. Mostly." He smiled, looked at Alex, and added, "However, *we* are going this way."

After a few minutes, they turned into a dark passageway, no more than the breadth of two men or Burhan alone, who now walked ahead. At the end was a wide paved square in bright sunlight, the left-hand border formed by a high windowless building with an open stone staircase at its side, which they climbed until they reached a landing near the top.

Burhan took a key out of his generous trouser pocket and opened a wooden door into a dark corridor that smelt of damp leaves. As his eyes adapted, Alex could see shelves of leather-bound books on either side. Turning right, they entered a day-lit room, a long narrow window on its left. This space was also lined with books, and there were maps lying open on a reading table. Burhan beamed. "Welcome to my library," he said.

Alex was invited to remove his rucksack and look around while his host took two loaves of bread from his plastic bag and made tea on a small stove. Most of the books were in Arabic, but some were in English. The one Alex pulled out seemed to be a grammar. Between the shelves were stacks of rolled-up charts. Burhan gestured Alex to a wooden chair opposite the window and gave him his tea in a glass.

Pointing at a nearby set of a dozen dark-blue volumes, Alex said, "May I ask what *those* books are about?"

"They're commentaries on religious texts."

"On Islam?"

"Not just Islam. On Christianity too. And Judaism."

Burhan sipped his tea and looked up at Alex. "And what is your field?"

"I'm an architect in London. Still training, really."

"How interesting. And you're in Muscat on business?"

"With some free time, yes," replied Alex, glancing sidelong at the window. "Have you always lived in Salalah?" he asked, wanting to change the subject.

"No, not quite," replied Burhan, smiling. "When I was a child, my father took the family to France, where we had some relatives. He thought we'd all do better there."

"And did you?" said Alex, feeling it was all right to ask.

"Yes, I suppose you could say that. For a while, anyway. He joined a small Arab trading company in Paris. A family concern, set up by our cousin, Faroukh." Burhan put his tea down. "My father was rather a timid man, in fact. Moving to France may have been the only courageous act of his life. But perhaps his timidity or even his silence was seen as wisdom. People trusted him, and they trusted his advice. So yes, he - and we - did quite well. Soon he was responsible for the onward despatch of any particularly valuable items, works of art and things like that."

They chatted on for a time, Alex describing his previous visit to Salalah, and Burhan telling him about his postgraduate research in London and his lectureship in English and linguistics at a college outside Salalah.

"So you've returned to your home town," said Alex in the pause that followed.

"Yes, like a salmon. Even to the house I was born in."

"Did your parents come back too?"

Burhan filled his empty tea glass with water from the jug on the table. "Actually, my father went missing in Paris, and after a year or so we gave up hope. It seemed better to bring the rest of the family back to Oman."

"I'm sorry," said Alex. "What happened?"

Burhan shrugged. "My mother and sisters had gone to London to visit some old Omani friends, so my father was looking after me. I got home after school one day to find the apartment door already open and no one inside. So I sat on the sofa and waited for him, but he never returned, and I haven't seen him since. This is thirty-five years ago. No one has seen him since."

"And your mother?"

"She never gave up hope, though she died last year."

Alex half yawned, despite himself, and Burhan smiled. "You look as if you need some rest."

Alex nodded. "It *was* a very early flight."

"Well, I may have a solution to that," Burhan said, "and to your accommodation problem in general. My cousin has a very small, very simple place a few minutes from here. He's gone to Muscat for a week. He'd be happy to know you were a guest there." Burhan read Alex's doubtful expression. "Of course, I'll call him this evening to let him know."

Alex balanced caution against fatigue, fear of what might happen on his return 'flight', and the possibility that any hotel he approached would ask to see his visa. "I can only stay a day or two..."

"Well, that's fine. Why don't you put a loaf of bread in your rucksack and bring your tea?"

At the other end of the library, a back door with a window opened onto some metal steps, a wide flat roof and, beyond that, desert as far as the horizon. Screwing his eyes against the sun, Alex followed his companion's diagonal path to the far side of the roof where, after stepping over a low wall onto the top of the next building, they found themselves by a wooden fence with a narrow gate. Burhan motioned him through, saying, "This is my cousin's property."

The rooftop dwelling ahead of them looked as though it had been constructed over a long weekend. Outside there was a yard with cactus plants, a washing line, and a large tarpaulin for shade; inside, a caravan-style kitchenette, a dark bedroom through an arched doorway, and a bathroom with a rigged-up shower and sloping concrete floor.

Burhan showed Alex how things worked, gave him a key, and told him where the nearest food store was. After that he left, saying he would look by and collect him when he came over to the library at seven that evening.

Alex woke after a long sleep, took a cold shower, made some tea, and set his watch to local time. Then he went outside into the yard, chewing a piece of bread. Beyond the shelter of the tarpaulin, the afternoon heat was an entity in itself, pushing down on the roof of the house.

So that's it. There are curves in the universe, and I have stumbled into one.

But what had happened to his carefully rehearsed wish? He certainly hadn't *intended* to be beaten up in his garden or dropped into a warm, syrupy sea. Nor had he asked for a cinematic review of his past misdemeanours. Should he attempt to summon the fairy back, or would that just invite another blast from her wand? And when would he dare to use his power again?

Alex walked farther out into the sunlight, where a slight breeze had got up. The questions could wait. Surely it was time to look at the positives? Whatever else he *had*, more or less, been granted his wish. So he decided to remind himself of the some of the things he had fantasized about on his way home from work – the joy of being able to take a walk in the Alps on a wet UK Sunday afternoon, or to sip an aperitif of chilled Californian wine *in California* before supper in London. The sheer kudos, though it would take a bit of explaining, of transporting a girlfriend to Xian for an evening stroll along the city walls.

Financial gain? He'd have to do some more work on that. Obviously he could sign up for a tour of a bank vault or something similar, returning at night to lob a few ingots into his rucksack. You still had to be careful, though, with DNA and CCTV. Not that a prison could hold him, of course, but did he really want to become a kind of outlaw ghost, unable to touch down on familiar soil for more than an hour at a time?

Perhaps he should settle instead for the quiet joy of a superhero's self-restraint? But if he *was* going down that avenue, would he need to draw up some kind of code? Should he think, say, about using his powers exclusively for the public good, or might that become rather dreary?

Alex walked past the yard's largest half-cracked pot and looked out across the desert. He was a 'curver' now. For the moment that was enough.

After getting some currency in town, changing his SIM card – he'd need to ring in sick the following morning – and looking up the times of return flights to Muscat in a café with Wi-Fi, Alex clambered back up the spiral fire escape on the other side of the cousin's flat to wait for Burhan to arrive, watching from the yard as the sun made its final, rapid descent into the desert.

At half past seven, assuming his new friend had become absorbed in a book or a map, he decided to wander over to the library himself, retracing his steps in the dark until he could make out the dimly lit window of the building's back door. Reaching up from the metal steps, he tapped on the glass and waited, turning to look over at the nightscape of Salalah, reckoning he could identify the floodlit, palm-fringed pool of the Holiday Inn, down by the beach. When there was no response, he climbed onto the final step and peered in.

The room was in chaos: the table overturned, charts and papers covering the floor.

Alex paused and then pushed his way in, stumbling over a pile of books, the kerosene lamp swinging in the wind until he had pulled the door shut behind him. It was only as he crossed the room, uprighting a jug by the sink, that he noticed the leg in the far corner, stretched out across the entrance to the corridor. Alex rushed over, Burhan groaning when he reached him, and lifting himself onto his elbows, before collapsing again.

Alex knelt by his side. "Are you all right?"

Burhan nodded. "Could you get me a glass of water, please?"

By the time Alex had found a tumbler and struggled with the sink's rusty tap, his companion had risen onto his knees, into the light of the main room, a trickle of blood at his temple. "Thank you," he said, taking a huge gulp and looking around him. "I had a visit, I'm afraid, from two rather overexcited gentlemen."

"What did they want?"

"Some information, which I didn't give them, and access to the paperwork in my library, which, after a bit of a struggle, I couldn't refuse them. But they won't have found anything."

Alex took his glass and helped him to the seat by the window. "Are you going to call the police?" he asked.

Burhan shook his head. "This is something I need to deal with myself. The end of the story, I hope," he said, looking around him. "They won't come back, by the way, the men, at least for a while."

"Can I help you tidy up, then?" asked Alex, wondering what the hell he had got himself into.

Burhan smiled. "Thank you. But afterwards you must go back to my cousin's and forget about all this. Enjoy the beach and return to Muscat."

At any other time, Alex would certainly have agreed. But today was different.

"No," he replied. "I want to hear your story."

3

Burhan picked Alex up at eleven the following morning and drove him the thirty kilometres through the desert to the hilltop where Job was entombed in a small gold-domed building. They sat in the Prophet Ayoub Region Restaurant, with a dish of curry and two Pepsis in front of them. Below them lay Burhan's town, Salalah, and beyond it, the Arabian sea. The restaurant was air-conditioned, with a few tourists inside.

Burhan's Jeep had surprised Alex by looking fairly top-of-the-range, but his driving style veered between periods of calm and bursts of reckless confidence, like an eccentric uncle who had invited you to tea, but was capable, at any given moment during the soothing rhythm of the event, of seizing the teapot and chucking it at your head.

And in the tomb itself, which he had entered alone while Burhan searched the roadside for the car keys he had dropped, Alex had been taken aback to see an actual grave, rather long perhaps, but built to contain a man's body. Looking down at it, he tried to imagine the day they must have brought Job's corpse up the hill, in the cool of the morning, he supposed, with a hundred mourners following, robes flapping in the wind and metal water bottles clinking on donkeys' backs. After that, centuries of darkness for Job himself, animated by the screech of buzzards or the rush of horses' hooves, but mostly silent until the tourists began to arrive.

When they had eaten, and Alex had texted Gemma with the flu-like symptoms that would keep him off work for the rest of the week, they found some trees between the mosque and the tomb, and sat in the shade against two rocks, bottles of water from the restaurant at their side. Burhan said, "My father brought me here as a child. So I know Job as a neighbour first, and Prophet second."

Alex nodded as two men passed in white robes with short curved daggers in their belts. There was a faint trace of perfume. "This is your backyard, then?" he asked.

Burhan smiled. "Yes, that's one way of putting it."

Alex picked up his bottle. "You were going to tell me your story."

"If you're sure," replied Burhan, smiling and lighting a cigarette from his soft pack. "And then you'll go back?"

Alex nodded.

"Perhaps," began his companion, "you know something about the Muslim occupation of Spain?"

"No, not really. I mean, I know it happened."

"Well, amongst the conflict, there was a short period of calm in southern Spain when Christians, Jews, and Muslims actually managed to live together without killing one another. A kind of golden age. It probably helped that the Moors – the Muslims – had built water courses so that farmers could grow fruit, vegetables, and flowers." Burhan drew deeply on his cigarette.

"Now imagine a square in twelfth-century Cordoba," he continued. "It's early morning and there are trees and a garden. According to the accounts, the Muslim philosopher Averroes has come to meet some friends, and as they talk, tilers are busy close by, renovating a building, taking advantage of the cooler temperature to get their work done. They've spilt some of their glue, it seems, and done their best to wipe it up with water and a large piece of cloth which they've stretched out to dry between two timber supports in a darkened room. Opposite this piece of material, however, there must have been a very small hole in the exterior wall overlooking the square." Burhan smiled. "And as the tilers stare in disbelief, an inverted image of Averroes and his friends is transmitted through this hole onto the cloth."

"Like a photograph developing?" said Alex.

"Exactly," replied Burhan.

"So what do the tilers do?"

"The younger one, the apprentice, starts shaking. But the older one takes stock. He may have started by considering the image a miracle but, by the end, he's looking at it afresh, as banknotes." Burhan burst out laughing. "He probably slapped his assistant a couple of times to calm him down and put a ladder up to obstruct the view of the drying cloth. He reckoned he had only to ask his apprentice to say nothing for word to get around pretty quickly. And at that point, he would begin considering offers."

Burhan stubbed out his cigarette and drank some water.

"And *did* the tiler manage to sell it?" asked Alex.

"No, not exactly," said Burhan, still amused. "He took a down payment in a coffee house from a merchant who was passing through Cordoba. I rather suspect, Alex, that he took several such payments, because the merchant in question knocked on his door that night, insisting on seeing the goods. So he took the man to the cave where he had hidden the cloth and they inspected the photograph by torchlight. I'm afraid to say the merchant never returned to town, and when they found the tiler two days later, he was gibbering like his assistant, saying that he'd been cursed."

"What had they seen?" asked Alex.

Burhan smiled. "You'll find out soon. Suffice it to say that the regulars of the coffee house thought it intriguing enough to assemble a delegation of three scholars - a Jew, a Muslim, and a Christian - and send them down to the cave to examine the cloth. When they got there, it had gone."

Burhan wiped his glasses. "Over the centuries to come, there were many rumours, of course, not only about its location but also about certain powers it was said to possess. But there are only two sightings I trust. The first was in Samarkand in 1397." He pulled a small and rather ancient-looking volume out of his jacket pocket, opening it at a bookmarked page. "This is an account of his travels by the Spanish envoy Ruy Gonzales de Clavijo. The chapter we're interested in deals with his time at the court of Timur or Tamurlane."

Alex took a mouthful of water and sat back against his rock while Burhan explained how the aging tyrant had been winding down the middle phase of his conquests, bringing treasures back to Samarkand from Iran, Iraq, Syria, and the Caucasus, and how De Clavijo, newly arrived in the city from Spain, was being given the regular tour, drawing in his breath or widening his eyes in the appropriate places as he was guided from room to room.

"As they passed the last of the giant guards," Burhan continued, "and entered a smaller, darker chamber near the exit to the treasury, De Clavijo caught sight of a wide cloth in the shadows and, because it had been suspended between two poles, must have been reminded of the stories he had heard amongst the community of collectors in his native Seville. Moving closer, pretending to examine some pots in beaten gold, he saw enough in the cloth's dim figures to persuade him that his hosts might have found the photograph without being aware its significance." Burhan paused, pulled out a cigarette, but took a drink of water instead.

"What did he do next?" asked Alex.

"If you like, I'll translate De Clavijo from his own words." Alex nodded, and Burhan found his place in the text. "'I knew I could not make further enquiries without drawing attention to my find. I knew also I would not be able to return...'" - Burhan searched for the phrase - "'by normal means, to the treasury. I knelt by my bed, therefore, and prayed for a plan. When I woke in the morning, God had given me one. That afternoon we had been invited to a banquet that would continue well into the night. There would be drinking and dancing girls but also, as a highlight, a long epic poem celebrating Timur's recent conquests, at which attendance was compulsory for all but the guards and the girls.'"

Burhan turned a page. "This next bit is illegible, I'm afraid. I rescued this volume from a cellar in Muscat, and it has been damaged by water. However, I know from what follows that amongst the envoy's men was a North African soldier called Abu Hamid Al-Ghaza, who seems to have developed remarkable skills as a female impersonator." Burhan ran his finger under a line of text, "Listen to this phrase: 'movements and gestures that were no parody, but rather an intoxicating and practised tribute to the finest seductresses of our age.'"

"And," Burhan continued, "halfway through the reciting of the epic poem, Abu Hamid, under instructions from the envoy, stole his way over to the small chamber, where he engaged the guard, who must have taken him for an inquisitive dancing girl. Here you are, in De Clavijo's words: 'Abu Hamid, dressed in a gold-edged robe that swung and caressed his belly and lightly muscled thighs, touched the guard so gently and skilfully with hand and mouth in secret parts of his body that the giant's heart soon raced with lust and love.'" Burhan turned another page. "According to the text, Abu Hamid enticed the guard into a dark corner, where he offered him drugged wine from a flask. While the guard slept, the soldier removed the cloth from the poles and walked calmly back along the main corridor of the treasury."

His host closed the book.

"So De Clavijo got the cloth?" asked Alex.

"Yes and no. They packed their bags the following day, relying on the guard being too frightened to confess the incident. But on their return journey, while they were camped in the foothills of Mount Ararat in Turkey, Abu Hamid must have decided he would get a better deal breaking free from the Spanish delegation and selling the cloth on the open market. He set off at night, travelling south to Syria and Egypt."

"Disguised as a woman?"

Burhan laughed. "Who knows? All we get, I'm afraid, is De Clavijo's lament that he never got a chance to appreciate the cloth in daylight." Burhan looked at his watch. "I'm afraid I'm already late for an appointment at college. Which flight are you on tomorrow?"

"The eleven o'clock," lied Alex.

"Well, if you can make it to my library again at nine this evening, I'll tell you about the second sighting, which includes a description of the cloth itself and explains what sent the tiler mad."

Back in the kitchen of his rooftop flat, Alex took a long draught of the weak beer he had managed to obtain in town after googling 'side effects of teleportation' in the teahouse, and discovering a rather unsavoury theory about the dispersal and re-composition of one's atoms, a key element in the process, apparently. In front of him was a tuna steak from the market, cut from a creature two metres long and so fresh it didn't smell of fish at all. When he had fried it in oil and lemon, he pulled the small table out beyond the tarpaulin and yawned, the day still hot at dusk.

Through a window on the other side of the square, a woman in a veil seemed to look across in his direction. Was she spying on him, in league, perhaps, with the guys who had searched Burhan's library? Let her. He was too tired to move. Too tired, in fact, to think in any serious way, though he had plenty to think about. Even at the best of times, Alex was a great postponer of *practical* thought, the sort that led to action. It had irritated his ex-girlfriend that he could pick up a problem as if it were a pile of paper, put it in his mind's spare room, and relax, not feeling the need to return to the room for weeks, months, or even years, as if he had the longevity of a Biblical character.

But at least he knew that quite soon he would be ready to tap his knee again. Looking at his watch, he wondered if he might be able to squeeze in a nap between finishing his tuna and returning to Burhan's library.

4

"The second sighting was in the Sahara Desert, in fact, south of modern Libya, at the end of the seventeenth century." Burhan stood and adjusted the wick on his kerosene lamp. "Have you heard of a book normally called, in translation, *The Road across Africa?*" Alex shook his head. "It's an unusual work for the time and place. A sort of *Canterbury Tales* or *Don Quixote* of the desert, but a true story. An account of six Syrian merchants who planned to cross Africa east to west from Port Sudan to Agadir."

Burhan poured the tea that had been brewing and sat again at the narrow table, showing Alex the route the merchants had taken. "They were a fairly lively crew, looking for adventure and profit, but there was also a writer amongst them, Abdul Jaleel. This is his account in Arabic. A second edition, which I was fortunate to get in Senegal." Burhan placed a surprisingly neat well-preserved volume on the table. Alex looked at it and then around the room. "You've built up a valuable collection."

"Well, perhaps. Valuable to me, anyway."

"*And* to the visitors you had yesterday?"

Burhan smiled and showed Alex a small journal with an eagle on its cover, saying, "This is what they may have been looking for – an aide-memoire, where I write down book titles, page references, and new findings. But we'll come to that later."

Alex sat back. "All right. Where did this second crew find the cloth?"

"Actually, they'd never even heard of it when they set off. But they *had* fallen in with a local prince and his retinue who were hawking in the desert. There was a little bit of trade to be done, and the prince was hospitable enough. Anyway, it was Saqr, the youngest and most daring of the merchants, known as the locksmith for his talent with keys, who had heard from one of the hawk handlers that the prince kept a piece of material secure in a trunk during the day, and would take it out at night to spread it on the sand under his mattress while he slept. No one had seen the material in the daylight but there were various rumours, of course, about its origins and purpose."

"The cloth," said Alex.

"Exactly. Though Saqr had got it into his head that this must be one of the legendary golden fleeces of the ancient world and was determined, along with Mansour, his quiet companion among the merchants, to acquire it, keeping their colleagues in the dark, as Jaleel discovered later, for fear they would find the plan too reckless or too dishonourable." Burhan sipped his tea. "One night, when they knew the prince and his servants would not be returning from a trip until the early hours of morning, Mansour engaged the guards in banter at the entrance to his tent, while Saqr stole through the adjoining servants' quarters, picked the trunk's lock, and put the cloth under his shirt."

"Didn't he take a look at it?" asked Alex.

"Apparently not. According to Jaleel, Saqr placed it straightaway in the saddlebag of his horse. Mansour then broke the news of their adventure quietly to their sleeping comrades, who were furious but agreed of course that none of them could stay. So they walked their horses to the edge of the encampment, slit the throat of a guard, and began to canter into the night. Soon they were galloping. They realized, you see, that the few hours' start they had was no guarantee of safety in a land they hardly knew."

"Did they continue on their original route?"

"No. They rode night and day until they reached Tripoli instead. They thought they might hide themselves amongst the crowds of the city for a day or two. In fact, they decided after some argument that they would split up in the city and make their way individually across the Mediterranean, meeting up in Marseille. They made a pact on the honour of each man's life that the value of their booty would be shared equally when Saqr finally sold it. All they wanted to do before parting, of course, was to actually see the cloth."

Burhan lit a cigarette and opened the window. "I'll let the author narrate the rest of the story. Forgive my poor translation," he said, finding his place in the text.

"'We believed we had earned a day's grace in Tripoli, before going our separate ways directly or indirectly across the sea. We chose a large, busy inn with a courtyard, and though it was located not far from the city, it had a country feel to it, with chickens running around and communal eating in the courtyard on long wooden tables. The place was owned by a fat man and his thin wife. It was busy, which was to our advantage, but we still arrived in two separate groups – a pair of us first and an hour later, the remaining party of four. We agreed to meet at nine that evening in Saqr's room. Afterwards we would eat, sleep, and part at dawn. We were in good spirits, despite our differences. Our trip across the desert had gone without...'" Burhan hesitated, and Alex added, "Without a hitch?"

"Of course. One of those expressions I always forget." Burhan rested his cigarette in the ashtray, poured them both some more tea, and returned to the account. "'When we had assembled in Saqr's room, we used the two lamps available to make the light as strong as we could. Music and eating had begun in the courtyard below, so we closed the shutters. Saqr took the cloth from his bag and began to unwrap it on the bed. Before he had even unfolded it, we were all aware that it wasn't anything like a golden fleece. When it was laid out, I would say it was about six feet wide, and four deep. It wasn't a plain cloth, however. Indeed, it had an astonishing design upon it. As I write this account now, thirty years later, I close my eyes, and as surely as the sea still ebbs and flows along my little stretch of Syrian coastline, I can recall what we saw that evening in Saqr's room. Therefore, I will describe it to you, reader, as my youthful eyes perceived it, without the small portion of knowledge I have since acquired.'"

Burhan looked up, exhaling smoke. "I'm not sure he quite succeeds in that, Alex. But let's see what he says." Burhan frowned, as if for the first time straining to translate. "'To begin with, despite some damage to parts of the design, we were amazed by the clarity of the image. We assumed it was a kind of painting, though it lacked the characteristics of a formal composition, being more like the view from a window. The colour, if there had been any, had faded completely, yet I cannot imagine a full palette offering a better description than those infinitely fine gradations of black to grey, amidst the bleached white of sunlight.'

'The scene itself was set in a courtyard, with orange and lemon trees and a modest fountain in the centre. On the left stood a tall, bearded man in a robe, clearly engaged in conversation with the men – and a woman – around him, one of his arms outstretched, palm upwards, as if he was weighing the air. I could not tell what their various robes and headwear signified, but there seemed to be no obvious hierarchy amongst them, or if there was, the animation of their conversation had suspended it. My friends and I stood in silence for a moment, marvelling at the lifelike detail. Then Mansour pointed to the bottom right-hand area, which was more in shade than the rest.'"

Burhan turned a page but didn't look up. "'At first it was difficult to make anything out, other than the trees and a kind of mist at ground level that suggested a hot day to come. But soon we became aware of a figure partly obscured among the leaves and branches, in a light robe and hood. I couldn't tell if it was a man or woman, but there was something about this person's posture and presence that held your eyes and then sent you back to the group near the fountain that he or she was watching. A kind of miraculous calm came over the six of us. I don't know how to explain it, but we all knew that the figure was God.'" His host looked up and smiled.

"So that's what drove the tiler mad," said Alex.

"He believed himself cursed for trying to sell it," said Burhan, stubbing out his cigarette and closing the book.

"Could I hear the ending?" asked Alex.

"Of course," replied Burhan, "though I must warn you of the sensationalism of the passage that precedes it."

He picked the book up again. "'We were soon torn from our contemplation by a hammering at the door. The thin woman had come to tell Saqr that he and his comrades would miss dinner if they didn't come down to the courtyard. We folded the cloth up reluctantly, put it back in the saddlebag, and agreed that Saqr should keep it with him. The meal went well, in fact. We were in good spirits. The meat was excellent, and the wine was spicy and cool. Though our comrades had taken a great risk, forcing us to abandon our original itinerary, we knew we had obtained a valuable addition to our booty. We were careful, however, to remain in our two groups. I was in the party of four; Saqr and Mansour took a table on the other side of the courtyard. There were perhaps forty diners in all. I suppose the evening reached a climax shortly before midnight when the fat man put down bowls of a liqueur that burned with blue flames. Good-humoured shouts went up from a group of sea traders when their bowl overturned and a fiery blue river ran across their table. Later, the thin woman got her husband to play the fiddle. My table was a little drunk, it has to be said. I tried to stay watchful, but with people standing up to sing or to shout to their companions, it wasn't easy. For a moment or two, I ignored the fact that my view of Saqr and Mansour was obscured by a group of diners who seemed to be amused by a dancing dog. Then I got up and casually made my way over to where they had been sitting. Both were gone.

'I was able, however, to obtain from two of their smiling neighbours the information that they had left together a few minutes before through an archway twenty feet behind their table. So I took their route. To begin with, the tunnel they had entered was pitch-black to my eyes, but I was able to feel my way along the wall until it led me into a cobbled street, dimly lit by moonlight and lined on either side by short, thick trees. I took a few steps to the left and stood still, letting my eyes and ears adjust. Slowly I was able to make out shapes in the shadows and against the trees. There was a gasp and a burst of laughter behind me. A man staggered backwards, exposing a woman's white rear, covered almost immediately by her falling petticoats. I realized I had entered an open-air brothel!'"

Burhan looked up from his book for a moment, and then continued reading.

'"As I surveyed the street, I could see that almost every tree had a man and woman at its trunk, copulating in their chosen fashion, the rhythm of their movements indicating which stage of the act they had reached. And as I watched, a warm hand touched the inside of my thigh from behind, so I turned, this time to see a young black woman, her white shirt open to her jewelled navel and her breasts held tight by a dark silk band.

'Reader, it is not at all in my nature to indulge myself in the street like a tomcat, but I am ashamed to say I had drunk too deeply and felt such a rush of compelling lust that I let her lead me to a nearby tree, where she lifted her skirts and placed my hand between her thighs. Never in my life, not even as a seventeen-year-old, had I felt such an urgency to penetrate and release myself, and though, after loosening my clothing for the initial upward thrust, I held as still as I could within her, it was only a matter of seconds before the spreading pleasure made me oblivious to the street, to the world, and to life itself.

'At the last shudder, however, I heard a strange and muted masculine gasp some yards ahead to my left and turned my head despite myself. Two figures, almost in total darkness, grasped each other in a tight embrace, the one nearer to me lifting and holding his partner against the wall. I turned back to my own concerns, tidying myself and reaching for my purse. But as I took two coins out and paid off my girl, I couldn't help but notice the man lowering the slumped body of his partner to the ground. And as the girl walked off, the figure's limp head fell out of the shadows and into the moonlight. For a second I was looking into Saqr's blank eyes, and then upwards at Mansour emerging from the shadows, turning without seeing me and running up the street with the saddlebag. I sprang the few yards to Saqr and put my hand to his chest, wet with flowing blood. He was dead already, dispatched by deep cuts to the heart. Though I have no proof, I suspect that Mansour planned all along to make the cloth his own, luring poor Saqr into the street, or forcing him at dagger point.'"

Burhan closed the book.

"And did they search for Mansour?" asked Alex.

"For a while, but without success. Our narrator himself, Jaleel, finally returned to Syria, where he began his research into the origins of the cloth."

"And it was never heard of again?"

Burhan smiled. "Well, what do you think, Alex?"

Alex shook his head.

"I'll rephrase my question, then," said Burhan. "*Where* do you think?"

After a pause, Alex said, "Paris."

Next day at nine, they were in the Jeep once again, Burhan having insisted on driving his guest to the airport. The suspicion that his friend actually drove better when he was engaged in conversation, glancing sideways at his passenger, rather than focusing on the road ahead, was confirmed as their small talk came to an end and the Jeep began to pick up speed, veering to the right on the outskirts of town and skimming the edge of a soft-fruit stall. Turning to watch a mango roll across the road, Alex realized it was time to distract his companion.

"So your father had the cloth, ready for despatch," he said. "Did he know what it was?"

"I'm not sure," replied Burhan.

"And the men who came last night. They think you know where it is."

Burhan shook his head. "Not now. I believe I managed to convince them otherwise. But the thing is, Alex, I don't regard this third episode in the cloth's history as finished. The whispers continue, you see. I'm coming to London in a week's time, in fact, because of a whisper. More of a shout, actually, I'm glad to say."

"Really? I'll give you my phone number."

Burhan stared at the road. "I'm not sure you should."

The conversation fell away, and soon they were racing into the airport car park, pulling confidently into a space that looked somewhat narrower than the Jeep itself.

Burhan switched off the ignition. "You know why the cloth is important, don't you? Not because of its miraculous genesis, though that would be enough, but because of the message it contains." He rested his right hand on Alex's forearm. "God, you see, has chosen to appear in a place where Jews, Christians, and Muslims have come together in peace."

Alex took out his wallet and gave Burhan his business card. "We can meet, at least, and you can update me."

A throb on the left indicated that the black Honda was pulling out of its space, so they both got out of the driver's side and walked across to the airport building, Alex relieved they were able to say their farewells before he got to the check-in desk, his new friend disappearing around the other side of what looked like a visiting basketball team.

Making his way to the Gents, Alex flexed his knee-tapping hand like a gunslinger, preparing himself for the pummelling to come, or a second psychotherapy session, or anything, really, that would get him home to his garden flat and a very large glass of wine.

5

Back in London after a suspiciously quiet second journey, like nodding off in a Friday-afternoon maths lesson, Alex did a Google search, various combinations of 'miraculous', 'photograph', 'Cordoba', and 'God' producing nothing more meaningful, however, than a face in a cloud above Norfolk that was either divine or Sean Connery.

Then he went a bit mad, flying about everywhere.

He began by transporting himself to France, tapping his knee three times and saying the line, imagining a spot in the woods near a campsite his father had brought the family to when he was a kid. In fact, a kid caught sight of him as he appeared from nowhere to sit on a log, and ran off when Alex made a ghoul gesture with his arms and pulled a solemn, vacant face. God knew what the kid thought, or would go on to do.

Next, he flew to Tokyo to the square behind a business hotel he had stayed in with his boss, arriving in the dead of night and not much bothering a nearby tramp or recently downsized salaryman. He went for a walk in the old part of the district through narrow streets, past tiny scrubbed-out fishmongers, and later in a red-light area where polite Japanese girls gave out business cards and squat men in black T-shirts and beige suits were ready offstage to see the niceties observed. Alex got a hot can of sweet coffee from a vending machine and came home.

His final trip was triangular, to check he could go from one destination to another without returning to his flat. First he went to Brighton for a brisk walk along the rain-swept sea front, and then straight on to a sports bar in Seville. After cold potatoes, olives, and a sharp house wine, he made his statement and disappeared home.

The journeys themselves, however, were never as straightforward as his wish had stipulated. After the brief respite of his return from Oman, each seemed to want to make its mark. On the flight to Tokyo, for example, it felt as though he were doing cartwheels through a sunlit sky that soon turned black and starry, and from the south coast to Spain, he found himself shrink-wrapped in a moist opaque membrane, which he managed to tear his way out of somewhere above Seville, the remainder becoming an organic parachute for the descent into the back street he had visualized.

And all the flights were accompanied by violent emotions attached to episodes from his early life, whose importance he had clearly undervalued. On his way to the French campsite, he had found himself murderously angry once more with a friend who had refused to take Alex's detour on a school hike. Flying to the south coast, no less taxing a journey for its proximity, he was hopelessly, weepingly, in love again with the girl from the last year of primary school who had kissed the back of his neck in the playground. The fairy, it seemed, had booked him in with an old-school Viennese psychoanalyst, who wasn't going to let Alex go until he had put his hand up to *everything*. But why?

Whatever the reason, he was probably in better shape by Sunday, four days after his return from Salalah, than he had ever been as an adult – brisk and positive, as if he were a geezer in a sixties movie leaving his Chelsea mews flat in topcoat and black velvet collar, breath steaming in the morning air and diamonds of frost winking up from the pavement.

Surely it was time to visit his ex-girlfriend?

Céline herself opened the door, and not Paul or Jessica, her two flatmates.

"It's you," she said. "Why didn't you text me first?"

"I'm sorry. I was just out and about."

Céline put on her look of not being convinced, so Alex continued, "Had I better come in?" But Céline had already retreated down the hallway, leaving the door open for Alex to follow.

Though the three flatmates had a decent shared kitchen and bathroom to which Céline had access, her large well-lit room was in fact completely self-contained. When you opened the shutters on one side of the room, you found a sink and cooker unit with utensils hanging from hooks; and on the other side, a tiny shower, wash-basin, and toilet were concealed behind a folding door. The whole thing appealed to Alex – the idea you could almost live indefinitely in one room. It made him think of a spy in a safe house or a wartime Jew in hiding.

Céline, though, was clearly getting ready to go out for the evening. She took off her dressing gown, unselfconsciously revealing dark-green knickers and a matching bra.

"Why don't you help me if you're here?" she said.

"What do you want me to do?"

"Iron that shirt, please."

Alex turned the shirt inside out, put the iron on a medium heat and got to work. Céline, meanwhile, sat at her dressing table and leant forward towards the mirror to do her eyes. In the background the radio stopped talking and began to play a big band show tune, which Alex found he could iron in time to.

"Would you mind switching that off, please, Alex? I hate that stuff, don't you?"

As he turned the volume down until it clicked off, Alex reflected that in the thousands of conversations they must have had while they were going out together, they hadn't actually covered big band music. He looked up over his ironing at Céline.

"Stop looking at me," she said. "Don't you see girls in their underwear anymore?"

Alex didn't really. "I'd just forgotten what a long back you had," he said.

Céline didn't reply, as if unable to decide if she liked being thought of as having a long back. When Alex pulled a new bit of shirt towards the top of the board, she picked up a nail file and her eyes glazed over. Perhaps she was thinking about who she was seeing that evening. Alex had to find out, of course, deciding, but only halfway through his question, that it might sound more casual to sound less casual. The change gave a curious Scandinavian lilt to his voice. "Have you got something *on* tonight?" he said.

"No, not really. Just seeing a friend," replied Céline, turning back to her mirror.

That didn't help. "Whereabouts are you going?" he tried.

"We're having a natter in a posh new restaurant, to see what it's like."

Alex rested the iron. Was 'natter' designed to make him think it was a woman?

"Really? Is it anyone I know?" he finally asked.

"La Scala, it's called, in Bayswater," said Céline, deadpan, spinning round on the dressing table stool with a black ball in her hands.

As Alex took the shirt off the ironing board, the ball became stockings, Céline draping one over her left leg and bunching the other up until there was no more than an inch of material for her right foot to push at. Soon all her foot and most of her calf were in, so she leant back on the stool, straightening her leg to negotiate her knee. Halfway up her thigh, the rubber circle at the top began to meet resistance and, when it was finally in place, she pulled it out at both sides, letting it ping back in a way that suggested novelty, but not absolutely *new* novelty.

Alex had never seen her wear stockings before.

"They're quite comfy really," said Céline, looking up.

Alex closed over the legs of the ironing board.

"Do you want a cup of coffee?" she continued.

This, translated from Céline-speak meant, 'Would you like to make *me* a cup of coffee?' so Alex opened up the shutters and got to work again as Céline finished dressing. Then they sat. Having coffee together was something they did quite well. After all, they had been together for five years.

"How's Marge?" she said.

"Fine. She bought that second-hand moped in the end."

Céline, smiling, was still close to his adoptive mother, meeting her when she returned from France, where his parents lived, happily it seemed to Alex, on a vicar's pension and Marge's magazine column.

"And what about you, Alex?"

"Good, thanks. Well, actually, no. I've got to go to hospital the day after tomorrow. I had a blackout."

Céline's concern was palpable at least. "What happened?" she asked.

"I don't know. I was on my way home from work, and I just blacked out. I'd had a few drinks because it was Gemma's birthday and I suppose I *was* working pretty hard."

"You'd probably strained your eyes, staring at Gemma's legs. Or her breasts. How long were you out for?"

"Not long. And I'm okay now. They just want to check it out."

"Well, you'd better let me know what happens, hadn't you?"

For a moment, it occurred to Alex to blurt out his whole story, including Burhan and the cloth, and he probably would have done had they still been an item. Later, on his way home, however, he was glad he had resisted the impulse. Céline seemed in a hurry to get out anyway, and was soon taking her brief but cheerful leave of Alex in the main kitchen of the house, where her flatmate Paul was very keen indeed to describe to him a recent success he had had at work, designing something he called a 'third-generation financial product'. He was roasting a large chicken, so he had plenty of time.

6

Alex tried his best to be excited by his job, reminding himself that his boss seemed to trust him, his team appeared to like him, and that architecture, in general, mattered, sort of. What worried him was not so much that life at work was all a bit of an act (this was obvious to him) but that, although he mostly got the lines right, he'd never really managed to get into character. Wasn't it odd how the signs of childhood - in his case, an ability to draw better than the next kid along - could now determine a working life? A little like navigating the oceans not by sextant and stars but the first passing current.

Opting for a conventional journey to work, Alex took advantage of his position in the centre of the carriage to observe his fellow passengers as warmly as he could. They were, after all, his ride companions not only on the Monday morning Tube but also, for a time, on this spinning, looping ball in space. The men, reading their newspapers or listening to music, were twitchy and pallid but protective of their slot of bother-free time. The women in their makeup were pleasanter to contemplate but more difficult to decipher.

Alex fell in love, of course, as he usually did on Tube journeys. This time it was a smartly dressed brunette with a carefree though private look about her, four seats to his left on the other side of the carriage. She had caught his eye twice now, but what could you do? Trying to chat her up en route or following her off the train were obviously out of the question, unless you were looking for a smack. So the only other option was to enjoy the fantasy while it lasted.

He looked across at his 'glancee' once again. My God, was there was a smile too, or at least a parting of the lips? Alex turned back, his gaze met by the very old man opposite, a black hat on his head and a somewhat startled expression on his pale, narrow face. Alex examined the floor. There had to be another way. What if he were to pass her a message as he left the train? Given the circumstances, it would have to be memorable, though, wouldn't it, if it were to stand any chance of success, or better still, *reckless*. You couldn't, in the circumstances, just ask her out for a drink.

Euston station. Alex checked his wallet and found a business card from a Japanese Embassy official he had recently met with his boss. Crossing through the front of the card with his pen, he turned it over and, since it was all he could think of, wrote out the opening lines from a poem he had memorized at school, followed by a brief invitation to meet. Afterwards he sat back in his seat, smiling to himself and shaking his head. What on *earth* was he doing? And how did it fit in with his new status as a flier, as a curver? Was it a kind of mad pride, perhaps, that though he owed his powers to the fairy, he could still intensify his own life?

The train slowed into Warren Street, and when the glancee reached to her side for her handbag, the prospect of her disappearing forever amongst the crowds of central London caused in Alex a sensation he had never felt before, a kind of lurch, as if one of his internal floors were collapsing. As her neighbours got up to leave, however, she remained in her seat, unclasping the bag, bringing out an old-fashioned powder compact, and allowing Alex half the length of Tottenham Court Road, at least, in which to act.

When the train moved on, Alex pulled himself out of his seat and took a step towards her, his heart pumping, his card hand extended, his plan not only absurd now that he was on his feet, but creepy too, and rather offensive. He had just drawn level with the glancee, deciding to crush the card softly in his palm, preparing a smile instead that was likely to turn into a ghastly leer, when there was a screech of brakes and his whole world jolted forwards.

For a moment Alex wondered why everything had turned brown. Then he realized that a large woman in a mac had caught and clasped him to her chest and now, with a hand to his elbow, was manoeuvring his dazed body backwards into an empty seat. He thanked her and bent to rub his ankle, the sole part of his anatomy, it appeared, that had resisted his impulse to continue travelling in the stationary train. It was only when the woman decided to move off to the left that Alex became aware of the glancee's stockinged calves, directly opposite now, elegantly crossed and within touching distance of his own, an opportunity he felt it wise to forgo.

As the train revved up and shuddered forward, Alex, under cover of massaging his forehead, began to lift his head, until he was finally able to take in a full view of the object of his desire. There she was, poised as ever, brushing her lapel and straightening her skirt – before attending to the crumpled business card that fallen into her lap.

A fine coating of sweat rose up through Alex's glands, covering his body like a second skin. In his numbed mind, he read the lines with her:

> *'What would I wish for ere I die?*
> *To kiss the skin of your naked thigh.'*
> *(Why don't we meet at 3pm today in*
> *the lounge of the London Edition hotel?)*

As the last drops of control drained from Alex's cup, a strange sense of relief came over him, as if the ancient liquids of his body - the blood, bile, and phlegm - had decided in their confusion to join forces like the gently bubbling waters of a Jacuzzi. With the train picking up speed, and the man in the hat bowing his head, the glancee looked over at Alex for a moment without expression before getting up and making her way to the doors to wait for the next stop. When it came, she vanished.

Alex's own exit, at Tottenham Court Road, was less easily accomplished. Even with his left leg taking most of the weight, his right ankle refused to play ball. About to collapse back into his seat, once more he felt an arm under his elbow. This time, however, it was the old man, who seemed determined, despite his age, to see him off the train and guide him to a platform seat.

"I should rest it for a while, if I were you," said the man in the overcomposed English of a dedicated second language learner. The skin of his face was deeply wrinkled and worryingly white.

"Thanks, but I need to get to work."

"Then I will help you," the man replied, clamping his hand to Alex's arm. They walked together to the escalator, his companion continuing, "I used to be in medicine myself for a time, until I reached its limits."

It was an odd sort of comment, but Alex felt he owed it to the man to be civil. "Really? What did you do?" he asked.

"Oh, you know, bones and that kind of thing. I wasn't what you would call a conventional doctor."

Alex thought, I bet you weren't, as they reached the exit and the old man guided him towards a taxi. When he had got in and thanked his minder, the man reached into his suit jacket, pulled out a business card, wrote a few words on it - not a proposition, Alex hoped - and said, "Take this. I'm more interested in the human mind these days, but come to the appointment if you're still having difficulties. You're missing a card now anyway, aren't you?"

By the time Alex's taxi had pulled up on Fitzroy Street at the door to Schaeffer and Schaeffer, it was ten o'clock, so he would have to work till two thirty, making his way down to the London Edition in a late lunch break. He limped straight through to the open-plan office, where his team, Gemma and Lewis, were working on the design for a villa in the forests of south-west France. His boss, of course, was in charge of the overall vision of the thing, with the client, Jeremy Knowles – owner of the delicatessen chain Avanti – changing his mind as often as his upmarket customers had gnocchi kitchen suppers.

Alex had just about got his jacket off and made his way across to his board, where he was working on the villa's bedroom extension, when his boss rang down. Rod never introduced himself on the phone, and though his mild Ulster accent, sprinkled with Americanisms such as *Noo* York, was pretty much a giveaway, the absence still had the power to unsettle you at the crucial beginning of the transaction. Other things Rod did that may have been aimed at producing the same effect, included answering the door to the small flat at the top of the building – where he often stayed overnight – in the nude, which was okay-ish, before making you coffee in the same state, which somehow wasn't.

"Can you come upstairs for a moment if you're feeling well enough?" said Rod. "Knowles is here."

Alex agreed and put the phone down. He hadn't actually met Jeremy Knowles yet. When he got to the door, he heard Rod's secondary laugh, a bit of a cackle but deployed at least in expected places. Much more common was a kind of smile with short hisses through the teeth and a bit of shoulder activity, which Rod seemed to employ almost at random, drawing you temporarily into his countercultural perspective.

His boss opened the door, finishing off his cackle in the way someone else might still be chewing a piece of toast. "Alex. You'd better come in."

The thing Alex always noticed about Rod was how incredibly clean he was, his beige chinos and white T-shirt freshly laundered and pressed, his pale skin pampered and plumped up. There was a faint tang of a scrubbing soap like Wright's Coal Tar about him, overlaid by the stronger scent of a high-end eau de cologne.

Jeremy meanwhile was half rising from a brown leather armchair on the right of the office, so Alex went over and shook his hand.

Rod, with a brief hissing smile, said, "Alex Harrison here is my right-hand man," and Jeremy replied in a camp voice, "Wish *I* had one." Jeremy's was a good-looking, biggish head, with a tanned pock-marked face and energetic eyes. His casual clothes were soft and very expensive.

Rod, leaning on the front of the black desk by the window, sucked on his vaping device, blowing a large cloud of vanilla-scented smoke into the room. "Do you *wanna* go into the food business with Jeremy?" he asked.

Alex laughed and sat on a bench to the left of the desk, while Jeremy lifted his right hand from the arm of the chair and waved it from side to side against Rod's encroaching vapour. "I might not stay in food much longer, though, Rod. I can't make the same kinds of margins as I used to."

Rod suspended his device six inches or so from his mouth and did the conspiratorial-smile part of his main laugh. "Get on! What do you pay for those one-foot salamis? Five quid at the most?" Jeremy half nodded, and Rod continued, "And what do you sell them for, when they're all sliced up real thin and gift-wrapped? Fifty quid? Come on! You're milking us! You're picking our frigging pockets!"

Jeremy was smiling now and putting on a slightly hurt expression, saying in his deep, well-textured voice, "The costs, my boy, the costs! The wages, the health and safety, the deliveries! It's not like your business! What do you do? I'll tell you what you do!" He paused, raised his shoulders and turned both palms upwards. "You draw stuff! Not even creative stuff. Just straight lines with rulers."

Rod cackled. "But I've got to keep people like Alex here in sun-dried tomatoes and truffles!"

Jeremy looked over at Alex in a pleasant but business-like way. "Rod says you've been working on the new bedroom extension."

Alex nodded. "Yes, I wanted to ask you. Have you decided what kind of windows you'd like?"

"Another sliding panel, Alex, so I can watch the mist rising in the morning. Which reminds me, Rod. I'd like you to put in a small gallery for paintings, with a kind of large skylight ceiling. I've just seen one like it in Edinburgh."

Rod pulled an imaginary piece of tobacco from his tongue, a hangover from his roll-up days. "You're joking," he said.

Jeremy ignored this and turned to Alex. "The gallery would have to be above the living space, with the entrance designed so that when you closed it, it would disappear. That way the focus is just on the paintings."

Alex looked at Rod and then back at Jeremy. "And the roof of the gallery would be more or less all glass?"

"That's it exactly," replied Jeremy. "Can you do that?"

Rod shook his head, smiling widely, balancing his vaping device upright on the desk. "You haven't got any goddamn paintings! I thought this meeting was supposed to be about books, anyway. You remember, the *library*."

Jeremy, relaxed, said, "I haven't got any books either, have I? That's why it's called a *project*." He got up. "That reminds me. I've got a landline now in France, even if I haven't got a mobile signal, and some new business cards with the address on them."

As Jeremy passed these around, Rod reached for his leather jacket, indicating the end of the meeting. "I've got to go out, but why don't you have a chat with Alex, Jeremy? Later on we can all have some whitebait next door."

Rod was convinced, Alex remembered, that a plate of whitebait in a Wisconsin diner had once saved his life after a bad acid trip, when his brain and his car pulled in at the roadside restaurant almost at the same time, both of them wrecked.

Taking a seat in a winged black leather armchair opposite its empty twin, Alex ordered a pot of Earl Grey tea for two. It was ten to three. As he viewed the hotel's rotating door, he considered the various routes the drama could take. Firstly, nothing. He would wait, and she simply wouldn't show. He was honest enough with himself to see this as overwhelmingly the likeliest option. After half an hour and a couple of cups of tea, he would return to work.

Secondly, she would show but with the police, at which point he would be hauled off and charged with harassment. With a criminal record and the intriguing story written up by a bored court reporter, he could always make a new start in Venezuela, teaching EFL in the mornings in a slightly grubby suit, but able at least to sip cheap white wine for the rest of the day, and possibly to wear one of those straw trilbies.

Thirdly, he thought, as the waiter unloaded his tray, she would be Russian and, instead of coming herself, would send her twin brothers, ready to escort him to the nearest alley, where, to the clash of pots and pans from the window of a restaurant kitchen, his face would be comprehensively ground into the brickwork. A fourth scenario was vying for life when the hotel door rotated once more, this time zephyring the glancee into reception, where she sailed her way around the chairs and tables, gloves in one hand like an actress from a fifties movie, finally arranging herself opposite him in the black armchair, leaning forward and saying pleasantly, "Is this tea for me?"

"Yes," said Alex, lifting the pot and swallowing to moisten his vocal cords. "You had no trouble finding the hotel, then?" he asked.

"No, I've been here before," she said, directing her cup towards him. "I take it you've got a room?"

Alex shot a small jet of pale-brown tea into his companion's saucer.

"What for?" he asked.

"Well, I don't really think I can let you kiss my naked thigh in the middle of reception."

Alex put the pot down. "I'm sorry about that card. I should never have written it."

The glancee laughed. "Perhaps not. I assume it was intended for me."

"Yes," agreed Alex.

"And I accepted it, don't you see?" she said. "I mean, I could have given it back or torn it up." Alex nodded, his skin tingling now with energy and fear. "So we have a contract, don't we?" she concluded, extending her hand. "It's Carol, by the way."

After a frankly embarrassing discussion with the receptionist over his 'delayed' luggage, Alex perused the mini-bar of Room 355 in what he hoped was a worldly manner, while Carol took her jacket off and hung it in the wardrobe. The room itself was filled with grey London light.

"Would you like a drink?" he said.

"Scotch and soda please," she replied.

Alex fixed her drink and, after a bit of should-I-have-this-or-should-I-have-that, took a small bottle of sparkling white wine with a plastic cap for himself, finally joining her by the window. A church-like calm descended on the room while they sipped their drinks and looked out over central London. Then she said with a smile, "Do you mind if I take charge, purely in the spirit of getting things done, of course?"

Alex shook his head, reasoning that he had already answered the question, and followed her to the dressing table, where they put their glasses down, Carol turning the wooden chair to face the bed. After removing her shoes, she placed a stockinged foot on its seat, looked Alex in the eye, and pushed the air down with her right hand as a signal for him to kneel. What else could he do?

When he had removed his jacket and got into position by the chair, she pulled back her skirt until it exposed three or four inches of white thigh above her stocking and, as she gazed down almost distractedly at him, Alex had time to reflect on the disturbing sensation he had that with each move she made, years, decades and even centuries were passing by in the world outside. Alex was convinced that, had they still been standing by the window, they would have seen time *rush* on the streets below.

While she arranged her foot on the chair, they would have noticed the first wild grasses sprouting up amongst the flagstones of Berners Street and watched department stores around them begin to decay and crumble. As he knelt before her, they would have gasped as the earth began to bake and tigers set about the chasing of gazelles from Marble Arch to Holborn Circus.

While she pulled back her skirt, they might have listened in wonder as the light, hot winds carried towards them the distant ballads of London's last gung-ho survivors. And afterwards they would have felt, palms pressed against the glass of the window, the beginning of the Great Freeze.

Inside the room, Alex had moved closer, close enough now to draw from Carol's thigh a musky scent of soap and tobacco. This perfume seemed to spread inside him until he sensed it in the tips of his fingers and rolling down like smoke inside his calves. Outside, great cracking sounds broke the silence as ice fought ice in sheets the size of counties. A kind of white buffalo with shaggy jowls had evolved, and penguins with fishing lines on their snouts worked Mayfair and Belgravia.

Carol, meanwhile, stood perfectly still, but her distraction, it seemed to him, had deepened over the millennia into something resembling sorrow or compassion, and her face had tilted, making the white parts whiter and darkening the shadows. Alex was so close now that all he could see was the milk-coloured flesh; all he could hear were the vessels that pulsed oxygen below the surface of her skin.

In the country outside, cool gases - cadmium blues, dusty white silvers, and fire-flecked oranges - prowled cautiously around each other, sometimes combining peacefully and producing new shades of themselves; sometimes drawn into violent liaisons that would raise English sand from the poisonous wastelands high into the sky in thunderclaps and twists of air.

Alex's lips met Carol's naked skin. A tiny jolt shot through her thigh and into his kneeling body. After a moment - ten or fifteen years, perhaps - of contact, he began to withdraw his mouth, unsticking his lips atom by atom from the white flesh. When the separation was complete, he stood, and Carol, removing her foot from the chair, returned to the window, where rain had begun to beat the glass.

In the dimmed room, Alex found himself asking, "What do you want from me?"

Carol turned and looked at him, her arms crossed, her back against the streaming window. "When it rains like this," she said, "you could see that I have shelter, I suppose. And you might also offer me food when I'm hungry. You know, wild salmon or deer or fruits that taste of themselves; when I'm thirsty, cool water and dark red wine.

"Can you build fires?" she continued. "I hate to be cold or fearful. And always, when I'm tired, let me sleep. Let's not have friends to see or things to do." She pushed the toes of her stockinged foot deep into the carpet. "Might you take me to a place, perhaps, where the shopkeepers laugh and you can smell mint in the air; where everyone except us has children; where no one is afraid to talk or pray? We could eat in the garden and when night falls, you could tell me something new from astronomy or mathematics.

"You would contain yourself, though, wouldn't you?" she concluded. "I want to be able to understand the world in my own way, you see. It isn't random. We all have a place in things. We just need time to align ourselves. Then we can *transcend*."

Alex raised both legs out of his bath and arranged them on either side of the taps. Now he could bend his knees and submerge his head for a moment or two, taking care as he re-surfaced not to shoot a gallon of water over the back.

With a re-run of the day's strange events almost complete, he found himself in the hotel room where Carol had picked up her jacket and agreed to give him her phone number – a landline – the only moment when he seemed to have any control over the situation. It also had to be admitted, of course, that it was the jamming of the Tube brakes that had actually propelled him over the chasm, from the country of hopes and dreams, where it is always autumn, to the dazzling snow-capped land of consequences.

But when he stood, shaking the water off himself and pulling a towel down from the top of the bathroom door, he couldn't quite suppress a smile. It had, after all, been a bit of a day, hadn't it? A bit of a fortnight, come to that. But what did it *mean*?

After pouring himself a glass of white wine, Alex sat on the garden step to cool off. Now that the afternoon's rain had gone, it had turned into a fine evening of high white clouds, long shadows, and the tangy smell of barbecue smoke drifting over the lawn. After inspecting the bruise above his right ankle, prodding its purple heart and tracing its yellow penumbra, Alex had just closed his eyes, Carol on his mind, but a dying world, too, and a speech that, though certainly original, seemed somehow familiar, when his phone rang out from the living room.

His towel in one hand and Samsung in the other, Alex began by negotiating a lunchtime rendezvous with Bill for the following day. Then, on checking his voicemail, the first to emerge was a polite female's, apologising and confirming that his appointment in the morning was indeed for an X-ray and not for the prostate biopsy their letter had indicated.

And the second, as the closing of a door finally muffled a medley of traffic sounds, was a male's, transmitting in a light Arabic accent the fact that Burhan was in town and would be free to meet in a day or two, should Alex have the time.

7

Alex only had two modes of arrival for lunch or any other rendezvous – early and so early it constituted a mental health problem. He considered this as he waited, at length, for Bill, cutting at the branch and foliage of his attitudes until he discovered with a shock that it all sprang from his underlying ideal of life as a clearing where nothing ever happened, a nirvana of unbothered existence. A meeting, therefore, or anything else for that matter, even when it was arranged by him, was *always* an intrusion, a form of minor assault. Thus, he concluded, it must be that he arrived early to arm himself, to claim the high ground.

Alex sat back in this train of thought and looked out over his empty half-pint of beer at the passing countryside, where an eastern European barmaid turned to milk an optic, her woollen dress, pulled in at the waist by apron strings, accentuating the line of a perfect figure, nurtured, he imagined, by cold dry winters, root vegetables drawn from the Baltic soil, and long farm summers with outdoor evening dances.

He was just completing his own waltz with Carol, under the stars, when Bill showed up and got them both into lunch mode, ordering meals, pints and extra half-pints in case the hot food arrived when their drinks were at a low ebb. Soon he was saying, "What's up with *you*, anyway, Alex? You don't have the dead-fish eyes of a man who's done a morning at work."

"I've been up at the hospital. I had a bit of a dizzy spell a couple of weeks ago."

"Really? And what did they say?"

"They're going to send the results to my GP."

"Are you worried?" asked Bill, taking a gulp of his beer.

Given the circumstances in Regent's Park, Alex would have been concerned if he hadn't fainted. So he told Bill instead about the biopsy letter he had received from the hospital.

"You know what that is, Alex? It's not a mistake. It just came twenty years early!"

Bill was very amused by this thought, almost choking on his beer. "Anyway, while we're at it, how do you define 'prostrate cancer'?"

Alex wasn't in a mood to be drawn.

"The one that always floors you!"

Bill *was* in a good humour.

"Why are you so cheerful?" asked Alex.

Whirlpooling the second half of his first pint, Bill smiled. "I managed to get Jessica to go out with me yesterday lunchtime."

"I thought she'd shut the front door in your face," said Alex.

Bill looked wistful. "True. But it was nicely done. I took it as her way of beginning a dialogue. And she let me keep calling."

"She contacted the police," said Alex.

"That was a bit of a misunderstanding. Anyway, things seem to be on the right track now."

Alex wasn't convinced. "You asked her out to lunch and she said yes?"

"Actually, she said she was hungry."

"And it went okay?"

"It was lively," said Bill, taking a contemplative pull on his beer. "I don't think she likes me much."

Alex couldn't quite think how to continue the conversation. And then the barmaid brought the food, smiling and retreating, swinging her way ahead of him on a country lane in Latvia, leading them all to the dance.

Bill meanwhile was cutting into a sausage. "Jess told me about Céline. She says she's seeing someone called Mike."

"Mike?"

"He's a colleague of Paul's."

"What, Paul, her flatmate?"

Bill nodded.

"So you're going out with Jessica, who doesn't like you, and Céline's seeing Mike, who's a colleague of Paul, who can give you a full two hours on the beauty of a stock option scheme?"

Bill looked up. "He's done that to you too? He said I could share his roast pork dinner, but the pig must have been alive, pretty young, and eating acorns somewhere when our conversation started."

"Mike," repeated Alex.

Bill pulled a face. "Your problem, Alex, is you don't want anything to change. You're the ultimate conservative. You want every girl who's ever fancied you still to fancy you, and be available in some parallel universe where anything *could* happen but nothing actually does."

They ate on in silence, Alex already hugging the shore of a different island. He picked up his glass and held it above the table. "Bill?"

"Yes."

"If someone gave you a speech about needing shelter and food, and of not being afraid, or afraid to talk, does it sound familiar?"

"Roosevelt?" said Bill, spearing a chip.

"What?"

"We studied it at school, don't you remember?" replied Bill. "The four freedoms speech that led to the setting up of the UN."

"Vaguely," said Alex, chewing on a piece of battered fish.

"Freedom from want, freedom from fear, freedom of speech," continued Bill, counting on his fingers, "and something else."

"Freedom of worship," said Alex after a moment, recalling Burhan with his Jews, Christians, and Muslims in Cordoba. "I think she mentioned that, too. Or prayers, at least."

"*She?*" asked Bill.

"This girl I met."

Bill looked up.

"Though I'm not sure I want to talk about it yet," continued Alex.

His companion put on a mock-surprised expression. "And there I was, preparing for a blow-by-blow."

"But there is something else," said Alex, ready for once to distance himself from the far end of the spectrum of reticence, where guys in greatcoats stamped their feet and smoked.

"Go on," prompted Bill, through a mouthful of peas.

"I took a break by myself a couple of weeks ago," said Alex, "and went abroad."

"Oh. Where to?"

"Oman, where I had that work placement. I fancied doing nothing for a while in a business hotel by the sea."

Bill pushed his plate away. "Quite a long way to go, but it sounds all right, I think."

"I met a chap there called Burhan, who's a lecturer with five kids. He collects old books and maps and has spent quite a lot of time looking for a kind of antique print. Seems a bit obsessed about it, actually."

Alex felt the usual mix of things when he tried to describe a significant event from his personal life: inadequacy in conveying the flavour of the experience, a kind of boredom and something else besides, close to a sense of betrayal.

"What's the print of? Is it valuable?" said Bill, sitting back, looking at his watch.

"It's biblical. Quite unusual, I think," replied Alex, going as far as he wanted to, as far as he could go, in fact, without endorsing Burhan's claims. "He's in London at the moment, actually, continuing his search.

I'm meeting him tomorrow."

Bill looked at him for a moment, before pushing his chair back and straightening his tie. "Let me know how it goes," he said. "It might be interesting if you don't get dragged in too far. Are you ready to walk?"

Burhan, it turned out, had got a two-week deal from a budget hotel near Russell Square, handy for the bookshops and also for the School of Oriental and African Studies where his old friend Don Millman worked as a researcher in Islamic studies. Alex had arranged to meet them for an early dinner in the canteen of the nearby School for Tropical Medicine. Now they were halfway through dishes of fish in chilli sauce and a salad that was so comprehensive as to be a kind of Noah's Ark of the nut and raw vegetable world.

Burhan was grinning and wearing a smart navy-blue V-neck jumper under his jacket, while Don looked gaunt, as if he had gone a few rounds with cancer or TB, but raffish too, like David Niven in the first *Casino Royale*. For ten minutes or so he had been quizzing Alex on architecture, taking a surprisingly measured interest in what Alex knew to be his half-baked replies.

Burhan was telling them both about seeing a fox the previous evening coming out of the graveyard of Southwark Cathedral with a rat in its mouth. "Can't we make it into a metaphor for something?" he laughed. "Don, Alex?"

"It sounds like the name of a pub," said Alex. "The Fox and Rat."

"Of course!" said Burhan. "One of those dark pubs by the river, where you think you'll see water seeping into the cellar bar."

Don covered his mouth for a cough that, though it didn't come, made his eyes glisten. "I don't know about a metaphor," he said, pushing his plate away, "but you could argue that every city has a period when it becomes most essentially itself. Athens in the era of Alexander ..."

Burhan smiled at Alex. "... Cordoba in the time of Averroes ..."

"Exactly," said Don, "except that London has two, the periods of Shakespeare *and* of Dickens." The cough came, and Don covered his mouth with a handkerchief.

"So?" said Burhan, emptying the last of the water into his friend's glass.

"Well," said Don, wiping a tear from his cheek, "according to Isiah Berlin, Shakespeare was a fox, a diffuse thinker, rather than a hedgehog, which links all its thoughts to a single world view, while Dickens ..."

"... had a morbid fear of rats," laughed Burhan.

"That's right," said Don, turning to Alex. "He could never put his hand in his coat pocket without worrying he would find a rat."

Don got up to get some more water, and Burhan reached out to touch Alex on his sleeve. "Can I tell you something?" he asked. Alex nodded. "I think, after a significant piece of good fortune, I've finally caught up with the photographic cloth."

"Really? Where is it?" asked Alex.

Burhan grinned. "Where else? In the basement of the British Museum."

"Can we see it?" said Alex, a flash of excitement in his chest.

Burhan was about to respond when Don returned, placing a jug of water on the table and narrowing his eyes at Burhan. "The miraculous cloth, I presume."

Burhan smiled. "Don's going to help us," he said.

8

Alex was afraid of the British Museum. His memory from early visits was of a fairly interesting collection of practical or pretty objects, infiltrated throughout by images of living creatures grotesquely made up of human and animal body parts. In his mind the past became a place where you might be going about your daily business, throwing a clay vase or watching your stick-spear bounce off a bison, when some obscene character with a man's body and a jackal's head would emerge from between the rocks, swaying slightly from the strong sweet beer they brewed for themselves, and force you to engage in a painful and one-sided act.

Jackal head aside, daily life for the ordinary person in any of the Museum's geographical or chronological zones seemed very much on the dour side to Alex. Freezing cold, of course, if you were herding yak on the tundra, but even in places like Egypt you tended to find yourself breaking your back working eighteen-hour days, hauling stuff around. And then in the evenings, wherever you lived, there seemed to be a mad idea that the pleasantest thing you could do was to get into a smoke-filled shack with most of your neighbours.

On the plus side, he supposed, there must have been the odd moment of truly primal sensation, wandering the veldt at dusk as a fiery sun melted the top of an anvil mountain, or waking to a pair of dawn buttocks pressed gently into the groin, under the animal skins of the communal dormitory.

Sipping weak museum tea, Burhan and Alex waited for Steve, their guide to the storage labyrinths that lie beneath the floor of the main building.

"How did you meet him?" asked Alex.

"He's a friend of Don's. Apparently, they drink a pint of beer together on the first Thursday of every month in a pub on Coptic Street."

Burhan looked round as Steve loped towards them in the kind of tan coat that ironmongers wear. "You're both security-friendly, then?" he said with a grin, tags and badges flapping on their clothing as they stood to greet him. In his early sixties, with long teeth you could floss with string, and combed-back hair the colour of a nicotine-stained finger, Steve nevertheless struck Alex as a man who seemed as comfortable as you can be in the semi-porous fabric that binds bone, blood and vital organs.

Alex and Burhan followed their guide along a public corridor until they reached a concealed door between two display cabinets. Selecting a key from the bunch on his belt, Steve led them through – the portly scholar from Oman that Don had vouched for, with his research assistant in tow, both allowed to view the recent delivery from Indonesia.

The first room they entered from a short, dark corridor was a high-ceilinged workshop with arched windows, divided into small studios. It smelt of shoe-repairers' glue. Steve looked around lovingly. "This is where we mend things," he said. "You'd be surprised by how much gets broken in transit. We can't own up to all the damage, so people like John here put it back together again so as you wouldn't notice."

Alex wondered to what extent Steve was joking as John, acknowledging the visitors with no more than a twitch of the head, continued what appeared to be the work of attaching an arm to a small stone archer. Perhaps Alex had got it wrong in laying the blame for the animal hybrids on the ancient world? What if, as late afternoon slipped into evening, John stayed on, sipping Polish vodka, high also on glue, letting his imagination unfurl, sticking this onto that?

They walked on past farther studios, similar in layout, reckoned Alex, to one of those tedious living craft museums in Devon or Jersey except much dirtier, where the artisans looked up if at all with a scowl rather than a welcoming smile. Steve was chatting to Burhan as they finally got into a trade lift with battered green doors, and began their descent to Level -4, interrupted only once by the entry of a woman carrying a bronze head under one arm and a bucket in the other.

Here they were led along a corridor by Simon, a short man in a baggy suit, who had an odd way of stretching his head up or weaving slightly to the right or left, as if he were discreetly replaying a classic football match, until they reached a large room, lit by strip lights, filled with opened crates of different sizes, their contents removed but covered still in brown dustsheets and plastic padding.

"Here we are, gentlemen," said Steve. "The inventory's been checked, but the real work won't start till next week." He chuckled. "Most of it will never see the light of day, of course." Alex surveyed the collection, which was heavy with the smell of dust and resin. Here and there a human arm or animal leg had broken free of its wrapping, or a wild eye stared back at him.

Burhan meanwhile strode forward, disappearing between two of the largest crates, Steve grinning and nodding at Alex to follow, Simon with his eyes on the ceiling, tracing the trajectory of a free kick perhaps, but at least not raising any sort of bureaucratic objection. By the time Alex had joined him in the far left-hand corner of the room, Burhan had set three cylindrical tubes to one side and was examining the tags on the remaining two.

"This is the one," he whispered, his plump hand on the sealed lid.

"How do you know?" asked Alex, wanting to reach out and touch it himself.

Burhan smiled. "I memorized the number from the copy of the catalogue I acquired."

"Are you going to open it?" said Alex.

Burhan shook his head. "No. We're going to leave it here and report back inconclusively to our companions. I'll explain later."

'Later' took place in Regent's Park, which Alex and Burhan had entered from Baker Street at around seven p.m. Now they were crossing a bridge over the narrowest part of the boating lake. Though a breeze was getting up, it had been a hot day on the streets, and there was a feeling of release amongst the passers-by, of unlived life bubbling to the surface in the warm evening air.

Burhan had other things on his mind. "If I say nothing about the cloth," he speculated, "perhaps it will just linger forever in some storage area of the Museum, obscure but safe."

"But if you know it's there," said Alex, "won't someone else eventually, like those two men who visited your library? How did you hear about it coming to the Museum?"

Burhan smiled as they continued their way around the lake. "Don't worry. There's no epic tale attached to this. There had been rumours for years that the cloth was 'somewhere in Indonesia.'"

Alex shook his head. "Not a very helpful phrase."

"Quite. But a month ago I got a phone call from a Malaysian dealer who knew about my interest in the cloth, though nothing of its origins. He said that the widow of a Sumatran businessman, an Englishwoman, had recently donated her late husband's collection of artefacts to the British Museum and did I, for a price, want to see a copy of the inventory their solicitor had drawn up?

"I couldn't believe my good fortune," he continued. "When the document arrived, it was immediately clear to me that the cloth had been included in the gift. For the moment, I felt I might be the only person in the world who knew its whereabouts *and* its true significance."

Alex motioned Burhan to go first through a small gate into the park's Inner Circle, saying, "In an ideal world, what would you want done with the cloth?"

Burhan stopped and turned. "First, I accept that its provenance would need to be investigated." He smiled and rubbed his hands. "But once we're all agreed, I would want it to be secured for public viewing in Spain near its original site, protected from its enemies." Burhan lit himself a cigarette. "Under its banner, so to speak, scholars could discuss the common points of the world's great religions. Now and again the cloth might tour to Egypt or New Delhi or even, one day, to Rome." He smiled again and looked at Alex. "I know, I'm a hopeless idealist."

They walked on in silence for a while. Then Alex said, "Who do you think sent those two men, and how did your father get involved? Surely you must know by now."

"Yes and no," replied Burhan, drawing so heavily on his cigarette that he almost set it alight, "but don't you think *you* know enough now? Too much, perhaps, for your own safety?"

Alex smiled. "That's not fair, is it?"

"Very well," replied the scholar after a moment. "But I'll need to tell you a little more about my own origins first." They had entered the Broad Walk, and were making their way towards the zoo.

"Until two hundred years ago," he went on, "my family were a pretty undistinguished lot. Some sheep farming, a bit of stonemasonry, and, after that, as far as I can work out, a line of cobblers and assistant butchers. In 1842, however, my great-great-grandfather was betrothed to Mumtaza, a woman who seemed on the surface to be as timid as any of her peers. One day, soon after they were married, she set out for a walk along the river, saying she knew where some special herbs grew, and would be back in an hour. In fact, she was away for two days. When she returned, the village was in uproar, of course, but she wouldn't say where she had been. I don't know how she explained this to Azhar, her husband, but fortunately he supported her right to silence, and the furore gradually subsided. But Mumtaza had changed. Over the next few months, she taught herself to read, insisting on setting herself apart from the family for an hour a day with her books. Believe me, this was quite an achievement at that time. And when her children were born, three boys, she read to them, too."

"And her husband remained supportive?"

"I think he was a little frightened of her, actually. People talked of her having powers, though I suspect this was simply because she chose to be different. They said she must have met a spirit on her walk."

They had reached an ornate water fountain, not far from the spot where Alex had had his blackout. Feeling a dull ache in his ankle, he said to Burhan, "Shall we get something to eat? There's a place near here where they do noodles and things, if you like."

Soon they were sitting outside the New Culture Revolution near Camden Town Tube station, plates of stir-fry chicken in front of them, now half-eaten. Burhan removed a piece of noodle from his beard. "Of Mumtaza's boys," he resumed, at Alex's request, "Bashir, the first-born, became a teacher, Sabri a traveller and writer, and Ibrahim, the youngest, a businessman. Bashir is my side of the family, four generations of badly paid academics and librarians. My father attempted to break the mould, of course, by going to Paris and trying to make some money, but that didn't last long, did it? With Sabri, the details are less clear. We know he went to university in Shiraz and then made a trip to Afghanistan and India, because he wrote a short account of it. But after that there are only rumours. My father told me he had a son who married an Irishwoman. Who knows? Sabri's descendants are a kind of ghost-line between the two halves of the family."

Burhan re-lit the cigarette he had extinguished when their food arrived. "Ibrahim's story, though, is well-documented. After all, it is the beginning of a dynasty. He started out as a traveller like Sabri but eventually made a base for himself in Alexandria and began trading in anything that would turn a profit. Though I have no talent in this area, Alex, I can appreciate the skills and the nerve. Imagine standing as a young man in the docks of Alexandria in the latter part of the nineteenth century. You're about to risk a portion of your precious capital on something like saffron. The ship comes in, the unloading begins, and the bidders arrive. All of them to the last man, of course, look sharper, more experienced, and more ruthless than you. But you have a hunch, and, in your eyes, it gives you an edge. You argue and bargain, but stop at your limit because your margin is going to mean everything in the weeks that follow. And as you walk away, you think the seller will never call you back, but he does."

Burhan poured himself some more Fanta. "The saffron gets put in a warehouse, and now you wait. How long you hold onto your goods matters vitally. Two weeks later, perhaps, a source you half trust in a teahouse near the port says that the price of saffron is high and rising in the markets of Esfahan. So you negotiate transport by sea past Haifa, along the coast of Lebanon, up to Latakia, by barge down the Euphrates to

Baghdad and by mule across the Zagros mountains to Esfahan. But you're a businessman now, of course, not a traveller. You don't make the journey yourself because you need to remain at base, making the next deal. Instead you entrust the saffron to Jules, say, the son of a French sailor you've met. But even if you knew the boy well, it wouldn't help. It's not based on loyalty with these types. It relies on self-interest. All you can do is hope that at this moment in Jules's life, it suits him well enough to work steadily for one master and make a regular wage. If you're right, he'll return in six weeks with profit and a consignment of Persian musk oil for the perfume makers at nearby Ismailya." Burhan sucked the remainder of his Fanta through his straw. "And in this way, and with these talents, Ibrahim became rich."

"What did he do with his money?" asked Alex as the waiter collected their plates and left the bill.

Burhan cupped his hand against the breeze to light a fresh cigarette. "Well, he'd made enough by his early thirties to marry into Alexandria's minor aristocracy and soon they had a daughter and two sons. I think the rot set in with the elder boy, Hisham. Ibrahim, of course, had planned to bring his sons up to respect application, discipline, and so forth – all the things that had worked for him and made their family life so comfortable. But, unless a child has some innate sense of these things, what can you do if he knows he's set up for life? With Hisham, it was a kind of fecklessness that brought him down, a butterfly movement throughout his life from one scheme to another." Burhan shook his head. "Even in his seventies, there is a record of him trying to interest the military in some bizarre new type of weaponry. The only practical thing he did, however, was to appoint a day-to-day manager who succeeded, despite Hisham's best efforts, in investing most of the family fortune in property."

Burhan knocked the ash from his cigarette and looked at Alex for a moment. "Faroukh, Hisham's only child, was different but, as I've discovered, much worse."

"Faroukh, who set up the trading company in Paris?" asked Alex, downing the last inch of his beer.

His companion nodded, taking cash from his wallet and refusing Alex's contribution. "But I've done enough talking for today," he said, pushing his chair back.

"Will you finish the story tomorrow?" asked Alex.

Burhan agreed. "But tell me about *your* family now," he said. "You mentioned in Salalah that your father was a vicar."

"Adoptive father, actually," replied Alex, as they made their way to the

Tube station, his mind still on Ibrahim at the docks. "My mother died when I was a baby, and my natural dad had a kind of breakdown. He couldn't cope, anyway. So I was fostered and then adopted."

Burhan stopped and turned to him. "Alex, I'm so sorry."

"No, it's fine. I had a good upbringing," said Alex, shrugging, though his companion's sympathy had a new, slightly unsettling effect on him.

They walked on, crossing Parkway.

"And are you in touch with your natural father?" asked Burhan.

"No," replied Alex. "He wanted us both to make a fresh start, apparently." He strode ahead, Burhan following as they turned onto the high street. "I may try to contact him one day, though," continued Alex over his shoulder, doubting the words as he said them. "When I'm ready."

"Of course," said Burhan as they approached the station.

After leaving the scholar at the Tube, Alex doubled back to Regent's Park, thinking first that he might find somewhere quiet to tap his knee, but then, as soon as he had entered through Gloucester Gate, making his way instead to the spot where the fairy had appeared three weeks before, daylight fading now with the approach of dusk.

What if he waited there? Might she re-appear and answer some of his questions - why she had half killed him with her wand, for example, or made his early flights so tortuous? And whether it was she who had led him to Burhan, even to Carol?

As he reached the spot where the path rose before dipping down to the Broad Walk, Alex looked over towards the bushes that had concealed his wrecked body and took up position, glancing theatrically at his watch as a bloke in a T-shirt and khaki shorts strode past him towards Camden. "Fairy, please," he finally muttered, looking up at the sky, "where are you?"

"Alex Harrison?" came a voice behind him, far too low for the fairy.

He turned.

"My name is Khalid," said a man, Middle-Eastern in appearance, with a neat moustache, a black jacket, and smart dark-blue jeans.

"How do you know *my* name?" said Alex, sweat itching at his armpits.

"Through your association with Burhan, of course," replied the man.

"What do you want?" said Alex, his tapping finger ready.

"I need to tell you a few things, my friend," replied Khalid, folding his arms and smiling. "Charming though Burhan undoubtedly is, he's also a liar and a fantasist. Hadn't you realized that?"

Alex shook his head.

"He picked you up on the beach and offered you a room, I suppose?"

"We met on the beach, yes," replied Alex.

"And now, with his absurd stories, he's enlisted your help."

Alex didn't reply.

"What were you doing at the museum?" asked Khalid, looking downwards, kicking a twig from the path.

"Nothing," said Alex, his armpits now unambiguously wet. "Just visiting."

Khalid stepped closer, well into Alex's personal space, remaining there in eye contact until a young woman in a red tracksuit had jogged past them towards the zoo. He placed a hand on Alex's elbow. "If you care about Burhan," he said, "or yourself, for that matter, you'll want to make sure that the article in question, the thing that has brought us all to London, is returned as swiftly as possible to its legal owner, who happens to be my boss."

"Who is that?" said Alex.

"So when you have information," continued Khalid, reaching into his top pocket and producing a business card, "I'd like you to call me. After that, we can all get back to our own lives, can't we?" He smiled again. "Architecture, isn't it? A noble calling."

Stepping to Alex's left, Khalid walked onwards a pace towards the zoo. "Salah is the name of my boss," he concluded, turning his head. "And we'll keep this evening's meeting to ourselves, shall we?"

9

The first person to enter Alex's half-waking mind the following morning wasn't Khalid – or Carol, as he had come to expect – but Mark.

This was Bill's fault. He had told Alex in a late-night phone call that their old drinking pal, apparently muddling along at British Gas, had in fact been writing a play that was about to be premiered at the National Youth Theatre. Now Mark would join the chorus line of characters who danced their way across the landscape of his pre-waking psyche, taunting him with their achievements. David Austerley, for instance, the school über-performer, rugby captain with a place at medical school already in the bag and recently, Alex was appalled to discover, part of a research team poised to eradicate some heart-rending kiddies' disease. Or Scott Wolff, a north London actor four years Alex's junior, seen regularly on YouTube riding Kawasakis in Africa, or messing about with guns on a ranch in Texas.

Alex pushed his face deeper into the pillow in a subconscious attempt to suffocate himself awake. With the process hardly begun, however, he finally came to, a chill settling on his chest as he remembered Khalid, but something else also, some notion that must have been at work in his sleeping mind, because now he realized what Burhan, friend or fantasist, must do with the cloth.

After meeting at Embankment station, Alex and Burhan had stopped halfway across the Hungerford footbridge to look downriver towards St Paul's. The sky was blue and the air fresh. Seagulls glided, flapped, and sometimes screamed above them. Passing Londoners looked scruffy and weekendish. Tourists were brisk and more purposeful.

"Look at that dome," said Burhan, who was sporting a generous tweed jacket. "With a coat of blue paint, it wouldn't be out of place in Samarkand, would it?"

After Alex had done so, he cast a glance sideways, wondering how close Khalid might be. If he mentioned him to Burhan, of course, the scholar would surely clam up. So they walked on in silence towards the South Bank, Alex with a careful lope on his bruised ankle, stiff in the mornings, and Burhan with a slow swing of his shoulders. "Shall we get a cup of coffee?" said the scholar finally, pointing in the direction of the British Film Institute.

With their cappuccinos in front of them on an outside table, Burhan lit a cigarette.

"What date are we up to?" asked Alex.

The scholar smiled. "Faroukh was born in 1915, but we're going to press forward fairly rapidly to an evening in 1985. My mother was holding a party to celebrate my older brother's marriage. It wasn't long since we had returned from France, in fact. The weather was fine, and most of our guests were in the garden. At dusk, when people were thinking of returning to the house, I saw the back gate open and a tall figure move inside. I thought it must be a late arrival or someone coming to meet a guest. I tried to catch my mother's eye, but she was busy collecting people's plates. So I went over myself. When I got to the end of the garden, the stranger had folded his arms and was leaning against a tree. The light was fading, and he wore a hat with his western suit. But I'll never forget his sharp eyes and white teeth, nor the short conversation we had that evening."

Burhan lifted his cup and put it down again without drinking. "I said, 'Are you here for the party?' and he replied, 'Don't you want to know what happened to your father?' I asked him who he was. 'You can call me Faroukh,' he replied. 'You and I are cousins, after all.' 'Yes,' I said, 'of course I do.' He laughed, Alex. Then he said, 'He wasn't cut out for business, was he? And he certainly shouldn't have taken a personal interest in my merchandise. But you don't know what I'm talking about, do you, cousin Burhan?' I shook my head, wondering how he knew my name, and asked him again what had happened to my father. 'Well, that's for you to find out, isn't it?' he replied, looking over towards the remains of the party and adding, 'Your brother seems to have other things on his mind.'

"At this point, my mother called out to me. So I asked Faroukh about the merchandise itself, hoping that might give me a clue. This time, instead of replying, he reached into his pocket and gave me a small book. I have it still in my library, Alex. It's an anonymous work published in French in 1910, which contains a lot of fanciful rubbish, including a chapter that describes the cloth and talks of the power enjoyed by anyone who owns it. Before I could examine it properly, however, my cousin said, 'You'll hear many things about me after my death but the only thing that matters is that I am a *collector*, but a collector with a purpose. I probably won't get that piece of merchandise now, because of your father's little fit of integrity, and my son Mahdi is useless to me, but fortunately there is my grandson. He's four years younger than you, Burhan, but already shows the right attitude.' He grasped my arm, making me accompany him back to the gate, where he leant towards me, 'There are pleasures in this world, my cousin Burhan,' he said, 'but you need to be hard, like a diamond, to take them.'"

Burhan knocked the ash from his cigarette.

"Your father was handling the cloth as part of his job, then?" said Alex.

His companion nodded. "I've wondered, of course, what his 'fit of integrity' was, and whether it led to his disappearance. But I never saw Faroukh again, despite trying to contact him. The last few years of his life were given over to the legal proceedings taken against him for events that occurred at his so-called dining club, including the death of a young female servant. Things my father wouldn't have known about when he took the job."

"I still don't understand why he chose to visit you," said Alex.

"It was a gamble," said Burhan, stubbing out his cigarette. "Soon he knew he would have two of us pursuing the cloth, his grandson and me, and if I found it first, well, my young cousin would have the means and the will to take it from me."

Alex nodded. "Have you met him, the grandson?"

"Only once."

Alex stood. "Shall we walk on a bit?" he suggested.

They had passed Gabriel's Wharf by the time Burhan returned to the subject.

"It was at Faroukh's funeral in 1988," he said. "My cousin had moved from Alexandria, where he was no longer safe from prosecution, to central Iran. I was the only member of our side of the family to be invited to the funeral. I'm sure it was Faroukh's wish. My mother thought it might be a belated gesture towards unifying the family and said I should go. So I flew from Dubai to Esfahan where I was met by Faroukh's son, Mahdi, who drove us to his late father's villa, two hours west of the city. It was, and still is, I'm sure, a remarkable building, a kind of Moorish fortress in the mountains. Mahdi and Faroukh's widow were both polite with me, perhaps a little surprised that I had come at all. But I didn't meet my cousin at that point. He was still travelling back from school in Tehran."

"The following morning, I was left to my own devices and did some exploring in the villa. Most of the building was structurally sound, but it all had a rather neglected feel to it. Chickens had been allowed to run free in the grounds and some of the small irrigation channels were blocked so that most of the plants had died. Vegetables that should have been pickled were growing mould in storage. And the few staff that I saw had a kind of sly look about them. I can only assume that in the last months of Faroukh's illness, Mahdi had let things go."

They stood aside to let a small surge of tourists, heading for the Globe, pass them by, Burhan pulling out his soft pack of cigarettes and finding it empty.

"Shall we get some more?" said Alex, but Burhan shook his head.

"I think Fate requires me to take a rest for a while. Rushing towards an untimely death is as undignified as outstaying your welcome, don't you think?"

Alex smiled. "How did the funeral go?"

"Later that day," said Burhan as they both looked out over the Thames, "I watched them bring Faroukh's body, wrapped in white cloth, into a shaded courtyard of the villa, where an Imam led the prayers. Afterwards, about thirty of us, all men, made the slow walk to the cemetery. By the time we got to the burial ground, it was almost dusk.

"Two holes had been freshly dug in the ground, a narrow one, the length of a body, in the side of the main grave. After the bearers had placed the corpse in the smaller hole, there was a moment of silence. Then a kind of commotion broke out in the group opposite me. A young man, really a boy, had worked his way through to the front and began to climb down into the grave. Once inside, he took a flat stone out of his pocket and placed it under Faroukh's head, standing back afterwards in a pose of respect, before climbing out again. When he got to the top, he rubbed the dust off his clothes and looked over to where my group was standing. For a second, he caught my eye, and someone whispered 'Salah' in my ear."

Alex and Burhan continued their walk. With the freshness of morning gone, Burhan had taken off his jacket and folded it over his arm.

Alex said, "So you've never actually talked to him?"

"No," replied Burhan, "but whenever I make enquiries about the cloth, I usually discover that Salah or one of his associates has been there before, or gets there shortly afterwards."

"He wants to continue Faroukh's collection, doesn't he?" asked Alex.

"Complete it, yes. I didn't tell you, did I, that I saw the collection on the night of the funeral? After Salah had returned to Tehran, Mahdi took me along an underground passage, and we entered a large, dimly lit chamber that seemed to have been built out of a cave. But what extraordinary objects it contained! Grotesque carved heads with bulging eyes; bloodstained swords with enamel handles; wild-eyed hunting dogs fashioned from silver; stone friezes with monstrous figures; rows of thick, leather-bound books. If I could see these things now, of course, I might recognize one or two, but I was eighteen, Alex, and we were only there for a few minutes. Mahdi himself was not very forthcoming. He almost seemed relieved to tell me that the whole collection, with an inventory that was locked away, was to go to Salah on his twentieth birthday."

Alex and Burhan had passed under Southwark Bridge and were walking in the shadows of Clink Street.

"How old is Salah now, then?" asked Alex.

"He must be forty-two," said Burhan. "He's done well for himself, of course. As successful in his way as Ibrahim. Although he trained as an art historian in America and made something of a name for himself in the area of provenance and authenticity, he soon realized he could make better money buying up failing businesses – farms, factories, even a chain of private colleges – and making them efficient, by sacking people, I suppose. He has interests across North Africa and the Middle East. I don't actually know where he keeps Faroukh's collection these days. I suspect it's in a temperature-controlled vault of some sort. But I know there's an empty space, ready for the cloth."

Burhan stopped as they emerged into the sunlight and a breeze. "You know, Alex, it isn't really a collection at all but a kind of twisted narrative that defends the darkest possible interpretation of our life on earth. When the cloth is installed as an object of mockery, the society that Faroukh founded, the dining club I mentioned, which Salah maintains, will finally come of age."

Alex led them towards the Old Thameside Inn.

"I imagine this doesn't really make much sense to you, my friend," concluded Burhan. "But take it from me that Salah the man is not a very pleasant creature. There are many victims of his fits of temper, and of the physical intimidation by his men in which, I'm afraid, he often chooses to play a personal role."

"Though not in your library?" asked Alex.

Burhan shook his head, an expression of deep distaste lingering on his face as they took a table by the river, Alex going inside to order sandwiches and drinks. When he returned, his Omani friend was looking over at the replica of Drake's *Golden Hind*, docked by the side of the pub, a *Private Party* sign on the gangway and people in suits on the deck. "Now that you know all this," said Burhan, turning his head, "I think you should retreat, don't you, grateful as I am for your company?"

Alex, wondering how his companion would react if he told him about

Khalid, took a glug of his wine. It was time to say his piece. "You were talking yesterday about what you should do with the cloth," he said. "Well, what if this is the moment?"

The scholar frowned. "What do you mean?"

"Go to the Museum. Tell them everything you know. Make it public."

"Won't they lock me up as a lunatic?"

Alex smiled. "From what you've told me, and the contacts you've got, they would have to consider a scientific examination. The age of the cloth alone would make it an object of special interest."

"Salah would find out."

"Yes. But now the cloth would be in the Museum's hands. Out of yours. There'd be no point in Salah threatening anyone." Including me, thought Alex. "And later on," he continued, "you could still pursue your plans for drawing attention to its significance, couldn't you?"

"I see," said Burhan, turning to watch a pleasure boat passing them by on the river. As a group of children waved from the deck, he stood, took a large white handkerchief from his pocket, and shook it in their direction. Finally, he sat again, leaning forward for a moment and rubbing his eyes under his glasses. "I think you may be right," he said, looking up. "It's been such a long journey. But I think you may be right."

After leaving Burhan at his hotel and arranging to meet him in the middle of the week to see what progress he had made at the British Museum, Alex was now on Store Street with his own unusually busy weekend agenda.

First of all, he needed to call in at the office to pick up - and later, do some more work on - the plans for Jeremy's attic gallery in France. Then, on Sunday morning, he had agreed - why? - to go to Céline's and let Jessica try out a new herbal cure on his bruised ankle. For the evening, Bill had managed to track down a rare screening of *Kopje*, a coming-of-age drama set on a Macedonian farm. And finally there was the target he had set himself: to call Carol and invite her out on the kind of date that somehow might appeal to her, but what?

He had turned into Fitzroy Street and was now unlocking the front door to Schaeffer and Schaeffer. There was a light on in the far corner of the open-plan section where he worked with his team, so he shouted hello, and Gemma's head appeared above the partition as he approached. "Alex. I thought it might be you. You got Rod's text?"

"Yes," replied Alex, advancing towards his desk and trying not to take in his colleague's low-cut cardigan, the top button undone, the second under serious pressure. "We need to work Saturdays again, he said, until the Knowles job is finished and out of our schedule."

Gemma smiled and shrugged. "He wants to see you in his flat."

On his way up with his plans, Alex remembered that on a Saturday afternoon any number of Rod's loose entourage could be visiting, taking refuge from families, creditors, or just the cumulative oppression of everyday life. As he reached the last step, he paused with his hand on the door knob to see if he could identify any of the voices: Max's, certainly – a freelance Austrian architect with a blond fringe and a pocketful of miniatures for the occasional swift shot – and Constance's, potentially, Rod's buxom Dutch partner, who came up to town only when Dulwich got 'really boring'.

As it turned out, Max and Constance were perched at opposite ends of the corner sofa and an additional pair of shoes, Cliff's probably, a defrocked lawyer, lying low and attempting to run an off-piste travel agency from his briefcase, hung over the side of the top bunk bed in the next room. Rod meanwhile was upright and holding forth by the mantelpiece, smiling widely and wheezing, saying to Max, "Be serious. You ain't going to make any money in Buckinghamshire."

Max, leaning forward and holding his cigarette hand flat in front of his mouth as if it were a mask, had thought it a good idea, Alex remembered, to have an English wife and new baby in the country and now needed to acquire serious cash and, along the way, a fibre of emotional commitment, to support them. "No, Rod, I don't gotta be serious because it's obvious I'm right. You wouldn't see a lion coming at you, seven feet in the air."

"Coming at seven feet. I haven't tried that," said Constance, smiling widely while continuing to knit what Alex noticed was actually the end of the patterned jumper she was wearing. Rod was cackling too, inviting Alex to sit, and lighting a small piece of dope on the end of a needle. When it was hot enough to produce its own thin, gently curling plume, he passed it to Alex, who thought it unsporting not to inhale as much of the bluish smoke as he could through his nose. "We're not in church now, Alex," said Constance, still smiling. "It isn't incense."

Alex, embarrassed, passed the needle to Max on his left, whose practised suck, like a clarinettist's, diverted the vapour with maximum efficiency towards his mouth.

"Fugging hell, Rod," he said, "where did you get this shit? It's top of the range without a doubt, I would say."

"If I tell you that, Max," Rod replied, "all you East European boys will be out there snappin' it up and selling it to half the population of Aylesbury."

"Come on, Rod," Max continued, "you never give me a break."

Rod was pointing at himself now, already well into his main laugh's hissing-and-shoulder activity. "I gave you two hundred quid for that Scotch last week, didn't I? What happened to that, you German baboon?"

Constance looked up at Alex. "Max got conned in the pub by a lorry driver with a crate of malt whisky to offload, only there wasn't any whisky, was there, Max?"

Max shook his head gloomily. "I don't think there was a lorry either."

While Constance comforted Max, Rod caught Alex's eye. "Can you come into the kitchen for a moment?"

Although there were two doors into the kitchen-cum-sleeping area of the flat, the bed was in fact the only dividing feature, so they had to pass Cliff's prone form on the way and now stood opposite him, Rod unscrewing a metal coffee pot at its waist. "How soon can you pack your bags, Alex?"

Alex gave him a blank look.

"Knowles wants you on site in France to sort out some details," continued his boss, "and I want you to make real sure he understands this is when the journey ends." Rod grinned. "It'll be a gas."

Alex put out some small cups. "When does he want me to go?"

"Next weekend," replied Rod, "if we can get Cliff out of bed to arrange the tickets. And he says you can bring a friend if you like, for the trip." Rod smiled, narrowing his eyes. "It's okay with me. As long as we get Knowles out of our hair."

They both looked round. Cliff, detecting the smell of coffee, had begun to rouse himself with an extravagant display of stretching and groaning. They watched him for a moment, Rod grinning and hissing in counterpoint, Alex pondering the weekend to come in France.

By the time he got home it was almost seven, but Alex reckoned that a swim somewhere exotic might be just the thing to help him plan his phone call to Carol. Looking at the Guardian World Time Zones map he had Blu-Tacked to the kitchen wall, he realized he hadn't knee-tapped his way to Brazil yet, probably because a disastrous two months of low-budget touring had cast a pall over most of South America.

He had gone with Céline, Bill, and Bill's then-girlfriend, Maisie. Apart from ordinary backpacking misery, some distant gunfire on the border with Bolivia that they had convinced themselves was playful, and a long black centipede that Maisie *knew* was sharing her rucksack, Bill had been going through his shamanistic phase, figuring that if he could just locate, pluck, and smoke the right combination of South American leaves, large fragments of the world's ancient wisdom would be conferred upon him and, once 're-born', he could set up somewhere in the jungle, shave his head, and write it all down.

Anyway, it was the calm of a small church in Ipanema, where he had dragged Bill to escape from a particularly persistent local dealer, that Alex remembered, so that was where he would return now, his trunks on under his trousers, ready for his swim. According to the map, it would be about four in the afternoon. Sitting back, he visualized the shadowy pew in question, tapped his knee three times and repeated the mantra.

The journey itself was comparatively smooth, a naked, webbed-wing version of himself flitting at treetop level through a vast forest at night, expertly avoiding the oncoming branches like an oversized bat. But when he landed in the church, instead of his usual momentary daze, a profound sense of loss engulfed him, rising into his chest from the pit of his stomach, the smiling face of a young, black-haired woman engulfing his vision, and, when he looked down, his left arm wrong somehow, too wide, the hand veined and weathered.

Before he had time to panic, a great pressure pushed inwards on his ribcage, removing the breath from his chest and launching him headlong towards the centre of the church, a desperate rushing sound in his ears. Only when his left arm, scrambling in the ether, had managed to fasten itself to a stone column in the aisle, did he realize that, for the briefest of moments, he must have shared the same physical space as the burly middle-aged man who now turned towards him, no more than a mildly puzzled expression on his face.

The wetness chilled under Alex's arms as he clung to the column. Who was the dark-haired woman he had seen? The man's niece or daughter? Someone who had died too young? There was nothing Alex could say or do, of course, so he staggered out of the building into the welcome sunlight of an Ipanema afternoon, sweat stinging his eyes. After resting by a gravestone, he made his way towards the beach, stopping to change a ten-pound note, and then sitting outside a café with a beer.

This was disturbing, wasn't it? Another example of the fairy stretching his safety clause to breaking point. What if, on an outward flight, he landed himself in a pillar or column recently erected on the spot he had chosen? Would his atoms mix with the stone, so all he could do for the rest of his days was whisper enigmatic messages to startled passers-by? And what about the grief-stricken man in the pew? Would some of his sadness now be part of Alex's life, too?

He needed a swim.

After finishing off his beer, he walked out across the beach to find a spot where he could lay his cairn of clothes, trying, as he made his way, not to watch the Brazilian girls go by, out of respect for the man in the church and the smiling face of his young relative, or for Carol, who now, despite the trauma of his arrival, required his full attention.

The sea when he got there was pleasantly warm, and Alex soon found his rhythm, breaststroking a twenty-metre lane parallel to the beach. He reckoned he could do this for the next fifteen minutes or so, by which time he would have the strategy for his date with Carol fully worked out, partly worked out, or possibly, given his ability to approach a problem from more angles than mathematicians had yet discovered, not really worked out at all. But at least he would have put in the time.

The venue for the evening – Kettner's Champagne Bar in Soho – old-fashioned yet sophisticated, came to him quite quickly, except he spent the next few minutes wondering whether 'sophisticated' might not automatically mean 'unsophisticated'. Where was Wittgenstein when you needed him? Not on Ipanema Beach.

Now for the day and the phone call. He ticked off the first without a great deal of fuss. Weekends were out (too much pressure), as were Mondays (too gloomy). This Tuesday then, with Thursday as a reserve. But when should he ring? Alex got ready to turn in the water. Once back in his flow, it struck him that six p.m. the following day, after Sunday's dead hours of three to five, and shortly before he was due to meet Bill, was just about right.

All that remained was a time for the date itself. Meeting in the champagne area of Kettner's might allow him to rule out a conventional dinner, keeping things short and thus reducing his scope for buggering it up. So, with eleven o'clock as a reasonable weekday finishing time, and two hours long enough for a foodless first date, it looked like a nine o'clock start. Eight forty-five, to allow for coat removal and retrieval, bill-paying etc., would have been perfect but might, Alex felt, suggest an off-putting level of calculation.

Alex slowed to allow a begoggled bald man, whose mouth with neatly trimmed beard and moustache resembled the image of a vagina dentata Bill had once shown him on his phone, to cross his path. Life might well look complicated, reckoned Alex, as the man raised his hand in thanks, but all you really needed in the end, was a shock, a beer and a swim.

10

Alex stopped contemplating his ankle and looked out of the window. Sunday-morning sunlight was finally shining on the brown beer bottles and silver take-away containers of the wet, now gently steaming, Earls Court pavements. If he twisted his head to the right, he could just catch sight of the square's inhabitants, overdosed on sleep, making their way like zombies to the Tesco Express on the high street. Could Khalid be amongst them? Twisting his head at least took his mind off the fact that Jessica had arranged to leave him on the living-room sofa of their flat with his right trouser leg rolled up to the knee, his foot stretched out on a kitchen chair and a burning-cum-stabbing sensation where her herbal poultice clung tightly to his ankle.

And it also gave him a moment to reflect on the dream he'd had in the early hours of the morning, a bit of a nightmare, in fact, to begin with. He thought he was back in the church, fixed to the pew and unable to breathe, sweat soaking his shirt, but when he looked up, he found himself instead in a packed outdoor stadium, vast, it seemed, a speaker at the podium half a dozen rows below him. And as he shielded his face against the sunlight, the young man in black - everyone else was in white or yellow - finished his speech and turned to look round, over Alex's head, an anxious expression on his face. After a moment of silence, a female voice rang out, saying a word in a language Alex didn't recognize, and repeating it as if to convince the speaker, who finally smiled and nodded.

Alex reached forward to scratch his ankle, another voice somewhere above him now but male this time, and too deep for Paul. Then a bath being run. Jessica perhaps? Having gone to fetch 'a final herb', she was quite capable of forgetting him completely in favour of a random soak. Next a word or two from the voice again. Alex looked upwards. Good God, this couldn't be Mike, could it, staying overnight with Céline? A drop of sweat fell from his armpit as he stilled himself to listen - a splashing sound now from the bathroom, and afterwards, surely not, the first few notes of a slowly rocking rhythmic creaking?

It was certainly very regular. Too regular, perhaps, to be of human origin? Could it be coming from the kitchen instead, the boiler or the washing machine? No. It was definitely upstairs, and, as the seconds turned into minutes, Alex was forced to unleash the first straining pack-dog of his imagination, a vision of Mike muscled like Apollo, his piston buttocks at their zenith locked tight against the bedsheets. Hard on its heels came a picture of Céline's animated face, as she knelt on the bed, Mike's sweating, red-faced head rearing above her. Alex was about to release his third hound, when the living-room door burst open and Bill walked in, barefoot, in jeans and a T-shirt, holding his phone and a half-eaten sandwich.

"Alex! What the hell are you doing here, like that?"

"Jessica's been fixing my ankle. But what about you?"

"I stayed over after our second date."

"Didn't she tell you she was expecting me?" asked Alex.

"No. I mean, she got up an hour ago, saying she had something to do, but she didn't say it was you."

"Didn't you hear me at the front door?" Bill shook his head. "Where is she now, anyway?" continued Alex.

"Asleep in the bedroom, last time I looked. I was going to run her a bath, but there's no hot water."

"And did you actually ...?" Alex enquired.

"Sleep with her? Good God, no. Far too soon for Jessica, even if we had a future, which she says we don't. I slept on a kind of foam thing she keeps under the bed. I mean, she pulled it out. I didn't actually sleep *under* her bed."

Alex put a finger to his lips. "Can you be quiet for a moment?" Bill did, and Alex listened again. The creaking hadn't stopped. "Can you hear that sound, Bill?"

"Sure. That's Paul. He's got an exercise bike linked up to a screen. On a Sunday morning, apparently, he cycles through the Black Forest, probably offering pension plans to grovelling peasants on the way."

"And where is Céline?"

"Away with Mike this weekend." Bill chewed his sandwich wistfully and added, "Getting shagged senseless, I would imagine, in some rugger-buggers' hotel."

"Thanks for that," said Alex. "Are you still okay for tonight?"

Bill nodded. "You've got your own bird now anyway, haven't you?"

"She's still in the bush."

"Bush? Or canopy of the rainforest viewed through a satellite telescope?" Bill smiled. "And what about that bloke you met in Oman, who's now in London?"

Alex nodded. "He found the print he was looking for, in a storage area of the British Museum. He just needs to get it authenticated."

"That's good, isn't it?" replied Bill. "End of story?"

Alex was about to reply when Jessica rushed into the room. "Alex! I'm so sorry. I just went back to bed to warm my feet. I must have dropped off. How's your ankle?"

"It's quite painful, actually."

Jessica began to examine the poultice. "It doesn't look great, does it? I wonder if I used the wrong mix." She produced a pair of scissors. "I'm going to cut through the bandage," she said, loudly and slowly, as if he were a Bulgarian pensioner with a hernia. "Let me know if it hurts."

Alex nodded, and various types of hurt began almost immediately, continuing until the poultice had fallen to the carpet, his companions contemplating the mottled colouring of Alex's lower leg much as you would a canvas at the start of a private viewing, when interest levels in the artwork are still reasonably high. Bill broke the silence with a hint of Australian twang. "I reckon you're on the mend there, mate."

The comment was so breathtakingly out of tune with the evidence in front of them and the pain written across Alex's face that no one seemed to know what to say next. In the end, Jessica picked up the remains of the poultice and made for the bin in the kitchen. As soon as she was out of earshot, Bill, without altering his position, or his accent, said, "I reckon your ankle is totally buggered there, mate."

Alex got up and staggered around the room while Bill checked his phone and polished off his sandwich, before exploding into a fit of coughing and spluttering. Alex watched dispassionately as a small piece of wet bread shot past him towards the window, satisfied that a tiny element of the morning's suffering had now been shouldered by his friend, and Jessica finally returned in going-out mode but with a glass of red wine.

"Bill's taking me for an early lunch, Alex, and then we're going shopping. I hope you don't mind. This," she added, passing the glass to Alex, "is from Paul. He heard you were here, and he's getting a piece of lamb ready for the oven. You're welcome to join him in the kitchen, apparently. He's invited Richard as well, a friend of his who's been feeling a bit suicidal recently. Are you going to put some shoes on, Bill?"

It was five thirty by the time Alex got home. The afternoon hadn't actually been so bad. The itching pain from the herbs had offered some distraction from Paul's talk, the lamb had retained a molecule or two of moisture, and Richard, emerging from his suicidal phase, was just very depressed but 'able to talk about it'. Alex, anyway, now had the phone call to Carol on his mind.

As he got out of the bath, he tried to picture himself in a brisk, James Bond-style hotel sequence: pouring himself a drink; crossing the carpet in his bathrobe; picking up the phone by the window; and finally, as he fingered open the slats of the blind onto the darkening Crab Key or Nassau nightscape, calling Carol's number. In reality, he rose to the challenge of the drink, carpet, and bathrobe bits. He just couldn't follow through with the call-making phase.

Instead, he walked twice round the sofa, sat in the armchair, got up, sat again, and finally lowered himself onto his knees, hoping he'd be ready by the time he had crawled across the floor. When he actually got to his Samsung on the window ledge, Alex loosened up his jaw by pulling the first two of his six or seven gargoyle faces. Then he pressed the call icon.

A man's voice, cold, said: "Hello."

"Hello. Um, is Carol there?"

"Anne Dewar?"

Alex was thrown. Was this an office or something?

"No, *Carol* please."

"Anne Dewar?"

What kind of an idiot was he talking to? Maybe he'd have a better chance anyway with this Anne person.

"All right then. Thank you."

The voice went from main part of the fridge to the freezer compartment.

"And. You. Are?"

"Oh, I see. I'm sorry. I'm Alex."

As the man's voice called for Carol, Alex tried to calm himself by returning to the state of high anxiety in which he had begun the call. Soon he could hear what he guessed were her footsteps approaching the phone across a tiled or wooden floor. Despite his nerves, the click of her steps, bearing evidence of the bodyness of the body above them, excited him. But who was frost-voice? Wasn't it a bit pointless asking her out if iceman was mixing her martinis?

"Hello, Alex. How are you?" she finally said.

"Um. I'm well, thank you," he replied from his position on the floor. "Are you okay?"

Carol confirmed that indeed she was.

Alex was enough of a discourse analyst to know this was the point where things needed to be moved on a little, but his mind had blanked out, so he prodded his herbally assaulted ankle, hoping to shock himself into focus. "Aaaargh!" he screamed.

"Alex! What are you doing to yourself?" she replied.

"Sorry," he said, "I twisted my ankle."

"But you're all right now?" she asked.

Alex caught a warmth in Carol's voice, which might have been satirical. "Yes, thank you," he said. "Look, I was wondering, you know, if we might meet up, on Tuesday perhaps? I don't know if you've ever been to Kettner's in Soho. They call it a champagne bar. We could meet there at about nine, say. In the evening. On Romilly Street. Sometimes they have music."

"Yes, I think I've got that."

"Um. Well?" said Alex, pulling gargoyle face number three while he waited.

"All right. I'll see you there."

It took him a few seconds to grasp the significance of Carol's utterance. Once he had done so, Alex signed off as quickly as possible to avoid the various opportunities he might easily take to blow the situation. Finally, he limped into the kitchen to see how much of the rest of the bottle of wine he could fit into his glass.

The warm glow from the wine and his success lasted as he dressed. Lasted too, as he travelled on the Northern line, walking afterwards through the streets of Bloomsbury towards the cinema. Lasted as he drank a swift beer with Bill, and continued to do so as the two of them realized they were in for a classic at the half-hour stage, when twelve-year-old Kopje began his third night on the mountainside, guarding the family sheep, with a faultless four minutes of wood-whittling, shot from three angles.

11

By eight twenty on the Tuesday evening, Alex had arrived at Kettner's to check out the basics: that the front door was where it should be, that it was open, and that there were people inside, drinking champagne. Now he was sitting in the nearby Bar Napoli with an espresso, wondering whether he should spend the next half hour in religious contemplation of the encounter to come, or instead permit his mind to wander, with whatever boost that might later give to his overall spontaneity. In the end, he weaved rather aimlessly between the two, like a monk on mead.

The side tracks included Burhan's phone call to him late the previous evening, as Alex had knelt on the floor with the plans for Knowles's house spread out in front of him. Apparently, his plump friend had made progress in his PR work on the cloth, drafting a short paper for the Museum and arranging an informal meeting with the deputy director of collections for today, which he would be able to tell Alex about in person when they met tomorrow. And on the ankle front, Alex noted only intermittent pain and throbbing as he stirred his coffee, remembering, too, that some of the new discoloration had gone. It was certainly worse, then, since he had seen Jessica, but at least the margin of worseness was diminishing.

In between these byways, Alex tried to organise his random recent thoughts on Carol into something coherent that might set him up for the evening. He sipped his espresso. She would have been attractive, of course, to anyone who had seen her on the Tube - glossy brown hair, dark-brown eyes, high cheekbones, and a self-assured though marginally kinky retro style of dressing. Despite her measured movements, Alex concluded, there was a kind of fundamental restlessness about her, a flux at the centre of her being as if the atoms and molecules themselves were in extraordinary motion, reaching out beyond her frame and returning, like bees to a hive. How had she come into his life? Alex ducked as a chicken sandwich was passed over his head. And what of the lines she had spoken in the hotel room after the rain? Rooseveltian, perhaps, lyrical, certainly, they seemed to consist entirely of a list of tasks to be fulfilled, like a poem co-written by Wordsworth and a Grasmere dominatrix. And then, of course, there was

Glacier Gary. Alex checked his watch and emptied his cup.

An hour later, he was looking at his reflection in the mirror of the Gents toilet at Kettner's. The evening had been going quite well. The excitement of seeing her again had carried him through the important first fifteen minutes. He realized, however, as he tugged at the blue loop of towel, that, agreeable though the rest of their conversation had been, they hadn't actually talked about anything significant yet. Walking across the crowded salon plus jazz band to where Carol was sitting, being gorgeous in a black jacket and sleeveless grey dress of a soft fabric unknown to him, Alex discovered his companion was thinking along the same lines.

"You haven't asked me yet about the man who answered the phone when you rang on Sunday," she said.

"Arctic Alan?"

Carol smiled. "John. But I know what you mean. He warms up a little when you get to know him."

"And are you, um, together?" Alex asked as lightly as he could.

"Yes, and he wasn't entirely happy I was meeting you in a champagne bar."

Right, thought Alex. Was she joking, or was that why she had given him the landline number – to make John jealous? "Is he a big chap, then?" he said.

Carol laughed. "He's muscular rather than tall. Is that better?"

"Much worse."

She laughed again. "I wouldn't worry, if I were you. I let him confuse you with my gay aromatherapist, who's also a friend."

As she looked towards the stage where a chanteuse in a blue dress had just joined the band, Alex poured her another glass of the mid-price champagne he had ordered, picturing himself in his aromatherapy salon with a bottle of lavender or myrrh, massaging the sweetly spiced liquid into her cool skin, all the way along from the stray brown hairs oiled to the nape of her neck to the short rise where the white towel met her waist. "I could do the therapy," he said when she turned back, "but I'd be shakier on the gay bit. I'm not at all strong on wallpaper or soft furnishings."

"That's a bit of a cliché, isn't it?" replied Carol. "I really don't think you've tried hard enough to understand the gay man inside you, Alex."

Alex smiled. Perhaps this was the moment. "In the hotel room *you* said you wanted to understand the world in your own way."

Carol frowned. "Can I just say first of all that I don't normally let strangers proposition me on Tubes?" Alex nodded. "Or kiss me on the thigh in hotel rooms, come to that."

Alex swallowed. "So why did you?"

"When I decided you weren't a maniac," replied Carol, "I thought I might give you a scare."

"And the speech you made?"

"I don't know where it came from, actually, but when I'd finished, it seemed to make sense. You need to be free to work out your own relationship with the world, don't you? You won't find it in a book, and you can't borrow someone else's, can you?"

Alex nodded, unhappily ruling out these two time-saving options as the singer took her applause. "And you talked about transcending," he added.

Carol looked at him for a moment, perhaps to check he was being serious, before replying, "Well, that *would* be the next step, wouldn't it? Once you know how you stand with the world, everything needs to change, doesn't it, into something new?"

Alex realized at that moment he didn't really have a philosophy of life. He just assumed you moved around reasonably autonomously, succeeding or not with things or people in a fairly random way, and repeating the successful moves whenever you could. "And did you have the sense," he said finally, taking a risk, "of time passing very slowly in the room, as if outside it might be, you know, *whizzing* by?"

Carol caught his eye. "Yes, perhaps," she replied, looking younger for a moment, before seeming to wise up again as something jollier began to distract her on the room's small stage, not quite Dixieland but involving two bald men extending and contracting their trombones like manically uncertain archers. As Alex turned to watch, she said, "What do you do, then, to earn our champagne?"

"I'm an architect. And you?"

"PA for a land agency, as it happens. What kind of buildings do you design?"

"Private commissions, mostly. We're working on someone's villa in France at the moment."

Carol leant forward. "But I would love to design my own house!" she said.

"What would it look like?" he asked.

"That depends on where it would be."

"On a hillside in the country, let's say."

"Wooden then, like a chalet but with an extra-wide veranda, where you could look out into the rain." She lifted her glass. "Actually, I've planned six or seven houses in different locations."

The champagne, her flushed face - and Jeremy's invitation - were beginning to give Alex a touch of that new destiny-changing impetus that led back along the Northern Line to the footpaths of Regent's Park and the featherweight fairy. "I've got to visit the villa on Friday, in fact," he said. "Why don't you come with me?"

"On Friday?" she asked.

"Yes," he said.

She span the liquid gently in her glass. Good God, she was actually considering it.

"I'd need to be back by Sunday evening," she replied. "And we are talking separate rooms, I trust."

"Certainly," said Alex.

"And what do you suggest I say to John?" she asked, looking at her watch and beginning to get her things together.

Alex picked up his glass and knocked back the remaining mouthful. "That there was a last-minute cancellation for a weekend aromatherapy retreat?"

Carol wrinkled her forehead. "Are you sure you haven't done this sort of thing before?"

Twenty minutes later, with Carol in a cab going west, Alex was allowing himself to wander the pavements almost at random but southwards in general, and therefore towards the river. A short line with 'nature' in it, possibly from school, definitely from Shakespeare, fluttered around the edge of his consciousness, never quite settling itself into a pattern of words. He walked past Charing Cross station and into Villiers Street. Three days in France with Carol. 'Eternity' was somewhere in the phrase too, wasn't it?

Crossing Embankment to the Thames, Alex leant on the wall and looked down into the water. A scene from the film came to mind, where the boy Kopje accidentally sees his mother naked, stepping out from the steam of the bath with her hair in a towel as if she were a woman in a painting.

The scent of fried onions beckoned him afterwards to the hot-dog stand by the bridge. And as he made his way along the pavement, he had the novel sense about him that, although the signposts might not yet be legible, he was actually beginning to walk along the pathway of his own life, *passing through nature to eternity*, in fact, just like the man had said.

When he met them at lunchtime the following day, Don Millman was taking his final drag on a flimsy roll-up and beginning a series of coughs that convulsed the top half of his body, continuing until the three of them entered the Pizza Express on Coptic Street, ordering a jug of tap water on the way to their table. Burhan was the first to take advantage of the calm. "I told Don about the new plans for the cloth."

Don signalled to them both that he wasn't yet ready to speak, so Burhan continued, "Anyway, I had a meeting with Michael Cross yesterday, the man at the Museum who makes decisions –"

"– advises committees," Don managed to interject, hand poised over his mouth. Burhan smiled. "Yes, of course. Well, he listened, agreed to read my paper, and said he would take a look at the cloth himself."

"That's excellent," said Alex, as the waiter brought their water.

Burhan nodded, adding, when they had placed their orders, "But he said that a second opinion from a mutually agreed expert will be vital before they carry out any tests."

"That won't be me, then," said Don, swallowing a mouthful of water and looking at Alex. "We had a row in a meeting over the provenance of a rather fine vase." He smiled. "To the extent that the charming Dr Cross will allow his voice to rise."

Burhan grinned. "No, but the person he *did* mention was one of my tutors at the School of Oriental and African Studies. Michael says he's retired now and raises free-range turkeys on a farm near Cobham."

Don nearly choked, this time with laughter. "Not Vivian Armstrong?"

Burhan nodded, and Don went on, "Then I'm afraid the turkeys will have ranged so free they'll be hiking on the North Downs. Did you ever attend a conference he organized or lend him a book? His office had to be sealed off periodically, Alex, for Health and Safety to attempt entry."

Glancing out of the restaurant window, wondering when Khalid might decide to drop by for an update, Alex listened as his companions exchanged memories of their colleague, Don finally saying, "But I see where Cross is coming from. You'll have your work cut out persuading Armstrong. Have you been in touch yet?"

Burhan looked sheepish. "I rang him this morning. After I'd explained why I was in the UK, he asked me if I had an international driving permit, which I do if I can find it."

"What?" said Don.

"I'm afraid I've agreed to pick up his car from a garage in Blackheath – don't ask me how it got there –"

"He'll have parked it on the way to London," said Don, laughing, "forgotten all about it, and taken the train back."

"... and drive it to Cobham tomorrow evening," concluded Burhan. "We'll be discussing the cloth on Friday."

"Don't you need insurance?" asked Alex, as Don smiled and shook his head at the arrangements.

"Apparently he has an 'any driver' policy," said Burhan, shrugging. "Actually, Alex, I was hoping you might be able to help me plan my journey, particularly getting clear of London." Alex agreed, wondering, as their pizzas arrived, if it were humanly possible to devise a route that would protect the citizens south of London from the scholar's erratic motoring skills. "I'll give you a ring, then," continued Burhan, leaning over his pizza, "as soon as I've got the endorsement from Vivian."

Alex smiled at Burhan's enthusiasm. "I'm travelling to France on Friday to do some work on a villa we're designing. There's no mobile reception yet, but you can call me on this landline if you have some news," he said to Burhan, pulling out his wallet and passing him Jeremy's business card, which the scholar pocketed after copying the telephone number into his eagle journal.

Don quizzed him on the villa as they ate their pizzas, amused by Jeremy's ambitions and describing a new museum he had recently visited in North Africa with a glass-covered courtyard, Alex finally having to tell him that the last thing Knowles needed at this stage was any kind of fresh idea.

Outside the restaurant, Alex watched his companions wander eastwards towards Burhan's hotel, Don's post-lunch cigarette provoking a new, now gently receding fit of coughing. Then he made his own way back to the office, planning to text Carol, on the mobile number she had given him at Kettner's, with the weekend itinerary Cliff had arranged.

Thirty hours later, with all the preparations made for his trip to France the following day, and having given up on the complex driving instructions he was due to deliver by phone, Alex found himself sunk low in the passenger seat of Armstrong's seriously dishevelled Ford Escort. They were well on the way to Cobham, where Burhan would drop him at the train station, Alex with a map on his lap, and a plan to keep the scholar away from most of the major roads. Although he had readied himself with a few topics of conversation, it was Burhan who had actually taken the lead, filling the first half hour of the journey with his news, including the fact that Cross, according to tobacco-haired Steve, had already indicated that the cloth would need to be moved to a lab, and that Safwaan, one of the scholar's associates and owner of a small IT business in Muscat, had said on the phone that he was close to locating some letters Burhan's father had written to an old school friend in the Omani capital shortly before his disappearance in Paris.

But now, in the lull that followed, Burhan was beginning to demonstrate around the car's main instruments of control the characteristic mixture of hesitancy and manic confidence Alex remembered from Salalah. He was also, Alex noticed, taking a particular interest in the rearview mirror. "That silver car has been behind us since London," he said. "Have you noticed?"

Alex hadn't, and was about to dust off his first serious piece of talk, when Burhan gritted his teeth and murmured, "Let's see if it follows us now," swerving out to overtake the battered blue transit van in front.

Re-centring himself on his seat, Alex took a look out of the window. Although the stretch of road ahead seemed straight and empty for the next half mile, he began to be concerned by the fact that the actual overtaking bit, the part where you really ought to be moving faster than the vehicle alongside you, wasn't happening. Either the Escort was losing power, or the van driver was trying to see Burhan off, Alex wasn't sure which.

Nor was he sure what to do. If he could talk to Burhan above the whining engine, it might restore the calmer driving mode that avoided this kind of situation in the first place, but it also risked losing them the maniacal bits of skill that now might be necessary to save their skin, particularly as the road ahead was set to turn to the right.

Alex looked across at Burhan, head down, smiling as he clung to the vibrating wheel, and then over to the van driver, his shadowy face fixed implacably forward. Both vehicles were taking the long bend reasonably well, and it wasn't until the road had straightened out again that Alex caught sight of the red tractor with its own retinue of delayed vehicles, still distant, but approaching the Escort head-on.

Retreating into his seat, Alex watched in alarm as the transit continued to match their speed, the gap between their rattling vehicles and the chugging tractor rapidly narrowing, until Burhan finally raised his head, not braking but pushing down so hard on the accelerator that his foot seemed to disappear into the fabric of the car, gaining distance on the van just as the tractor's giant wheels reared up before them, and then aiming the Escort at the car-sized gap to its left.

Alex closed his eyes.

When he opened them again twenty seconds later, Burhan had removed his foot from the accelerator, and was already indicating for the turn he would take into a minor road on their left, fifty metres ahead.

"Are you all right, my friend?" said the scholar as they made the manoeuvre, hedges on either side of them – the silver car long gone, reckoned Alex – and, as he nodded and looked upwards through the windscreen, a hawk or buzzard high in the sky above, cruising on a current of warm summer air.

12

Afternoon sun had turned the portion of the Loire that was making its way west towards the Bay of Biscay, six thousand feet below, into a channel of molten silver.

When Alex thought back to the early years of secondary school, it was actually bits of geography he tended to recall, perhaps because of the strange expressions that cropped up such as 'basket of eggs topography' and 'ribbon settlements', or simply due to the fact that the teacher, still in his PE tracksuit, would crack you on the head with a book if you looked like drifting off. Either way he was fairly sure that before turning westwards, the silver line below had already travelled two hundred miles up from the Massif Central.

Next to him, Carol turned another page in the book that her white gloves seemed to raise to the status of a relic. In fact, from what he had been able to make out from the back cover, it mainly featured Goethe making a walking trip through Italy. Alex, who had drunk most of Carol's wine as well as his own, spent the next five minutes idly wondering if there was a slim bestselling volume to be made out of someone else's holiday. Perhaps Beethoven had spent a few days fishing in Kent or Rembrandt had gone sailing off Corfu? Bill had been convinced, since a bloke his sister half-knew had knocked out a book on oranges, that there were easily researched pickings to be had in the world of non-fiction if you just got the subject and timing right. He was making a mental note to raise the vacation theme next time they were in the pub, when another warm wave of Carol's perfume reached him sharp and sweet, like a bowl of lemons and peaches ripening under the Calabrian sun, and he focused on that instead.

Someone sitting silently next to you, of course, offers very few visual opportunities, almost nothing in the way of touch and, unless he had overlooked an angle, even less in the sphere of taste. So you had to make the most of the other senses. In terms of smell, perfume aside, there was something bracing about her hair, wasn't there – perhaps a seaweed shampoo? And as for hearing, apart from the page-turning, there was also the rustle of her red silk dress and the occasional sound of her breathing. None of it was to be missed.

After taking a taxi from the airport to the railway station, Alex and Carol were soon on their way south to their hotel in Mont-de-Marsan. Carol had finished checking her phone, and Alex was sitting opposite her at the window end of their compartment, conversation all but ruled out by the full-volume chatter of the three passengers that had dived in with them as they pulled out of Bordeaux.

Right now the young couple next to Alex were being entertained in rapid French by their thin friend on Carol's side who, though only in his early twenties, was dressed like a spiv in a double-breasted suit. Could they have come from a wedding, the couple's, and be fairly drunk? At the moment the spiv was outlining with his arms the stereotypical curves of a woman, but as he got to the waist, he transformed his hands into fists and vibrated them with machine-gun sound effects. All three of them thought this was hilarious.

Alex looked over to Carol for some kind of a visual comment, but she was staring out of the window, mesmerized perhaps by the kilometres of darkening pine trees. From the ghostly image of her reflected face, he let his gaze drop to her lap, gloves in her left hand, her right, palm upwards, opening slowly like a flower in the light from the lamp on the window shelf. As she extended her fingers, he noticed with a shock that the lower part of the palm seemed to be covered by a paler square of grafted skin. Turning away, he wondered firstly why he hadn't seen it before and later, as they were pulling into the station, which new muscle in his heart had tensed at the sight.

"Of course, if I actually *was* at an aromatherapy retreat, I'd be drinking green tea now and eating muesli with bits of dried fruit the size of small horses." Carol paused to dip a croissant lightly coated with prune jam into her bowl of coffee. "And I'd be surrounded by people, well, women mostly, I suppose, dressed in those white kimono things."

"You sound like you're missing it," said Alex.

They were sitting on wrought-iron chairs at a small marble-topped table in the hotel's breakfast area. A beam of sunlight streamed through the high window of the narrow room, exposing a cross-section of dust in the air before falling onto the black-and-white chequered floor between their table and the buffet.

"I spent a day in fact in the place I'm supposed to be at now. It was a bit boring, actually. Nothing compared to the one I visited a few years ago in the Black Forest. That was wonderful. So serious. So *rigorous*." Carol's face glowed with the memory as she went on, "High ceilings, a boiler-room that hummed, and lots of treatments with German names in private rooms with metal doors. Quite invasive, some of them. And in the evening we all went into a kind of glass dome where there was white wine and, outside, just darkness and massive trees, and wolves, somebody said. You couldn't smoke, of course," she concluded with a smile. "Not that I do anymore, except occasionally at weekends."

Alex searched his mind for a holiday reminiscence with a dark edge to it or a wild animal, but he all he could think of was Bill's back and strangely undulating arms as he 'hypnotized' a snake on their path through the Brazilian Highlands, and his scream when the creature decided to launch itself through the air at them. Giving that one a miss, he pushed a last piece of croissant into his mouth and looked at his watch. Jeremy, who'd returned from Paris early that morning, was due to pick them up at the hotel at ten and drive them through the forest to the clearing where his house was being built, unbuilt, rebuilt, and generally mucked around with.

"Are you okay to meet me in the foyer in twenty minutes?" he asked. "You can smoke on the patio, by the way, if you want. I saw a man there with a cigar."

Carol pushed her chair back. "Thanks, but I've got my egg." Alex had seen the blue oval-shaped stone in the plane and now by her plate, but hadn't liked to ask. She rolled it with her finger. "When I want a cigarette, I touch it instead."

They stood, smiling at how much croissant was still attached in small flakes to their clothes. Alex brushed his from the smart jacket he had put on to feel business-like, and Carol from jeans and a pink blouse that made her look several years younger, quite untouched by tubes and brisk probing hands.

Once they were off the main road and driving through the pine forests, the trees seemed to thin out, offering more light than expected. There wasn't much to catch the eye on the flat ground, though – no wild flowers or streams, just dry grass or greener grass in the clearings. It went on like that for miles.

The sunlight, the trees, and the self-assured motion of the BMW had made Alex drowsy and quiet, which was all right because Carol was in the front with Jeremy, talking to him about how he had come to choose this part of France – childhood visits to an aunt – and afterwards about the house and the furnishings it needed. All right, but unnerving too, to see how immediately at ease she was with him in body language as well as conversation. Right now they were on to rugs – colours, materials, location in the house etc. – and it brought back to Alex the oppressive boredom he had felt in carpet warehouses with Céline, as if he were lying under six or seven layers of their product, his face flattened against the cold concrete floor.

Soon they arrived at a junction in the road that looked like any other except, astonishingly, for a full-sized stone Christ on a high wooden cross, set back no more than a metre from the roadside. The architect in Alex calculated the angle a supplicant's eye-line would make, straining up towards the slumped head and, as Jeremy turned right, the coward in him winced at the tight band of thorns piercing the man's temples, the pain replacing the thinking, Alex supposed, now that he was held to his destiny by nails.

The house, when they eventually saw it, didn't look as bad as Rod had predicted. The left-hand side, where a new bedroom was being added, was certainly going to bulge a bit and spoil the proportions, but the main feature, the rounded white walls that seemed to grow out of the green grass, still impressed.

And when you stepped inside through a modest central door, you actually got the small thrill of ambition Alex had hoped for in the plans. He watched Carol's face as she surveyed the light-filled space whose walls on the forest side were made of sliding panels of glass that gave onto the lawn. The focal point of the interior, though, three steps down to their left, was a lounge area with a white fireplace and funnel chimney that jutted outwards like a small stage.

Jeremy, in jeans, a black polo shirt, and a very light tweed sports jacket of a type not on offer in the places where Alex did his shopping, motioned them towards a wooden table by the glass panels. "What do you think, Carol? All the finer points are Alex's, of course."

This was true insofar as he had managed to restrain Jeremy from including a water feature, a porthole, and some ironic timber beams.

"I like it very much," replied Carol, still looking around. "It feels open and private at the same time."

Jeremy grinned as Alex and Carol sat at the table. "Alex and I had the odd disagreement, though, didn't we? I was going to say argument but Alex is much nicer than me, so it was all ..."– he put on a posh voice – "... very civilized." Jeremy opened one of the glass panels by a foot or so and a light smell of resin entered the room. "But we had to bring in Rod, Alex's boss, on one or two of the details, didn't we?"

Carol looked from Jeremy to Alex and said, "And what was his view?"

"He bloody well agreed with Alex. They're both a bit puritanical in their own ways, Carol. I think you'll find that."

"It was different with the picture gallery, though, wasn't it?" said Alex, slightly hurt.

"That's true," replied Jeremy, as he made his way towards the kitchen. "I think I'm going to get away with that. Anyway, shall we have an early lunch? I haven't got much, but I'll bring it in."

Jeremy's idea of not much, which Alex helped him carry from the kitchen while Carol stepped out onto the lawn, turned out to include two types of paté, three cheeses, smoked fish, white wine, fresh asparagus in a vinaigrette, and a dry sausage that Jeremy prepared with a penknife. Alex looked over at Carol as she came back in to eat and wondered if this was the kind of foodstuff that would meet the criteria she had set for him in the London Edition hotel room. He could always turn to crime.

Alex was still brooding on this when there was a hurried knocking at the door and Jeremy went over to let in a nervous, plump-faced man in an open shirt and blue woollen suit that looked too hot for the time of year. They talked in French for a few minutes, before Jeremy introduced him as Pascal, "the owner of the construction firm we're working with."

A minute later, almost to prove Pascal's status, a second man walked in, this time in blue overalls and a mouth-covering moustache that just about used up his current allocation of head hair. This was Gerard. Though he clearly worked for Pascal, there was a pleasant air of professional self-sufficiency about him that reminded Alex of tobacco-haired Steve, Don's contact at the British Museum. Jeremy invited both visitors to sit down with them and eat.

Pretty soon a conversation had got going that switched between English and French, the latter workmanlike from Jeremy, strange and literary from Carol, thought Alex, and present-in-class-but-not-really-paying-much-attention from himself. As their talk progressed through the peculiarities of the region, various hitches in the building process that Pascal was keen to smooth over, and which type of boosting device Jeremy could install to get a phone signal, Gerard, whose accent stretched *maintenant* into 'meng-tun-ang', introduced a series of innuendos featuring Carol, who needed 'feeding up', if Alex had got the French right, on various types of local produce.

Somehow, a schedule for the rest of the day got made that would see the four men doing business after lunch while Carol toured the area on an old moped that Jeremy kept among his bike collection. Afterwards, when the builders had gone, Jeremy and Carol would decide on some colour schemes while Alex, at his own suggestion, took a hot bath for his ankle, the idea of which amused Gerard into suggesting five or six perfuming additives that might prepare him for the evening.

Apart from the sexual tilts at Carol, the undermining of his own masculinity, and the strange habit Pascal had of putting his hand over his mouth as if he were about to cough and then inhaling deeply, presumably to lower his stress levels, Alex felt it was all going quite well, which was unsurprising since, not being in control of the supply, he had drunk his white wine less in pleasure than through an atavistic fear the source might dry up at any moment.

Two and a half hours later, arranging his legs on either side of the bath taps so he could submerge and soak his head for a minute or two, Alex reflected that it was only in these underwater moments that he actually felt completely himself. Perhaps he should have been a carp or koi.

Of his companions, he could hear Gerard directly above him, staying on to complete the final few minutes of light drilling and hammering required to move the picture gallery one step nearer to the compromise agreed at their afternoon conference. Carol and Jeremy, meanwhile, were disembodied voices occasionally picked out as they walked about the house, discussing which shade of what would match this or that fabric as it lay, hung, or covered various pieces of furniture. And Pascal, finally, would be at home resting his nerves, Alex hoped, though it seemed a long shot, particularly as his wife's parents had moved in, as he had explained, to help them with their myopic toddler.

Now, though, it was time to get out of the bath and sit still long enough by its side to cool down without sweating. He should be doing some thinking about something: his new powers or the way things were going with Carol, or about Burhan and the saga of the cloth, surely to be brought safely to an end by Michael Cross at the Museum. But he could also, he realized, simply shift all that into the lumber room of his head and enjoy instead the end-of-day draught from the window with its smoky pre-autumnal finish. The evening meal would be a pleasure too, as night fell in the forest and Jeremy took on some of the gentle pressure of Carol's intensity.

A car door slammed outside, and the engine of what he assumed was Gerard's van juddered into life. With his towel around his waist, Alex opened the bathroom door to check the coast was clear and walked along the corridor into his room, sliding back the glass panel and looking out into the silent forest.

"Where did you get to, anyway, on the moped?" he asked Carol twenty minutes later over lime juice on the three-sided sofa built into the fireplace, Jeremy in the bathroom, showering and humming something classical.

"I don't know really. I drove away from the house, past a small lake and a ploughed field. Then I got off the bike and walked into the forest just to see what it was like."

"How dark does it get?" said Alex, finishing his drink and hoping he could lean back for a while and just watch her as she spoke.

"Not like the Black Forest. But when I'd gone in a few hundred yards, I sat under a tree for a while. I couldn't hear a thing, not even birds." Carol took a clasp out of her hair, and Alex felt the skin tingle on his neck. "Then I thought I *could* hear something, a child's voice, so I walked in that direction. There was a kind of clearing and two kids playing around a small bonfire, with charcoal on their cheeks and legs. Behind them was a hut with an open door. I suppose there was an adult inside, a farmer or a woodcutter or something."

Alex smiled. "A woodcutter?"

"Yes. It's getting a bit Hansel and Gretel, isn't it?" she laughed.

"Didn't the kids see you?" he said, the tingle in his stomach now, rising again as Carol leant forward to put her glass on the floor, and expanding against the sides of his chest.

"I think so," she said, catching his eye, "but the odd thing is they didn't acknowledge me at all, the way you might have expected."

Jeremy burst into an aria, Carol smiling in the direction of the bathroom. When she turned back to look at him, Alex thought his chest might explode. So he leant forward and kissed her.

"Was that all right?" he said afterwards.

"All right to do it, or all right as a kiss?" she asked. He was about to reply when she smiled. "It's fine," she said.

The bathroom door opened, and they adjusted their positions on the sofa, stifling giggles like teenagers, before Carol pulled a mock-serious face. "I gather you've earned your trip by reaching some kind of agreement with the builders?"

"Sort of," replied Alex, looking over to where their host hadn't as yet entered the room and lowering his voice. "But Jeremy wants a cellar now."

Carol laughed. "He didn't mention it when we were doing our fabrics around the house. That's more work for you, isn't it?"

"Definitely not," said Alex. "Rod has called it a day. I mean, if Jeremy wants at some point off his own bat to get Gerard to dig a hole under the house ..."

"I suppose that in his line of business, Jeremy could quite easily get hold of a cellar's worth of good wine," said Carol.

Alex gave his ankle a rub and added, "I think he could probably get hold of anything he liked from anyone else's line of business too."

Jeremy walked in at this point, dressed and drying his hair, or rather his head, since there wasn't really enough hair left to keep a towel occupied. "What's this, Alex?" he said. "I hope you're not re-touching the delicate picture of myself that I've spent all afternoon painting in Carol's mind?"

He chucked his towel into the kitchen and went on, "Anyway, are you coming with me into town, Alex? I need to pick a couple of things up. We can leave Carol to her bath or shower or whatever, if that's all right?" Carol nodded. "And do you mind if we take the motorbike, Alex? It needs a bit of a run," said Jeremy, picking up a small rucksack and opening the front door for Alex.

After saying their goodbyes to Carol, they walked around to the end of the house where a red Yamaha sports bike rested on its insect leg. One helmet was attached to the handlebar, and Jeremy took a second out of the rucksack. "Do you mind putting this backpack on, Alex? I was an idiot not to get a machine that could take a proper pannier. Have you been on the back of a bike before?" Alex shook his head. "You'll enjoy it," Jeremy went on. "There won't be much traffic. The secret is to relax and move with the bike, particularly on corners. You can use the grab rail or you can hang on to me. Give me a dig in the ribs if you're worried, but I'll try to take things steady."

After ten minutes of Jeremy taking things 'steady' and, on flat stretches through the forest, pushing fairly hard at the word's definition boundary, they coasted into Mont-de-Marsan, Alex releasing his grip on the grab rail finger by finger while Jeremy pulled up outside a small shop with a sun-faded awning.

Inside, as Alex followed Jeremy, was everything an animal had to offer in death – black and white sausages, dark red cuts of meat, yellow tripe in one counter; a cooked tongue, jellied trotters, and a smoked ham in the second – and a few of the things it provided while alive: speckled eggs in a basket and a hotchpotch of ten or fifteen cheeses in the third counter, some alabaster-white, some marbled with veins, others wrapped in gold foil or rolled in black peppercorns. Jeremy's nostrils quivered.

"This is how it's done, Alex, alas. I wish I could get that wonderful aroma into *my* shops. I first noticed it when my aunt brought me here. This place must have been doing the same things again and again for more than a century – chopping, curing, salting, smoking." Jeremy smiled across at a small middle-aged woman, who emerged from the gloom at the back. "I'm sure if you gave Jeanne here a gentle rub, you'd smell it on her too."

The shopkeeper looked pleased and then suspicious, saying, if Alex was getting his French right, "What nonsense are you telling him?"

As the two of them chatted on, Alex closed his eyes, inhaling deeply but detecting only the earthy smell of a garden shed. Taking advantage of this solitary moment, he replayed his kiss with Carol, surprised he had more or less got it right, and noticing the ache in his chest that it had left behind.

Jeremy and Jeanne had now entered the serious phase of their encounter, prodding and sniffing flesh, exchanging coded words that presumably referred to age and origin. Something about the intimate offhand way they handled the products irritated Alex, almost as if a kind of natural boundary was being flaunted. The result of it all, anyway, was no more than three small packages in a plain plastic bag, which didn't stop them costing the best part of a fifty-euro note.

Outside again, they made their way to a café where Jeremy ordered them some Pernod. At the other end of the bar a small TV showed highlights from a local rugby fixture. Jeremy poured water into their drinks from a flat-sided Ricard bottle. "Carol said you hadn't known each other long?" he asked.

"Only ten days, in fact," replied Alex. "Did you mind me bringing her? Rod ..."

"No, no. That's fine," said Jeremy, shaking his head and continuing in the same easy tone, "How did you meet?"

What could Alex say? That he had accidentally propositioned her on the Northern Line with a lewd poem on the back of a business card?

"On the Tube, actually."

Jeremy looked up. "That's impressive. Did you make the first move?"

"The train braked, and we were sort of thrown together," said Alex, a flush rising from his neck.

"How interesting," said Jeremy, smiling. "Quick work on your part, then."

Two regulars entered from the street, the barman pouring measures for them and shaking their hands as they hoisted themselves onto their stools. Jeremy added more water to his own pastis. "Well, I think she's rather remarkable, Alex. She holds her own, doesn't she? Do you know anything about her background or family?"

"Not really," said Alex, as the Pernod navigated its way comfortably through his system. "Except she's living with a bloke called John."

"Oh. Always a fly, isn't there? Does he know about Carol being here with you?"

"No. He thinks she's on an aromatherapy weekend."

Jeremy laughed. "I've heard worse. Perhaps you should have taken a bedroom together at my place while you had a chance." Alex felt his face simmer as Jeremy continued, "Although I'm not sure how wise that would be after you've eaten everything I've got planned for tonight."

Alex managed a smile. "We're not actually an item yet," he said.

Jeremy shook his head. "You straights don't half hang about." He lifted his glass. "Actually, with Carol, you might find that the ball is not entirely in your court, so to speak."

Alex took a sip of his drink and looked for a way out. "So how do you feel about the villa?" he asked.

Jeremy smiled, either at Alex's clumsy change of tack or in contemplation of the project. "If it doesn't sound pretentious, and I'm sure on balance that it does, I'm getting ready for the third phase of my life. The final phase, without getting too gloomy. The house is part of that." He looked down at his drink, rather gloomily, thought Alex. Then he added with a smile, "Although I don't completely rule out a last mad period in my eighties with bad drink on Madagascar or somewhere."

Jeremy gestured to stop the barman refilling his empty glass after Alex's. "I want to do a bit of contemplating, if that isn't too posh a word," he said. "The villa will be ideal."

"Can I ask what you're going to contemplate?" asked Alex.

Jeremy winced modestly. "The business of dying, actually, or getting used to the idea. I've just begun a collection of books and things back at the house."

"Really? Could I take a look?" said Alex.

Jeremy raised his finger in mock warning. "Yes, but don't get too interested. We wouldn't want you trying to escape the obligations of experience, would we?"

With that, he got down from his stool, paid the barman, and, after acknowledging an acquaintance on the far side of the room, agreed to meet Alex outside.

As he finished his drink, Alex took a few moments to look around him at the men in the bar, struck for a moment by his chance inclusion in this community of habitual action, like a curious kitten among the mechanical figures of a Swiss-clock tableau: the same hands shaking each other on arrival; the same seats or standing positions taken up as one cog fell into another; the trusty barman swinging out on the quarter hour with the pastis bottle, ready to refill their glasses. These men weren't on the run from the routine of life, they actually wanted more of it! What they must be escaping, he concluded, and who could blame them, was the outside world's tiresome demand for innovation.

Alex wandered out to where some teenagers, looking bored but not achieving Anglo-Saxon perfection of the state, were loitering around the bike. He puzzled them slightly, he guessed, his helmet obviously connecting him to the machine but his manner somehow not quite driver-like. They moved aside, though, when Jeremy briskly appeared, one of the boys asking him a technical question and getting a ready response.

The wind felt cooler on the return journey, and the forest had got darker. On the final hundred metres, the track to the house, the roadside lights that Gerard had rigged up were already lit. Alex and Jeremy pulled round to the back, parked the bike, and buzzed at the front door. After a minute or so, Jeremy got out his key and let them in. Carol must be in the shower, they reckoned, or drying her hair - engaged anyway in some pre-dinner activity that Gerard would have considered entirely appropriate *for a girl*.

13

How long do you wait, was the question they asked themselves, for an independent-minded woman you've known for less than two weeks to return from an unadvertised absence, given she knows you're cooking her dinner?

Alex and Jeremy decided that an hour and a half, bringing the time to half past eight, was long enough. The first phase of the search, which they were still being sanguine and even jaunty about, was what Jeremy called 'a bike sweep' and would involve him driving about for the last hour of reasonable daylight in the several directions available from the house, including the tracks into the forest. Alex had closed the front door on him and was now moving across to the kitchen, where he switched off the oven and tidied up a bit. Neither of them had eaten much, just pieces torn from a baguette with some white wine and nothing from the rabbit casserole. The first course of elvers would only take a minute and remained in the fridge.

They'd checked that the moped was still in the garage, so an evening walk before dinner was surely the likeliest, wasn't it? She could have got lost. Or perhaps she was having to make some complicated call back to the UK and, rather than use Jeremy's landline, had gone out to try and find a signal somewhere. Maybe she was dumping John?

Alex walked into the centre of the room and looked out through the glass doors into the forest, visualising the phantom woodcutter as he chased Carol maniacally through the trees. Stumbling, she kept ahead, but his dark hut lay at the end of every path. Finally, he sat by the small fire Jeremy had lit, his host saying it got colder at night but really for its scenic value, Alex reckoned.

It could of course be an act of whimsy. How well did he know her, after all? There were people, weren't there, who just did things and sod the rest of the world. Alex remembered a girl at college, Virginia, who made stuff up and would disappear with some bizarre excuse in the interval of a play she'd been expensively taken to, and you couldn't really say straight out, 'What you're telling me could be true, of course, but I've made a rational decision based on experience and probability that you're lying.

Why do you do it?' She was stunning, anyway, and people - well, men not women - wanted her around even if it was just for half an evening.

Alex got up and wandered down the corridor towards what Jeremy called 'the wash-and-sleep zone', though it also contained his temporary office. They'd been into Carol's room once already and seen nothing unusual. But they'd been quick. Perhaps they'd missed something. Alex hesitated before going in again, not entirely convinced by his own motives. Once inside, though, he turned the dimmer switch high and moved around efficiently enough, opening drawers and peering in cupboards, impossible not to feel like a TV cop. But still there was nothing to explain her absence – no bags gone except her handbag and there, hanging outside her wardrobe, was the black satin dress she must have been planning to wear that evening.

Alex tried to be clever. The jeans, jacket and blouse she had been wearing were nowhere to be seen, and the jacket wasn't in the hall either, so at least they had a description they could give the police. He reached for her towel, hanging on the handle of the window. Damp all over. Then he walked back to the door, dimmed the light and leant on the wall.

So she'd had a bath or shower, returned to her room, and hung up her towel, temporarily perhaps because it wouldn't really dry like that, while she got into the silky white dressing gown that now lay on the bed. But what next? Why would she get into her day clothes again? Unless ... unless something had occurred to her, some reason to go outside. Perhaps she'd heard a noise? So she thought she might as well slip her clothes on, the gown being too flimsy, and investigate.

He let himself slide down the wall to the floor. Maybe another angle would occur to him later, unbidden. The scent of her perfume was stronger here, and there was a soapy damp smell too from the towel or from her wet hair. A feeling of foreboding crept up into his chest. Reaching over to the bed, he picked up the sleeve of her dressing gown and held it to his face. *Carol*.

Midnight was quite early for a police visit, since she had only been gone for five hours. But Jeremy had rung Pascal for some local advice and, after a fruitless call to the nearest hospital with an A and E unit, a combination of the builder's natural caution and his long-standing friendship with a detective of Spanish origin had brought the rangy frame of Santiago Olmo first to their door, at the end of his Saturday shift, and later to their table. Now he had finished a portion of rabbit casserole and was removing the napkin that had covered the trousers of his black suit.

On arrival, he had surprised them both by conducting a torchlight examination of all the building's entry points after only the briefest of conversations. Then, in precise English with the occasional French word or phrase inserted, Alex reckoned, as a kind of sub-Poirot comfort break, he had asked them for their account of the day, his quiet appetite for details sometimes beyond their capacity to satisfy. Did she take a bag with her both ways on her afternoon trip into the forest? Had she heard a voice from the hut? And how exactly had she seemed when Jeremy suggested she have a bath or shower while they were out? When one of them was uncertain about something, Olmo would look to the other to see if he could add some verbal shading or a new brush line.

On the other hand, beyond the basic information about inviting Carol to France despite her domestic arrangements with John, which Alex instantly knew he had to give up, he didn't seem fazed at their necessarily short description of the rest of Carol's life. The detective must be used to working with what he could get. Anyway, he had been at the house for more than an hour now. Surely it was time for some kind of interim professional view?

Pushing his plate away, Olmo took a cigarette out of a silver case, gestured for permission to smoke from his host, and then lit what smelt to Alex like the bonfire tang of a full-strength Marlboro. Jeremy got him an ashtray.

"I can find no obvious cause for her disappearance," he said, a trace of sympathy in his tone. "The strongest possibility, therefore, is that she walked out of the house of her own accord between six and seven o'clock this evening and has decided, for some reason, not to return." He ran his cigarette hand through his thinning black hair. "You have both tried her mobile from the landline, Pascal has contacted the hospital, and Monsieur Knowles," he said, catching Jeremy's eye, "has made a search of the area. All you can do now, I'm afraid, is wait. She is, after all, an *adulte*."

Jeremy turned to Alex. "She's got *my* number?"

Alex nodded. "I gave her a copy of my business itinerary."

"*Bon*," said the policeman, pushing back his chair.

"But what about the hut?" said Alex, looking at Jeremy and then at the detective.

"The empty hut?" said Olmo.

"There could have been someone inside," replied Alex.

"They're used by hunters, aren't they?" added Jeremy.

Olmo nodded. "*Bien.* Let us assume, then, that there was a hunter who had lit a fire, attracting two of the local children."

"They may be *his* children," said Alex.

"Perhaps," said the detective. "And now he has retired into his cabin?"

"That's right," said Alex. "He could be plucking pheasants."

Jeremy raised his eyebrows.

"What next?" said Olmo, sucking deeply on his cigarette.

"Well," said Alex, "he sees Carol, and when she moves off, he follows her."

"*Un type athlétique*," murmured the detective, amidst his fumes.

Alex looked at Jeremy, who said, "She's on a moped."

"Or he has a car nearby," continued Alex, the woodcutter, or pheasant-plucker, clearer now in his mind's eye, a lean face and a black woolly hat tight against his scalp. "Anyway, he finds out where she's staying, and waits until the coast is clear."

Olmo stubbed out his cigarette. "Many things are possible, Mister Harrison. Her partner John, for example, suspecting her of *une petite aventure*, may have followed her to the house, using the travel details you kindly supplied her with, and taken her back."

Alex, deciding this wasn't the cue for the elaboration of a new theory, took a gulp of his water instead.

"As I said, for the moment we must wait," concluded the detective, pushing back his chair and offering Jeremy his hand. "Thank you for your hospitality. I'll call in at eleven tomorrow on the way to my office. Let us hope that the matter is resolved by then."

"What if John *is* involved?" said Jeremy, after Olmo had left. They were sitting by the dying fire, each with a glass of cognac.

"You don't think he's in France, do you?" said Alex.

"I doubt it," replied Jeremy. "But there's one way to find out." He took a sip of his brandy. "Do you have his number?"

"John's, you mean?" said Alex, his pulse quickening.

"Yes," said Jeremy, rubbing his hands together.

Alex pulled out his Samsung, found the number he had used to make the call to Carol a week before, and looked at his host. "You mean a wrong number call?"

Jeremy smiled and shook his head. "We need to find out if John knows anything at all. But don't worry. I've had an idea," he said, putting his hand out for Alex's phone. "She's in estate management, isn't she?"

Alex nodded as Jeremy walked over to the landline. On the way, he loosened up his shoulders. Then he dialled and waited, finally speaking into the mouthpiece with one of those upper-class accents that's been shaped, since the initial act of robbery, by centuries of serious land ownership, "Terribly sorry to disturb you at this hour. Word of explanation. My name is Henry Norton, and we're in a bit of a pickle over a property injunction Carol's been working on. Can't get her on her mobile. People moving in overnight, police involved etc, etc. Who would I be speaking to?" Jeremy stayed in character as he listened and then said, "I see. Not readily contactable. All right, we've done our bit. No, no. No need to take it further. Well yes, fair point to you. Yes, I do take your point." He raised his eyebrows at Alex before bringing the conversation to an end, "Look, old chap, I won't keep you up any longer, and thanks awfully for your help."

"Shirty type, isn't he?" suggested Jeremy, once he was back on the sofa and pouring them both another drink. "Started to attack old Henry pretty forcefully on the subject of professional etiquette. Doesn't prove anything, but he seemed convinced Carol was at the spa hotel with her phone switched off until tomorrow evening."

14

Alex woke at eight the following morning, no buzz at the front door or phone call from Carol having disturbed his short night of sleep, a large smooth stone of melancholy settling in his chest as he stared out at the alien pine trees, waiting until the pressure on his bladder forced him to rise and dress. Pulling back the glass panels of his room, he thought he might get a breath of fresh air, taking a pee outside rather than disturbing Jeremy.

Crossing the wet grass, still within earshot of the phone, he had begun to undo his belt when he caught sight of something white, nestling in the tufts at the base of a tree three or four metres into the forest. He walked over to take a look. Closer up, it appeared to be a small handkerchief knotted to contain a lump. A child's shroud for a dead bird, or maybe Pascal had bitten into something he hadn't much liked at lunch and smuggled it out? But he wouldn't have gone round to the back of the house and lobbed it into Jeremy's bit of forest, would he?

As he found a small stick to prod it with, a disagreeable image occurred to him of Gerard coughing up some monstrous sputum. But that didn't work either, because he wouldn't have bothered with a handkerchief or if he had, it would have been the size of a small parachute, the kind that more or less covered your face as you gave your nostrils a good going-over. Anyway, the lump was solid to the touch of the stick. He picked it up and, unable to undo the knot with his fingers, managed to tear an entry with his keys, pulling at the material until Carol's blue egg emerged into the palm of his hand.

After peeing in the undergrowth, he was poised to share his discovery with Jeremy when the phone rang at last. With flapping trousers clasped to his belly, Alex propelled himself into the lounge to pick up the receiver. "Carol?" he gasped.

"Alex, is that you? Are you all right?"

Burhan's voice.

"Yes, I'm fine," said Alex, disguising his disappointment. "Did you get the endorsement?"

"Alex, I'm afraid the cloth has been stolen."

"What do you mean?"

"Vivian invited me to stay on until yesterday. We had a lot to discuss. It wasn't until I got back to the hotel late in the evening that I checked my phone messages, and found one from Steve. He said he had been due to show the cloth to Michael Cross on Friday afternoon, but when they got there, it was gone." He paused, before concluding, "I have a feeling they searched my hotel room, too. I wanted to let you know."

Shit and fuck, thought Alex, immediately blaming himself.

"Burhan, there's something I should have told you." He closed his eyes. "One of Salah's men, Khalid, approached me in London, the evening we had that meal in Camden. Asking for information, which I didn't give him."

"What? Why didn't you say?"

"I thought you would warn me off," he said. "And I had that plan for the cloth, didn't I?" Alex tried to relax his grip on the phone. "I'm sorry."

"Alex," said Burhan. "It's not your fault. It's mine. I should never have involved you in all this in the first place. The very idea that you would come into contact with Salah and his gang!" He paused. "Alex, are you still there?"

He was. It was just that the landscape around him had changed.

"Yes, but listen, the friend I brought with me to France, Carol, she's disappeared."

There was a moment of silence, during which Jeremy walked into the room, dressed already, and stared at Alex, one hand on the phone and the other at his crotch.

Then Burhan said, "Please go on."

"She went missing from the house last night some time around seven, while I was out with our client. We've spoken to a detective." He looked at the egg. "And now there's evidence she may have been taken against her will. What if they followed me to France?"

"It's not possible. But you need to tell the police."

"About Salah, you mean?"

"Everything you know," he replied, before adding, "It must be a coincidence, Alex, about the girl. She will surely re-appear, but please keep me informed at the hotel."

When Alex had finished talking, he found it impossible to read Olmo's face. They were sitting outside, the shade of the house protecting them from the late morning sun, and Jeremy, who had already confessed their late-night call to John, pouring the policeman some more black coffee.

94

After showing him the egg – surely, suggested Alex, some kind of signal from Carol, hurled out of her bedroom window as her captor gave her a minute to dress – he had indeed told Olmo everything: about his visit to Oman; about Burhan and the cloth; about the scholar's family feud with Salah; about the British Museum, and his friend's trip to London. And nothing, of course, about fairies or flying.

The detective, in a smart grey suit, white shirt and red tie, as if he might be en route to a country wedding, picked up his cup. "It's a bizarre situation, Mr Harrison. You would certainly have been advised to keep your distance," he said, swallowing the remains of his coffee. "But since it is in front of us, let us explore it a little."

Olmo got up and took a few paces towards the forest, his hands clasped behind his head. "We know from your account that this man Salah and his associates had been looking for this *antiquité* just like Monsieur Burhan, except that, quite wisely, they let him do the hard work. When your friend drove to, where was it, Mr Harrison?"

"Cobham," said Alex.

"Yes," continued the detective, "well, while he was there, they could have searched his hotel room for information. Up to this point, perhaps they believed your friend was arranging to pick up the cloth and hand it over to the Museum. Now they accept that it is already there."

"But you can't just walk into the British Museum and take what you like," said Jeremy, "or else we'd all be at it."

Olmo shrugged. "I agree, Monsieur Knowles. But remember that this item is not yet on public display. If they had a contact on the payroll, perhaps?"

"Someone they could intimidate, you mean?" suggested Alex.

"Or bribe," added the policeman. "There are even people," he continued, "who work legitimately in an organization like that for six months or a year and are ready to undertake an assignment to order if you know how to contact them."

"But why," asked Jeremy, "would they take Carol, if they've already got the cloth?"

"Exactly," said the detective, returning to the table and lighting a cigarette. "It doesn't make sense."

Alex reached over and picked up the egg. "What if Salah sees this as the endgame, and is making some kind of show of strength?" he suggested. "Searching the library in Oman and the hotel in London, stealing the cloth from the Museum and kidnapping Carol, all within the space of a couple of weeks?"

Olmo smiled. "Four places, three countries indeed, but essentially one *coup*, you mean," he said, resting his cigarette in the ashtray, raising and clenching his fist, "like a punch in the face, designed to knock you out so that you will relinquish any further interest in the cloth?"

"That's it, yes," said Alex.

"Surely not," said Jeremy.

"Making you both responsible, in effect, for the abduction of an innocent?" added Olmo. Alex nodded, though he wouldn't have put it quite like that. "Well, if your theory is correct," continued the detective, exhaling extensively, "we may have some advantages."

"How do you mean?" said Alex, not entirely convinced he was being taken seriously.

"Firstly, they would not have known that Carol was 'available', so to speak, until they had followed you to France, which means they are unlikely to have a house ready nearby. So they may have to move their victim quite a long way, even to Spain, Africa, etc. We don't know where, of course, but it puts them at risk, however good they are. And secondly," he continued, "I would be surprised if they left you to 'guess' at the reason for the abduction. In which case, they will have to contact you or your friend at some point. This too is a weakness on their side." The detective stubbed out his cigarette and looked at his watch. "Gentlemen, I will need to be going."

"But what happens next?" asked Alex.

Olmo got up. "If the young lady does not join you at the airport for your departure, or make contact with Monsieur Knowles by the end of the day, we will begin our normal procedure for a missing person tomorrow morning."

"But what about Salah and the egg?" said Alex.

"I assume that your friend Burhan will speak to the police in London as part of the investigation into the stolen cloth. I suppose they will run checks on this man, Salah. We may contact them ourselves, in case there is a connection," said the detective, doing up the middle button of his jacket. "As for the egg, it doesn't really prove anything, I'm afraid."

Alex was about to speak when Jeremy touched him on the arm. "Is there anything I can do, Inspector?" he said.

"Tomorrow, perhaps," replied Olmo, "if we begin a formal search of *les environs*. Meanwhile, Mister Harrison, do you have a photograph of Carol?" Alex shook his head. "Well, I imagine her friend John does," continued the detective. "You will need to ring him again, the sooner the better, but this time with the truth about her disappearance." The inspector placed a business card on the table and began to write on the back. "I'd like him to send a photo to this number."

After Olmo had left, Jeremy put his hand on Alex's shoulder and smiled. "I'll be in the kitchen, putting the finishing touches to lunch, while you make the call to John."

Alex looked at the phone, and rested his head in his hands. Carol gone, the cloth stolen. How had he got himself into this mess? The fairy of course was the point of departure. But rash decisions on his part had followed the wish, hadn't they? Getting involved with Burhan; suggesting they publicize the cloth; and both of them underestimating Salah and his will to act. He had stripped off his shirt and gone over the barricade like some mad-bastard officer at Rorke's Drift, inviting the Zulus to launch their quivering spears at his chest. Nothing came close, though, to the fact that he may have endangered Carol.

He looked over at the phone again, the scale of his situation vis-à-vis Carol's partner truly Himalayan. A quick breakdown might prepare him at least for the man's reaction. First, he'd gone away with John's girl. Simple, but bad enough. Second, though more minorly, it would become evident in the conversation that Alex was aware of the humiliating lie Carol had told her partner. And thirdly – the killer flourish – he had left her alone in an isolated house and was quaffing Pernod in a bar six miles away while persons unknown crept out of the forest to spirit her away. If imagination were stretched to pinging point, it couldn't get much worse. Actually, Alex realized, as he was about to pick up the phone, it *was* worse. He had also allowed his companion, on this number, to disturb John in the early hours of the morning with a preposterous story, delivered in a comic accent.

Alex went over to the glass doors, slid them open, and looked out into the forest. He could renounce his powers and run, he supposed. The forest was big enough. He might make a life out there, enduring the sharp pains that follow the transient satisfaction of filling his belly with nuts and berries. There would be sightings of him along the coast in the early morning with his useless fishing stick, or at kitchen windows at dusk, reaching in for bread and cheese.

Alex stepped outside, sucked in a measure of the warm pine-filled air, and shook his head. No. Rather than run, he would commandeer that mini-submarine from *Fantastic Voyage* and dive inside himself, a beauty and a cleft-chinned companion at his side, beginning the search, up veins and down arteries, around the spleen and appendix, into the briny air of the lungs, through the sulphurous storms of the stomach, until finally, somewhere on the soft slopes of the liver, perhaps, they would find a shallow-rooted flower with potential by nurture, his small emblem of nobility. Yes. He would use his gift to find and rescue Carol, restoring her, well, maybe not to John, but to whatever life she freely wanted to follow. He had to start. Pressing the keys on the phone, he waited. Then he said, "John, this is Alex here. I'm phoning from France about Carol."

By the time Alex had finished the call, Jeremy had laid the small table in the kitchen and was opening a bottle of white wine, beaded with water. "Chinese okay for you, Alex? You can have enough of the French, can't you?"

"Thanks," said Alex, knocking back his first glass fairly quickly, and Jeremy refilling it, before bringing over a series of small dishes of rice, pak choi braised in garlic, mushrooms, and finally, a trout in coriander and star anise. He cut the fish into pieces with a spoon and invited Alex to help himself, saying fairly neutrally, "You got through to John, then?" Alex nodded, and Jeremy went on, "And it wasn't as bad as you thought?"

Alex took a gulp of his second glass. "At first he just listened while I explained what I was doing in France, and how I'd asked Carol to come with me. Perhaps he thought it was a wind-up. By the time I got to her disappearance and the police, though, I don't suppose he was in any doubt I was telling the truth."

"He blames *you*, does he?"

"I don't know. But he said at the end of the call that he didn't want to talk to me again. So I gave him your number for the investigation. I hope that's okay." Jeremy nodded. "And he's got Olmo's now, of course."

"He's going to send a photo?"

"Yes. He's probably done it already."

"Did you mention the egg or your friend Burhan?" asked Jeremy.

"No. By this point anyway, he was returning to the subject of me and Carol, wanting more details in a very matter-of-fact kind of way – when we met, how often we'd seen each other etc."

"And how did he take all that?"

"It was strange. I thought at one point he might just say, 'sod you both.'"

"But?"

"Well, next he started talking about her as if she was a child, saying she'd done this kind of thing before, wandering off. That it was all part of their long-term relationship."

"Interesting."

Alex nodded and drank of the rest of his second glass, Jeremy pushing some more vegetables onto his, Alex's, plate, and both of them eating in silence. Then Jeremy glanced up casually over his food. "That's not all, is it, with the conversation?"

Alex looked at him. "No. How did you know?"

Jeremy shrugged and topped up Alex's glass.

"Before we finished speaking," continued Alex, "he said, 'Listen, mate, when this is over, when Carol is back with me in London, don't doubt even for a fraction of a second that I'm going to come for you and tear you apart so you'll be shitting into a bag for the rest of your life. Do you understand that?'"

Jeremy looked up, a forkload of pak choi halfway to his mouth. "It's bluster, Alex, believe me. I've heard that kind of thing."

Alex put his glass down. "If it's okay by the police," he said, "I'm thinking of going back this afternoon as planned. I don't see what more I can do here."

"Olmo mentioned your departure himself, didn't he, so I don't think he plans to detain you," Jeremy replied. "I can keep you up to date with whatever happens here. And I'll give you a lift later on."

"Thanks. I want to help Burhan with the UK police. Make sure they believe him. I'm sure there's some connection with Salah and Khalid and the car that was following us to Cobham. Even the van that blocked us. But if I'm wrong, I'll come back to France."

Jeremy pushed his plate aside. "Of course, you should both tell the police what you can. But I also think that Burhan ought to go home, and that you should stop spending time with him. I don't like the way he's drawn you into this. The police will find Carol, and you've seen yourself what this chap Salah can do, if it is him. So disengage yourself as soon as you can."

Alex picked up his glass and nodded, his thoughts unfolding already upon the opposite course of action.

15

Alex stopped thinking about Carol for a moment, contemplating instead the handsome, pudgy, younger face of Radovan Karadzic, who had finally been found guilty, twenty years after the Bosnian War, of crimes against humanity. With his teddy-boy quiff, he looked like the kind of man whose don't-write-me-off-yet swagger would be an embarrassment at his daughter's wedding. According to the newspaper profile, which Alex had been trying to read on the Tube home from his return flight, alone, to Heathrow, he had been a psychologist and poet before giving genocide a fair crack of the whip.

Getting to his stop, Alex manoeuvred himself up onto the street as decisively as his mostly recovered ankle would let him. After all, depending on what information Burhan had for him tomorrow, he might have to spring into action at any moment. Meantime, the walk to his flat would give him time to itemise, and if possible, minimise, his other commitments.

He'd need to go to the office, obviously, but Jeremy had kindly said he would phone Rod today, explaining the events in France. Perhaps that would gain him some latitude at work. Apart from that, he had agreed to go to Céline's late the following evening to help her move or remove something, he couldn't remember which. And why did it have to be him? Had Céline, in a rare moment of carelessness, forgotten to include 'moving things' in the job description of Mike, her probationary boyfriend? Anyway, that could be squeezed in after his rendezvous with Burhan. Then, on Tuesday morning, according to the receptionist at the surgery, Dr Patel needed to see him - though 'needed' was surely too strong a word for the mellow medic - to discuss a letter that had come from the hospital.

And finally, he was due to meet Bill in the evening of the same day, in a cocktail bar of all places, so his friend could have a dry run at the evening that would finally get Jessica into bed. Alex hoped that the realism of the event would stretch as far as his host's wallet but stop some way short of Bill's dingy bedroom. Whatever, it could always be postponed. Carol, now, was the only thing that really mattered.

Three hours later, after a takeaway Chinese and most of a bottle of wine, no news from Jeremy and no immediate evidence his flat had been entered or searched, Alex was sitting on the log at the end of his garden, looking back towards his kitchen and trying, for the benefit he might gain from a good night's sleep, *not* to think. Somewhere over on his left a bloke was either breaking the hosepipe ban under cover of night, or else emptying a bladder of Herculean proportions.

In this part of town, one set of back gardens led into another, so there was a good depth to the darkness and also a few frogs, the odd fox, cats, of course, and smaller creatures that made noises but didn't appear, or when they appeared, defied Alex's ability to define them, looking more like furry draught excluders than anything Noah might have welcomed aboard. It worried Alex how many words, *yew* or *geranium*, for example, or *tench* or *grebe* or *stoat*, clattered around in the natural world sector of his mental lexicon, unattached to any image. What if he turned up in a landscape, a wood or something, where he couldn't name a single thing below the sky, and even there the types of clouds would fox him? Would *he* too begin to fade away, examining through transparent hands the last unnameable insects crawling up the stems of unknown flowers?

Sod it. He was *thinking* again. In the garden to his right, a burglar light clicked on, pushing back twenty metres or so of darkness, and behind him on the other side of the trees, amidst an al fresco clinking of glasses, came a burst of laughter, followed by a posh female voice so close it might have been addressing him.

"The secret is to focus on your body."

Alex froze, fearing he was about to be exposed as a neighbourhood voyeur.

"The secret to not thinking, I mean," said the voice.

Alex turned to his left.

"Hello," said the fairy, sitting at the base of a tree, her arms clasped around her knees, this time wearing a black business suit.

"You've changed," was all Alex could think of to say.

"Well, that was four weeks ago. Isn't a girl *allowed* a change of outfit?"

"And your accent's different. It's English, not American."

"I know," she said. "I'm feeling very 'old country' at the moment. Do you like my hair? I think it's called a bob."

"Fine. I mean, it's nice. Why are you here?"

"Oh. I thought you might have a few questions. But if you don't, the night is still young," she said, raising her right hand in a fist above her head.

"Wait!" said Alex, his heart lurching in his chest. "Of course I have. Twenty or thirty."

"Um, let's see," said the fairy, lowering her right hand and resting her chin on it. "I'll give you three."

Christ, thought Alex, I didn't prepare for this.

"Try to be spontaneous then, if you can," said his companion.

"Is there a time limit?" said Alex, giving himself an immediate mental kicking.

"Uh-huh," she replied. "And I'm going to be extremely generous, and *not* count that as your first question. Two minutes."

She looked at her wrist, though Alex couldn't see a watch.

"First," he said, a drop of sweat forming on his brow, "how can I rescue Carol?"

"Good," she replied. "You got that right, at least. And the answer is, follow the egg."

"What?" said Alex, and then, "I'm sorry. That *wasn't* my second question."

She narrowed her eyes and nodded.

"Okay," he said. "Here *is* number two. Did *you* arrange for me to meet Burhan and Carol?"

"Clever," she replied, "but badly framed. And the answer is no, not me. Last question, please."

Alex looked down, pulling a gargoyle face and then, realizing that his ability to rescue Carol would depend on it, set aside her mysterious speech and the dying planet, the cloth and his strange dream, and asked instead, "How long will my gift last?"

"Until the star fades, if you use it purposefully," replied the fairy, holding her hand up in front of her face long enough for Alex to realize he could see through it. "It's an elm, by the way," she added, looking up at the branches above her and then down at her disappearing body. She laughed. "I must say, I preferred the puff of smoke."

"And what about the aphrodisiac I wished for?" muttered Alex finally, though by now he was talking to the tree.

"Just get the chef to give it a quick blast under the grill. If it tastes underdone, I can always send it back for another blast, can't I? But if it comes overcooked, there's nothing I can do, is there?"

The new Spanish waitress looked blankly at Rod's grinning face and heaving shoulders. To the rest of the Monday lunch party, Alex and Max, it was pretty clear she hadn't understood a word, but Rod, it seemed, didn't really believe in language difference, persuaded perhaps that his meaning would get through intuitively, in the course of the girl's return to the kitchen or even in the way she passed the order to Chris, the chef at Maria's who got bored, often wandering away from his pots and pans.

While they waited for their food – Rod's plaice, Alex's and Gemma's pasta, though Gemma herself would be a few minutes late, and Max's steak tartare, 'good for the blood,' he said – Rod and Max were keen to bring Alex up to date on their thinking over Carol's disappearance. It was clear that Jeremy had given Rod a decent report and clear also that Rod, Max, and probably Cliff, if he was on the run again, had spent the previous evening discussing the situation, drug-induced paranoia winning an early victory over rational debate, Alex suspected.

Rod leant backwards, which had the same gestural effect as anyone else leaning forward, and spoke quietly, "What you've got to realize, Alex, is that the cops on both sides of the Channel don't actually want to get your friend back, not for a while."

Max demonstrated his ability to nod, gulp wine, chew bread and now speak at the same time, so it was not surprising that sensitivity got left out of the bundle. "Fugging right," he said, "and by then it's too late."

Rod picked up his thread again. "There's this kind of missing-female graph, see, if she's over twenty. To begin with, the line is flat. Nobody cares because it could be anything – minor breakdown, just gone walkabout, or whatever. After a week, if she's British and there's a good photo, the line begins to pick up. Right now, the fuzz *are* getting interested." Rod smiled knowingly. "Not in getting her back though. They're beginning to feel a big case coming on." Rod was cackling now. "Big case means big *ree*-sources." Max's fringe flopped over his left eye as he nodded and, brushing it back with his bread hand, added, "That way, the super can get his liddle extension built. You see?"

At this point on the Rod-and-Max-track, you could attempt a pull on the reality brake. You could also stand in the path of an oncoming express train, blowing as if you were Superman. Instead, he said to Rod, "And when does the line on the graph reach a peak?"

They all took a break while Gemma entered in a dark-pink silk blouse and a very short black skirt. As she approached the table, three types of appraisal competed with one another. Max's was a frank 'continental'. Rod's, to be fair to him, was almost aesthetic. And Alex's, in a well-brought-up kind of way, sought by a variety of tics and subterfuges to combine maximum coverage with the minimum indication of interest.

When she was settled next to him and sipping her beer, Rod answered,

"Two weeks. It isn't just the extra cash they can pull in. It's also the fact that the longer the case continues, the wider the network of crooks they can finger. Believe me, they wanna keep that old graph peaking."

Alex strained to keep his eyes on Rod's chuckling face as Gemma crossed her legs. Meanwhile Maria herself, the brow of her thin face furrowed by thirty years of seeing off the three husbands her business acumen had attracted, brought Rod's briefly blasted fish and Max's raw meat.

"Maria!" shouted Rod. "How much money have you made this month?"

Maria scowled. "What bloody money? It's all rates and wages."

"You're joking," Rod continued. "You're stashing it away."

Rod and Max were convinced she was doing up the ancestral pile outside Verona. Max tucked into his steak mince. "What about those gigolos, those Italian boys you're going to keep in the palazzo? You got them on a retainer already, have you? You should feed them up on this stuff," he said, diverting his loaded fork two or three inches towards her.

Maria seemed unsure whether to smile or slap him and in the end gave way to her Spanish waitress, who had brought the pasta for Alex and Gemma. While they ate, Gemma told Alex about a new project that had come in, and Rod gave Max his latest theory on how Émile, or Mills, Constance's cat, had recently escaped from the top-floor flat. Then, as Max ordered another bottle of Orvieto, Rod looked over. "Don't you want to hear the solution, Alex?"

Alex swallowed a raviolo in readiness. "To finding Carol, you mean?"

"*Pree*-cisely."

Alex wasn't sure. "Of course," he said.

"Well, me and Max came up with it around two this morning."

Oh dear, thought Alex. Max, however, looked excited.

"Delilah," the Austrian said, mopping up his raw egg yolk with an inch of bread.

Alex wasn't sure if this was a person or some bizarre theory based on barbering their way towards Carol's captors. It was Gemma who cleared things up. "You mean the woman I let in with Cliff when Mills disappeared?"

"That's it," said Rod, as he refilled the chamber of his vaping device. "Alex, do you have anything that belonged to Carol?"

"Well, yes. A sort of china egg she used to rub."

Max's eyes took a surge in voltage as he turned to Rod. "My God. That's perfect!"

Alex was beginning to feel a bit left out. "Perfect for what?" he said.

"She's a psychic detective," replied Gemma, looking down at her pasta.

Half an hour later, stumbling into the sunlight with Gemma, leaving Max and Rod to their third espresso, Alex found he had agreed to bring the egg to work the following day for a 'compass session' with Delilah. According to Max, this would give the psychic a fairly good idea of the direction and distance of the house where Carol was being concealed. Admittedly, Delilah had only operated so far at pet and car-keys level, but Rod was convinced she was ready to be stretched. Alex shook his head. Was this really what the fairy intended when she had advised him to 'follow the egg'?

"And *did* Delilah give an opinion on the cat?" he asked Gemma.

His colleague put on a deadpan expression. "Apparently, Mills is making his way back to Dulwich but hasn't 'crossed water' yet." As Gemma turned to unlock the front door to Schaeffer and Schaeffer, drawing a backward glance from the last of her admirers, she continued, "Lewis says Rod and Max are planning to go down to the Embankment this evening, where they reckon Mills is waiting for the cover of darkness to make his way across the Hungerford Bridge."

She pushed at the door. "This is our *boss*, Alex. I do hope Lewis is joking."

16

Burhan and Alex had been together for ten minutes at the most, meeting outside the Devonshire Hotel and crossing the Bayswater Road towards Kensington Gardens, the scholar explaining how, on the Museum's advice, he had just made a statement at Holborn Police Station, when the silver car, its tinted passenger window descending, pulled up alongside them in the early evening sunlight.

"Excuse me, please," called a voice from inside, map held up against his face, horns already honking behind. It was only when Alex had got close enough to lean forward, putting a hand to the door, that he recognized Khalid, a gun in his lap, its short barrel elevated towards Alex's right eye. "Hello again, Mr Harrison. Please tell your friend to get in the back and then join him as quickly as you can," said Salah's man, adding with an easy smile, "before we cause a revolution behind us."

"Let Alex go," repeated the scholar, grey-faced behind the driver's seat as the car negotiated its way westwards. "None of this is his concern."

Ignoring the requests – but apologizing to Alex for his use of the gun – Khalid finally turned towards Burhan and made a response, saying something in Arabic, his tone measured and reasonable – saying quite a lot, in fact, if you included the scholar's angry interruptions, because by the time he had finished speaking, they had crossed the Edgware Road and were heading up towards Marylebone.

Alex swallowed to moisten his mouth, his right hand poised to reach out for Burhan and his left to tap them both back to his flat, assuming, of course, the fairy would choose to honour the passenger clause of his carefully worded wish.

"I'm sorry, Alex. I would do anything in the world not to have involved you in this," said his Omani friend, pulling out a handkerchief, removing his glasses, and wiping the sweat from his brow. "He says they have absolutely no intention of harming us. They're going to take us to an apartment near Regent's Park, apparently, where they have a proposition to make, a business deal that will be 'very beneficial' to all of us, in his words." He put his glasses on again. "He assures me the meeting will last no longer than half an hour, after which we'll be free to go." Khalid looked round and nodded at them in agreement. "But he won't answer any questions about Carol or the cloth," concluded Burhan. "He's leaving all that to Salah."

Apart from the two leather armchairs they were sitting in and the wide desk in front of them, the large room was empty, three windows on the park side to their left filling the space with daylight.

"Salah will be with us in a moment," said Khalid, looking across at the trees through the middle window, before turning towards them with a smile. "Do you have any idea what they are selling this apartment for?" Burhan, though closer, made no response, so Alex shook his head. "Two million pounds," said the man. "You could buy two or three *streets* in my home town for this money. Can you imagine that?"

Before Alex or Burhan had a chance to do any imagining, however, the door at the far end of the room opened, a young man, beefier and wider than Khalid entering first, followed by a small man in his forties with balding grey hair, a paunch held in by the belt of his comfortable black suit and a wide, cheerful smile. "Gentlemen, how good to see you," he said in a slight American accent. "My name is Salah, and this," he continued, touching his companion's elbow, "is my colleague Tarik."

Burhan rose, unsmiling, as Salah moved quickly towards him around the desk, and clasped his shoulder. "My cousin," he said, looking the scholar in the eye, "though we haven't seen each other for a quarter of a century, have we, not since my grandfather's funeral?" He turned to Alex, who had also got up. "And you must be his friend, Alex Harrison. Am I right?"

"Why are we here?" asked Burhan.

"Yes, yes," replied Salah, not unpleasantly, gesturing for them to sit. "I know you want to talk business. But let me welcome you to this elegant apartment first, which might have been mine. Guess what, though?" He burst out laughing. "I don't have two million in sterling to spare! Who does, these days?"

He walked round to the other side of the desk, pulling back the wooden chair and sitting down. "Before we begin, there's something I really want to share with you," he said, opening a drawer and taking out a flat brown parcel. Grinning, he removed the paper, lifting and turning the object, a small framed seascape with clouds, towards his guests. "This," he continued, "is a rather interesting oil sketch, recently attributed to Constable, which I have the good fortune to possess, as of today. Sublime, of course, which is why I wanted to show it to you." He paused to let them appreciate it. "But would you like to know what makes it genuine?" He crooked his finger. "Why don't you come and have a look, Alex?"

Glancing first at Burhan, who shrugged without expression, Alex rose from his chair, Salah beckoning him closer until he was leaning over the desk. "It was executed *alla prima*," said their host. "Do you know what that means, my friend?"

"I've no idea," replied Alex.

"The usual translation," continued Salah, "is 'wet-on-wet'. It's a process that involves applying one layer after another of wet oil. Unless you're a master, the result can be a bit of a mess." He smiled. "But that doesn't make it a Constable, of course," he said, taking a magnifying glass out of the inside pocket of his jacket and passing it to Alex. "The key to this attribution are the strokes around the clouds. Have a closer look."

Alex hovered the lens over the upper half of the sketch, tracing the lines of air that seemed to blow the clouds across the sky. "I can see it was painted fast," he offered, wondering where this was going.

"And thin," added Salah, nodding. "But the important thing is that these brush strokes pass what we call the handwriting test." He smiled at Alex. "Observe the way they loop upwards, in particular, at the end. No two painters are the same."

"All right, Tarik," he concluded, nodding his head, "take it away, please, and bring in the cloth."

For a moment or two, apart from the low hum of traffic and the distant pulse of a burglar alarm, there was silence in the apartment, Alex and Burhan leaning forward in their leather armchairs, Salah at his desk, Khalid and Tarik a few feet behind him on the park side of the room, holding the miraculous cloth taut by its corners as if they were the white-gloved assistants at an auction – allowing light from the windows to fall on the orange and lemon trees, the fountain, the scholars, and the hooded figure in the mist.

Then Salah rose from his seat, stepping towards the exhibit until he stood, back towards his guests, inches from its surface, appearing to inspect some detail above the fountain. Just as it seemed he was about to turn and address them, he put his hand into his jacket pocket instead, took out a small knife and thrust it into the centre of the fabric.

Burhan gasped and surged forward, Alex following him instinctively, but Salah already had both hands on the material, gripping with the left, and slashing with the right. As the scholar clung to his waist, he dropped the blade and began ripping at the fabric with his fingers until the two of them finally collapsed to the floor, Khalid and Tarik releasing the remains of the cloth so it fell around them, and Alex kneeling to attend to Burhan.

With one hand on Alex's shoulder, the scholar raised himself into a sitting position, reaching out for his glasses, the two of them watching as the prone form of his cousin, face down, slowly began to shake, its right arm blindly summoning Tarik for support.

"Burhan, you old ox," said Salah, turning towards them on the floor, his eyes wet with laughter, his bodyguard hoisting him onto his knees, "I never knew you had it in you."

"What have you done?" said the scholar, lifting the piece of cloth next to his legs.

"Alex," smiled Salah, wiping his eyes, "it's over to you, I think."

"I don't understand," said Alex.

"Well," replied Salah, "if I said I had actually done nothing much wrong at all, what would you conclude?"

Alex looked down at the cloth, torn but still in one piece, and then up at Salah. "It must be a fake," he replied, a sick feeling in his stomach as he began to realize what had brought them to the apartment.

"'Fake' is actually an unkind word," said Salah, once they were back in their seats and Tarik had brought in a jug of water and glasses. "There was no real intention to deceive," he continued. "It's more like the kind of copy you make for display while you keep the genuine article under lock and key." He smiled and shook his head. "The Museum would have discovered this, of course, if we'd given them a chance." He looked at Khalid. "That was a waste of our very useful contact, wasn't it?"

"I had no idea," repeated Burhan.

"No, I don't believe you did," replied his cousin, "but it leaves us with a problem, doesn't it?" He smiled and shrugged. "I may be wrong, but here's my analysis: we have entered a rare, critical period, perhaps lasting a few days only, when the real cloth is on the move, in the possession of whoever supplied the Museum with the copy." Salah sipped his water. "If you act now, cousin Burhan, using your enviable list of contacts and the purchase price that I will approve and wire to any account you name, I am convinced you can obtain the cloth within a week ..."

"Impossible," said Burhan.

"... and when you do so," continued Salah, "I want you to hand it over in Paris, just as your father should have done all those years ago. At that point, as long as there is no sign of the police," he added, looking across at Alex, "the young lady will be released without harm."

"Where is she?" said Alex, rising from his seat, Tarik taking a step towards him, but stopping at a signal from his boss.

"No longer in France," replied Salah, "but quite safe for the moment, and well looked after." He turned to Khalid. "Please give my cousin the details for the funds and our appointment in Paris."

As Khalid handed the scholar a slip of paper, Salah rose with a smile and a shake of his head. "We thought you might have run off to France with the genuine article in the trunk of your car, cousin Burhan. The last time we had seen you, of course, was on your drive south through Kent, after which we found Mr Knowles's business card in your hotel room and thought we'd make a visit. When my men saw Mr Harrison leaving the man's premises on the back of a bike, they were rather surprised to find the girl at the house instead of you." Salah turned to Alex in explanation. "The young lady, you see, had the misfortune to call herself your friend."

With his second large Smirnoff and tonic in front of him on an outside table, Alex watched Burhan return from the Gents at the Globe on Baker Street. In the thirty minutes since quitting the apartment - Alex making a brief but necessary call to update Jeremy - they had agreed, after further apologies from Burhan, on a division of labour that would see Alex attempting to locate Carol, while the scholar pursued the cloth, bringing it, if he could, to the stipulated rendezvous - the news kiosk under the departures board in the Gare du Nord - at five p.m. the following Monday.

Despite the vodka, it all seemed quite hopeless to Alex, his unspoken gift their only advantage. "Do you have any idea of where they might be holding Carol?" he asked as Burhan settled himself onto the bench and reached for his Coke.

"I'll be making some calls when I get back to my hotel room," replied the scholar, "but my initial guess is that there are three possible places where they could hide her safely. The first is a compound near Djelfa in Algeria. I know my cousin has had a property there for a couple of years. The second is Cairo, where Salah's company has a number of flats, and the third, of course, is Faroukh's Iranian villa, the one I told you about, in the Zagros mountains east of Esfahan, though I heard Salah is trying to sell it."

Burhan lit a filterless cigarette from his battered pack. "If you come to my hotel in the morning," he concluded, "I'll have the details ready."

"There's no chance, then, that she's in France or Spain?"

Burhan shook his head, picking a piece of tobacco off his tongue and exhaling an improbable amount of smoke. "From my knowledge of Salah, I'm convinced he would have got her out of France and into more familiar territory as rapidly as possible. If they drove down through Spain on Saturday night and Sunday, they could have taken a boat to North Africa and driven her to Djelfa by yesterday evening. Or they might have paid someone to fly them from Algiers to Cairo or Esfahan." He took a sip of his juice. "You'll need the help of the police, whatever Salah said."

"It might be safer to contact Olmo, the French detective I told you about, rather than the London police," said Alex, downing his drink.

"There's so little time," said Burhan, smoke rising to obscure his glasses.

"But you *do* have leads, don't you?"

His companion nodded. "Yes. In that, my cousin was right." He pulled out his eagle journal and flicked through the pages. "The Malaysian dealer ... the widow of the businessman ... the lawyer who drew up the inventory ... who knows what they might say, with Salah's money on the table." He looked up at Alex. "And there are my father's letters, too, that Safwaan said he might be able to locate."

Burhan stubbed out his cigarette and lifted himself from the bench, not smiling for once. "Perhaps we should get started?" he said.

17

Six days to find Carol, Alex said to himself as he took a seat on the Tube for Céline's. But where to begin?

Once he had the addresses from Burhan, he'd ring Olmo. Retracting his legs to let a backpacker go by, Alex did his best to visualise the French authorities going into immediate overdrive with their international counterparts: computer databases searched; suspects rounded up; eager detectives taking their seats as plans of Salah's properties were projected onto screens – all on the say-so of an amateur scholar and a junior architect. It wasn't going to happen, was it?

 So he would have to do it himself. But which of the addresses to visit first? 'Follow the egg', the fairy had said. Did that really mean taking his cue from Delilah, who was holding her compass session at midday tomorrow? If so, he would probably have to get a visa (with Cliff's help?) and a regular flight from London. Spain was the closest he'd been to North Africa, and Oman the only place he'd previously visited in the Middle East.

And once he'd got to a property in Algeria, Cairo, or Iran, what was he supposed to do? Break in at night? What if there were guard dogs? Should he take poison with him, perhaps, or a knockout drug he could mix with meat? Then, to actually get inside, he'd want one those short metal things with a curved end that you could also use to prise up floorboards, a 'jemmy', wasn't it? Good God, it was beginning to sound like an Ealing comedy. But he had to try.

And what about the *human* guards? Even if he got his hands on a gun, would he really be able to shoot someone who was kipping in a chair outside her room? Alex thought for a moment. But maybe he could knock *them* out too. Some kind of anaesthetic on a cloth was normally the way, wasn't it? The guy would be stronger than him, of course, if he did kidnappings professionally rather than, say, architecture, but all Alex would have to do was hang on for dear life till the man slumped. He'd still need a gun, though, as a threat or last line of defence.

As the train rattled south from High Street Kensington, Alex checked off his list: dog drug, jemmy, anaesthetic, and gun. The last two were obviously the trickiest. But wait a moment. Bill's brother was a pharmacist. He'd been in the back of his shop once, when Mel was showing off about the various pharmaceuticals he had access to, so he could easily fly back there at night and pick up a bottle. That just left the gun. The only person he could think of was Rod. Hadn't he once offered to get Cliff 'tooled up', the man having a well-grounded fear he was about to be assaulted? But even if he did manage to assemble all this stuff, how on earth was he going get it through Customs?

Alex levered himself up for Earls Court. Of course. Once he'd got close to the property by normal means, he could immediately knee-tap his way back to London, pick up the gear and return. This was the way forward, then, wasn't it? An artful combination of curve and convention.

Deciding he would say nothing about Carol to his ex-girlfriend until he had contacted Olmo, Alex had stepped out onto the darkening streets and turned into Céline's square, early for his appointment. Now, with no one in or the bell not working, he tried her mobile but got no response. Picking out from his bunch the front door key he should really have returned six months ago, Alex let himself in.

There was a garlicky smell downstairs of something cooking or having been cooked, but no lights on at all and, when he stopped at the end of the hall, a faint chugging sound coming from the first floor. Alex climbed the stairs softly to investigate. Halfway up, he could see through the landing banisters that Céline's door was closed. Jessica's, on the other hand, was open enough to be giving out a dim bluey-pink glow. It was also the source of the strange noise.

When he got to the landing, Alex tiptoed towards the light, stopping outside Jessica's room. Now there was a new sweet smell, like candyfloss. Leaning forward, Alex heard a muffled gasp from inside and a short intake of breath. Feeling that a silent retreat to a safe distance was definitely in order, he lifted his left foot from the carpet and was putting his arms out for balance when the floorboard made a long, moaning creak. Freezing as if he were a Greek dancer in a holiday snap, he heard the sound of a body gliding up the duvet. "Hello," said Jessica, "is there anyone there?"

In shame, Alex hesitated, and by then it was too late. Now he had no choice but to muscle this one out in silence. He guessed she would be sitting up in bed, leaning forward, straining to listen, but at least there was a door between them. If it came to it, he could cut and run, he reckoned, wondering how recognizably Alex-like he would look, disappearing down the stairs in the darkness.

More duvet sounds, and the chugging had stopped. Was she lying down again in a lucky return to the pre-creak state of affairs? Or was she getting up, ready to spring at him with a lamp or a hockey stick? Folding his aching arms, but not daring to lower his left foot to the treacherous floor, Alex was leaning closer for a listen when he felt his entire centre of balance lurch forward, launching him into Jessica's bedroom with the swift crack of a head-butt to her door.

She stopped screaming when she recognized his face. "Alex! What the hell are you up to?"

Lifting himself up onto his knees, he winced and rubbed his head. "I'm sorry. I tripped on the landing."

"But why didn't you say anything when I spoke?"

Jessica was sitting up on the bed, wearing only what seemed to be a knee-length black silk dressing-gown. On the table next to her there was a pink box with a hole in the top and a lamp cloaked in a translucent material that cast a pattern of red and blue orbs across the interior of the room.

"I'm sorry," said Alex again. "I didn't know you were talking to me. Where's Céline?"

"I've no idea. I was the only one in the house when I came back with this."

She was looking at the box.

"What is it?" asked Alex.

"It's for burning powders. The vapour comes out the top. I'll put it on again if you like. Look, you'd better sit on this chair. I think you're going to have a bump on the head."

Alex got up and sat on the wooden chair by the bed. The chugging had begun again, and now the machine was producing small rings of smoke at two or three-second intervals, as if it were inhabited by tiny Native Americans with blankets. They both watched it for a moment.

"Is it making that candyfloss smell?" asked Alex.

Jessica nodded and seemed to be smiling. Her face had gone a little hazy. She was lying on the bed again, her left arm hanging over the side and her right hand resting on her stomach. Alex sat back, watching the red and blue circles on the ceiling, wondering if he was about to pass out, his eyes drawn afterwards to Jessica's lipstick-red lips, the rise of her breasts, and the outline of her thighs under the black silk of the gown. He tried to swallow. When his voice emerged, it was slightly slurred. "Where did you get it?" he asked, though a wand-shaped answer had already begun to form in his mind.

Jessica turned her fuzzy head towards him. "Strange, isn't it?" she said. "A new guy on the market sold it to me. The machine and the powder. Said it would help me relax after work. He looked a bit Peruvian. How do you feel?"

Jessica was observing the ceiling, concentrating perhaps, but probably just *feeling*. And, whether she knew it or not, she was beginning to ease her hips upwards and downwards on the bed. Alex, meanwhile, had become rather lost in desire, as though a small alien hand within his bowels had begun to squeeze and release his slippery vital organs. If this was fairy lust, it was so primal that, as the moments passed, all he could think about was breaking the fragile cords of civilization that bound him to his chair, opening the black silk at Jessica's thighs and pushing his face so firmly between her legs that she would widen miraculously, drawing him inside.

"A bit weird," he replied.

"It's quite powerful, isn't it?" said Jessica, "And it's only one of a range, the man told me. There are some other ones which ..." At this point, she seemed to lose the power of speech as a slow shudder moved down her body from her shoulders to her feet. "... which you can use for backache and that sort of thing. But I think I had better come over and look at your head."

Oh no, don't come any closer. What about Carol or Bill, defenceless against what he assumed was the fairy's belated gift? But Jessica was already swinging her legs down from the bed, moving unsteadily towards him. When she got within a foot of his knees, she tried to lean over him, laughing tipsily and reaching out for his shoulders, tumbling forwards until he drew his legs together, thereby encouraging his companion to open hers on either side in order to approach his wound. This was an enormous mistake.

As her legs touched his, he jerked instinctively, but Jessica just kept coming, bending over him now to inspect his head, exposing her dark brown nipples, her soft hair brushing against his face. And as she placed a finger to the bump on his head, the warm perfume from her body seemed to combine with the sweet smell in the air to produce a new hypnotic drug, drawing the red and blue spheres inwards from the walls and the ceiling until they seemed to be planets, spinning around their heads.

Alex untied Jessica's dressing gown, opening it at the waist and placing his hands behind her thighs while she, in turn, rapidly undid the buttons of his shirt, hoisting the rest of the material out of his trousers, catching a fingernail and smiling as she drew its broken edge across his chest. Loosening his trousers, he felt no pain, and together they worked his jeans and underpants over his knees. Alex reached out afterwards and pulled her buttocks towards him, Jessica resisting and then giving in, finally beginning to lower herself into position – one hand on his stiffened penis – when the lights went on outside the room, and they heard the voices of Céline and Paul in the hall below.

"Jessica!" cried Céline, as she climbed the stairs. "Have you seen Alex anywhere? Paul and I had to do some last-minute shopping."

Jessica and Alex looked at each other for two seconds. In the first, Alex reckoned later, they had both considered carrying on anyway. They might cry out as they dug in their nails or pulled at each other's hair, but they would complete the act whatever the consequences, even as Céline and Paul stood gazing from the doorway. In the second, however, they both must have realized that if they were resourceful, their position was still recoverable. "Céline. Just a moment. I'll be right with you," said Jessica, in a don't-come-in-yet voice.

Quickly she dismounted, turned off the machine and opened a window. Alex, meanwhile, pulled up his trousers, buttoned his shirt, and sat up straight. Then he looked to Jessica, feeling the need once more for the kind of unilateral action that she seemed closer to taking. "Alex is in here, Céline," she shouted. "He fell over, and I'm taking a look at his head."

Ten minutes later, as he and Paul were attempting to swing Céline's chaise longue over the banisters and wishing it were a bit shorter, Alex smiled to himself that he had been able to use his ex-girlfriend's own furniture-shifting plans against her clear and immediate need to interrogate him on his sweaty presence in Jessica's bedroom. He was also trying to put aside the dreamlike images of his recent activity, not because they were unwelcome, but because the side of Paul's head was currently being crushed against the stair wall by the wing end of Céline's chaise.

"Hang on, Paul," said Alex, still a little high on vodka and aphrodisiac, "I'm going to rest the legs on the banister so I can come and help you."

"Gum rung bung," Paul replied, as the pressure on his face momentarily increased, Alex ducking under the chassis of the sofa until he was able to get to his companion's side and lift the legs by their wheels, temporarily pushing the sofa backwards up the banisters.

With the chaise parked in the hall, Jessica, Alex, and Céline took their places around a candlelit table in the kitchen as Paul put the finishing touches to a Bavarian duck stew he had been working on for the best part of a week. His jaw not yet fully operational, he seemed anyway to have sensed that ten o'clock might be pushing it as a time to discover any gaps they had in their pension plans. "Are you hungry, Alex?" he managed to ask. "Would you like a couple of thighs?" Catching Jessica's eye across the table, Alex gritted his teeth and nodded. She still had the look about her, and something sly besides, despite having changed into jeans and a sweatshirt. "You seem to be bleeding," continued Paul to Alex, pointing at his guest's shirt front with the wooden spoon before bringing it back to the pot for the second bit of duck.

Céline glanced sideways at her former boyfriend.

"Perhaps it was a nail," said Jessica lightly, Alex looking up and across at her, pursing his lips. "From the sofa, I mean," she continued, a tremor in her voice, adding, as Paul turned to serve his housemates, "I could get the tea-tree oil, I suppose, but you really ought to be more careful, shouldn't you, where you put yourself?"

Good God, thought Alex, smiling into his stew, she's actually trying to break me.

"Is that what you gave him for his head, Jess, tea-tree oil?" asked Céline, who was a long way from laughing.

"No, his hair's too thick," she replied. "I couldn't find the spot."

A quaking began somewhere deep in Alex's stomach. But he was damned if he was going down alone.

"Sorry, Alex," interrupted Paul, reaching for a serving spoon, "I haven't given you any of the vegetable medley."

"Fine, but I'm not that hungry, Paul," replied Alex, pointing at the plate opposite him and managing to add, "I'll just have what Jessica's got."

Pressing the palm of his hand into the upturned prongs of his fork, Alex was pleased to see Jessica lower her glass and raise a napkin to her trembling chin, turning her head from the table. He was on the offensive now. Serving Céline, whose investigative glance moved between the two of them, with a potato, he looked over at Jessica again. A tear glistened in her eye, but she took a deep breath, bravely bringing her napkin down.

The moment was perfect. Picking up the dish of potatoes with a shaking hand, he observed, "They're rather big, Jessica, but can I give you one?"

They both cracked up, Jessica bending forwards, weeping into her plate, and Alex sobbing his way off his chair, onto his hands and knees.

In the minicab home, which Paul had arranged for him, Alex hoped Jessica was now in as much pain as he was. It felt as though he'd dislocated his left shoulder, every intake of breath like the stab of a stiletto. But at least they had managed to finish the meal in something approximating civilized behaviour, thanks to Jessica asking Paul for a few quick tips on the best way to invest the four thousand pounds she had inherited from her aunt, a strategy that more or less removed the need for further conversation.

He also had the vial Jessica had slipped him as their paths crossed on the way to the toilet, a concentrate of greenish liquid that you collected inside the pink machine, according to the man at the market, to be used in a conventional burner or applied with caution to any warm surface in the household, against the stresses of modern life. They could try it out separately, she suggested, and compare notes.

18

By ten next morning Alex was feeling a little better, the guilt he felt at giggling while Carol remained a prisoner diminished by the fact that he had already picked up Salah's addresses from Burhan's hotel, bought them both plane tickets for the rendezvous in Paris, *and* rung Olmo in France, the detective seeming to take the new developments in his stride, indicating that his department would begin their investigation of Salah in Algeria while his English colleagues (whom he would contact later in the morning) made enquiries in Egypt, but that things were bound to be *un peu plus difficile* in Iran.

Now, though, Alex was once again among the off-colour and the off-kilter, the stoics and the skivers, as they waited outside his surgery for the good Dr Patel. Most of them knew which approach his Bentley would make and were craning their necks towards the brow of the hill between Franklyn Road and the cemetery. When he finally appeared, however, it was from the opposite direction through the sports ground, and the reaction from the people around Alex – a short gasp of shock, followed by silence – was not at the absence of a cheroot or his elegant topcoat, but at the fact he was still sporting both as he glided along on the tiny wheels of a bicycle.

"Good morning," he said, pulling in sharply, dismounting, and grinding his cheroot into the pavement. "It folds up, you know. My son does that when I get home, and puts it away in a cupboard."

Alex, who had managed to secure the first appointment, followed the GP into the surgery and was soon taking a seat in his consulting room.

"Did you know, Mr Harrison," said the doctor, his intense scrubbing-up at odds with his otherwise relaxed approach to his craft, "that hand-transmission is *the* critical factor in the spread of bacteria, pathogens, and nosocomial infections?" Alex shook his head, taking a rare opportunity to seize the conversational initiative as the medic silently completed his rubbing and rinsing. "That's a useful-looking bike you've got," he suggested.

"The bloody wife, that is," replied the GP with affection, chucking several paper towels in the bin and making his way to his desk. "Said I was getting too fat for anything useful." He pulled an X-ray out of a large brown envelope. "I'm afraid I haven't had a chance to open this, old boy, so we'll have to look at it together." He furrowed his brow. "They gave you the all-clear at the hospital, didn't they?" Alex nodded. "I don't know why they've sent me this, then," he continued, summoning Alex towards a white screen by the hand basin, before adding, "Remind me, you got drunk, didn't you, and walked into a tree. Had a pain in your jaw afterwards?"

"Not exactly."

"Still, that kind of thing." He put his hand on Alex's shoulder. "Don't be ashamed. You need to take a few risks when you're young. Surprising how robust the body is. A chap about your age was taken into A and E yesterday, having fallen out of his bedroom window. Nothing but a few breaks. He'd had a drink or two, of course, which helps." The doctor attached the X-ray to his screen. "You don't recall them taking the pictures, do you?" he asked. "Only they don't seem to have got round to doing your head."

"Really. That's odd. I mean, I don't remember them not doing my head."

Dr Patel looked at him for a few seconds while the syntax sank in. "I don't know how strong you are in anatomy, Mr Harrison, but you may be able to work out that they've sent us the chest instead. Mind you," he said, turning to the screen, "there's quite a bit of TB about at the moment, so it's always worth having a butcher's at the lungs."

"You haven't seen something, have you, Dr Patel?" asked Alex, after a moment.

The medic looked at him in a curious way and then pointed towards a white mark, just above the image of his heart. When he had got close enough to inspect it, a chill settled on Alex as he stared at a silver star, the shape of a sticker on a child's homework, but rougher, more organic. "I don't really understand," he said finally. "What is it?"

An hour later, with a double espresso in front of him, Alex was at his desk, sifting through his in-tray, catching sight occasionally of the silvery object in the corner of his eye and wondering, despite the doctor's clinical assessment that the hospital must have got a 'bit of fluff' stuck in their machine, whether this could be the star the fairy had told him would fade, and how would he know if it did, when the doorbell rang.

The knack with the front door was to pretend you were pushing it firmly shut and then surprise it by pulling the lock jamb back with your left hand, while simultaneously turning the knob anti-clockwise with your right. By the time he had done all this, the tall North African-looking woman on the other side, in maroon jacket and matching skirt, had already turned to watch something more interesting farther up the street.

"Hello," said Alex. "Can I help you?"

"Yes," said the woman in an upper-class accent, "why do you think that fat chap over there has bought up every rose in London?"

Alex looked across the street at the man. "That's Philip," he said. "He's hoping to marry the owner of the local Italian restaurant." He paused. "Can I ask who you've come to see?"

"Of course," she replied. "Rod, and my name's Delilah."

Once they were both settled on the corner sofa in the flat above the office, Rod himself finishing off his shower and Max nowhere to be seen, Delilah gently interrogated Alex on the subject of Carol. "I think she's the calm type," was her final comment.

"Yes, I would say so. Does that make a difference?"

Delilah held his glance. "Well, I might have to distinguish her from other presences," she replied as Rod entered the room, a short towel around his waist, his little finger shaking the water out of his left ear. "I'll make us some of your tea, Lila," he suggested with a smile, continuing into the kitchen before she had replied.

"How long have you known Rod?" asked Alex.

"God, years. He designed the tea-room I set up with my ex-husband in Chalk Farm." She rummaged in her handbag. "Here's our card."

"My first independent commission," shouted Rod. "Leonard, her ex, was so tight-fisted he would have chopped his own wood in Epping Forest for the fittings. When's he coming out this time, Lila?"

Delilah ignored this, smiling at Alex and rubbing cream into her hands until Rod, wearing a white towelling dressing gown and giving off his usual smell of Coal Tar and cologne, brought in the tea tray, lowering it onto one end of the coffee table next to a ruler and pencil, before joining them on the sofa. "A Lila special, Alex, black tea Jamaican-style with fruit and plenty of sugar," he said, adding in an all-purpose Caribbean accent, "Sweet as de virgin's dreams."

"Good for the memory, too," said Delilah.

"Helps you to find dat insulin syringe," beamed Rod, taking a jab to the ribs from Delilah, and then turning to Alex. "You got the egg?"

Alex took it out of his pocket.

"Good," replied Rod, reaching under the sofa, "cos' ah got de map."

"Can I hold it, please?" said Delilah to Alex, extending her hand and wrapping her long fingers around the egg, not swooning or closing her eyes, but placing it, once Rod had spread the world map on the table, in the North Pacific, a hundred miles or so west of San Francisco. Next she put her hands palm-down on either side of it, thumbs touching, her left hand covering South America and her right, the Indian Ocean.

"I think I'm ready," she said. "Are your phones off?"

Alex and Rod nodded.

Finally, Delilah did close her eyes, beginning to breathe deeply through her nose. From the street below came the muted sounds of cars, car speakers, shouts and occasionally laughter. Rod, meanwhile, had rested his head against the back of the sofa and was staring benignly at the ceiling.

When Lila opened her eyes again, Alex noticed she had made her Indian Ocean hand into a soft fist. Reaching for the ruler and pencil, she drew a line originating in the south of France, bisecting Italy, Turkey, and Iran, clipping the north of India and the south of China, and ending somewhere in the sea near the Marshall Islands. Looking up, she confirmed to Alex, "Your friend is somewhere on that line."

Rod pulled a face. "You can't be a tiny bit more precise, can you, Lila? I mean, she's not going to be on a dinghy in the Pacific Ocean, is she?"

Delilah's calm expression didn't change. "I can tell you, as a matter of fact, that she's on dry land."

Alex leant forward, his newly viewed heart juddering into action. "My friend Burhan has given me three likely locations, and one of them, Esfahan in Iran, is right here on the line."

Walking south with Alex to an appointment with a supplier in Villiers Street, Rod, now in a white T-shirt, black jeans, and trainers, had also started to get excited. "What are we going to do next?" he asked.

Alex shook his head. It was good to have an ally, but he had to focus on what was actually going to work for Carol, and in cannon world, Rod wasn't just loose, he was up there flying with the ball. But perhaps he could be useful.

"A gang of mercenaries is what we need," said Rod, as they were about to turn from Old Compton Street into Charing Cross Road. "I'll have a word with Cliff. He used to represent a guy from Dundee who got arrested in the mid-nineties in Syria or Lebanon trying to blow up a dam."

Well, that's fine, thought Alex, if we can get a Scottish bloke who didn't blow something up in the Middle East twenty years ago. Then he took the plunge. "Do you think Cliff could get me a plane ticket instead? I was thinking of going over to Iran myself in the next day or two, if you can spare me at work," he said, rubbing the back of his neck with his hand. "If there's any sign of Carol at the address near Esfahan, I can alert the police, can't I?"

Rod caught his eye and grinned. "You sure about that?" he replied. "You'll need a visa as well as a ticket, but if anyone can do it, Clifford can." He stopped, bending down to tie his laces. "Leave it with me, why don't you? I can also find out more generally how the land lies in Iran."

Allowing Rod's latest parry in the battle against meaning to hang in the air, they sauntered on until Alex felt ready to complete his conversational agenda. "There's one other thing," he said. "I know this sounds weird, but I was thinking of getting a gun just to keep around the flat in case any of Salah's guys decide to pay me a visit."

Rod scrutinized him with a narrow-eyed smile as they entered Cambridge Circus. "It's not a great idea, Alex. You'd probably get yourself done for possession before you even got home with it. But if you really think you need something," he added, taking a card out of his wallet, "Sammy here owns a car repair business in Clapham with a rather *dee*-manding clientele. Tell him I sent you and ask for a Taser. If they catch you with a stun gun, at least it doesn't look like you're planning to waste anyone. Max'll probably buy it off you later, anyway. He's looking for something for his wife," said Rod with a cackle. "To give her for self-protection, I mean, not to sting her with."

Six hours later, Alex was allowing himself to relax into the black leather sofa in the dark far corner of Sophie's in Kensington, a Randini (gin, vodka, lime and coconut milk) on the table in front of him. Back at his flat there was a bag at the bottom of his wardrobe that now contained a 'floorboard' jemmy from a branch of Robert Dyas, a torch, a penknife, two sachets of large-dog sleeping powder from Abbey's Pet Products, a can of Tesco corned beef to mix it with, a guide book from Stanford's that included a pull-out map of Iran, and Carol's blue egg. While locked in his desk was a Taser C2 from Sammy's and a voucher from Cliff – exchangeable at a first-floor travel agency on Mortimer Street – that might or may not give him access to a visa and plane ticket for Tehran (via Rome and Istanbul) on a flight scheduled to leave at five p.m. the following day.

With an eleven-hour journey and a time difference of plus three and a half hours, it would be Thursday morning before he was in the Iranian capital, and early evening by the time he had made the train journey to Esfahan. The best he could hope for, then, was to be setting off for Faroukh's villa on Friday morning. Not great, particularly if Burhan and

Delilah were wrong about Iran in the first place, but what else could he do?

Alex took a long pull on his cocktail, stretching his legs, trying to picture himself in action, blacked-up and being technical with his weaponry, but seeing instead a sinewy dog sniffing the air as it woke prematurely from its drug-drenched beef, or a bearded guard clutching his Tasered chest theatrically and shrieking with laughter.

"How was France?" said a familiar voice behind him.

When he had completed his description of the trip and subsequent meeting with Salah, Alex knocked back a quarter of the contents of his second glass and watched as his friend, opposite him now in an armchair, made the small but significant change in his world view that the situation required.

"Bloody hell," said Bill. "No wonder you're piling in the Rondinis. Is there anything I can do?"

"Randinis. No, I don't think so."

Somehow, explaining it to Bill, who wasn't a gay expatriate millionaire, a French policeman, or a boss who had comprehensively seared his brains with acid during the late eighties, brought it all into a starker and rather terrifying light.

"Surely, they're messing around," said Bill. "Burhan and his cousin. I mean, they might be in it together."

Alex tried to think clearly, but the Randinis weren't helping. "Why would they do that?" he said.

"I don't know. Perhaps they're a fantasist family, playing with your mind."

"But what about Carol? She *has* disappeared."

"She could be hitchhiking around Spain, couldn't she, contemplating her life or whatever?"

"I'm wasting my time tomorrow, then, flying to Tehran."

"You're what?" said Bill, choking on his cocktail. "It's you who's mad, Alex. You can't just wander around Iran. They'll lock you up as a spy or something. This whole thing started when you flew to Oman, didn't it, and met this guy on the beach? What kind of person talks to people on beaches, anyway?"

You, actually, more than me, thought Alex. Perhaps that was what was upsetting Bill. "I'll only be away for a couple of days," he said. "And if I find anything out, I'll let the police know, of course."

Bill shook his head and they both looked around them as a pianist, live-sounding but not visible from their corner, started to play.

"Tell me about Carol," said Bill.

"What do you mean?"

Bill put on a look. "Describe her, of course."

"She's good-looking. Brown hair. You know."

"And have you...?"

Alex shook his head quickly. "There's a complication."

"You mean, apart from her being kidnapped?"

"She's got a partner called John," said Alex.

"Oh dear," said Bill. "I mean, if he was called Steve or Jeff."

Alex smiled, realizing as he did so that John must have been in touch with Jeremy or Olmo by now. Bill meanwhile had knocked back the rest of his first Randini, caught the waitress's eye and was asking for two more.

"Anyway, aren't we meant to be talking about your evening with Jessica?" asked Alex.

"At least *your* life's got interesting," said Bill.

That was true, thought Alex, even in respect of Jessica. "When are you taking her out?" he said.

"Friday."

"Bringing her here is a good start, I reckon, particularly if you get her a couple of Randinis," suggested Alex.

Bill looked depressed, though. "Every woman I meet," he said, "seems to have a reason for not going to bed with me. They're just coming out of a major relationship, like Mirabelle, or hospital, like Anne, or they just want to slow things down because they moved too quickly last time. I mean, why can't they move too quickly with me?"

Alex pushed Bill's new drink towards him. "Where are you going to eat after you've brought her here?" he asked.

Bill brightened and leant forward. "It's a classic. A small old-fashioned Italian, of course, but a new one I've found. The waiter will give us their special table."

"They know you already?"

"No, I'm going to bribe them."

"And then back to your place for coffee?" said Alex.

"Well, the Italian's not far. The key, I think, is not to finish the meal too late, or she'll say she has to get up early or something."

"It sounds perfect."

Bill half nodded. "I've even taken the afternoon off work on Friday to clean my room up." He leant backwards into his armchair, looking around him and sighing. "It's all a bit of an effort, isn't it?"

Alex agreed, but all he could see, on closing his Randini-weighted eyelids, was Carol. Despite everything, it didn't actually *seem* like an effort. When he opened them again and took a gulp of his drink, his companion was yawning and loosening his tie, looking rather drunk, in fact. "What would *your* perfect night be anyway, Alex? I bet you've got it worked out."

Alex smiled as a spurt of pure alcohol shot its way to his brain. "I'm on a walking-trip in the Carpathian Mountains," he said. "It's dusk, and I'm looking for somewhere to stay. In the distance, I can see a castle and when I get there, the ancient butler lets me in. Following the local code of hospitality, he shows me to the guest quarters, a large bedroom with a connecting bathroom. There's a fire going in the grate and I decide to have a bath. Afterwards I feel amazing – relaxed and hungry.

"So I find a fresh white shirt in the wardrobe," he continued, "get dressed and make my way down the stone stairs to dinner, arriving in a sort of baronial drawing-room with a massive fireplace, chandelier and that sort of thing. After a moment, the old man re-appears, this time bringing me a glass of champagne on a tray."

"Not a Randini, then," said Bill, stirring his last inch of spirits and melting ice and glancing at his phone, which had throbbed on the table.

"Over the next twenty minutes," Alex went on, "a dozen or so other people – young, old, men, women, all dressed for dinner – join me in the room. They're from different countries, but the conversation and the movement between the groups is easy and light, like a dance. When our host arrives, he comes straight over to my group, a Spanish couple and a young woman with black hair and a limp, and kisses the girl in a fatherly way. We all know, of course, that it's Count Dracula."

"Remind me," said Bill, "that this is your perfect evening."

"Anyway, six of us, including the count and me, but not his daughter, go up to dinner in a gallery-cum-dining area that overlooks the main room. During the next couple of hours, as the waiter brings delicious courses and fine wines, the conversation ranges from science to art to music and history, the count somehow drawing out the best from each member of the party, adding flourishes of his own." Alex stopped as the waitress put a bowl of tiny sandwiches on their table. "After the meal," he went on, "there's a short recital of Mozart or Schubert, and then we retire. Back in my bedroom, I open the window, blow out the candle, and watch the fire die. An hour or so later, when the castle is quiet, the door to my bedroom slowly opens and the count's daughter enters in her nightdress."

"Christ!" said Bill, "it's just a bloody sex fantasy!"

Alex laughed. "I feel great the next day. There's bright sunlight, a decent breakfast, a good library, and a lake to bathe in."

"But you can't actually leave, can you?" said Bill.

"No," said Alex.

"And there's a terrible price to pay, isn't there, after dusk?"

Alex nodded slowly.

"And you must have known that all along."

Alex scratched his ear. "Yes, I suppose so."

"In fact," said Bill, "I would guess that the punishment is a key ingredient."

"Oh, I see," said Alex. "And what does that mean?"

Bill saluted his friend with the last of his cocktail. "It probably suggests you inhabit that place on the other side of the mountains, beyond the land of therapy." He looked at his watch, picking up his phone and the bill. "Shall we go?"

Alex nodded. "But there's one more thing for your evening with Jessica," he said, taking out a small glass container into which he'd transferred a portion of the fairy's aphrodisiac. "If you do get her back to your room, put a drop of this in a burner."

Having left Bill at his bus stop, Alex turned right, passing the Tube station and hiding himself in a shadowy side entrance to the Barker's Building, where he tapped his knee and flew to the pharmacy. Mel had obviously done some re-arranging since they'd been given the tour, but it didn't take long to locate the bottle of Forane that Bill's brother had boasted about, and siphon off into his empty hip flask enough of the transparent liquid, he hoped, to flatten a small elephant.

Back at his flat, he had just put his Samsung down after texting Burhan with his travel plans when it rang.

"The best that Cliff could do," said the voice, Rod's, "was a seven-day transit visa for an onward flight to Delhi. You know what that means?"

"No," said Alex.

"Well, once you've arrived, you'll have to get it stamped at an office in downtown Tehran. Better buy a SIM card locally while you're at it."

"And afterwards I've got to fly on to India?"

Rod cackled. "No. Not unless you fancy taking in a tour of the Taj Mahal," he said. "It's kinda complicated, but basically your trip to Delhi gets cancelled, and then Cliff's associate transfers a pre-booked return from Tehran into your name." A bit of a hiss from Rod. "Makes you want to stay in architecture, doesn't it?" concluded his boss.

19

Dawn must have broken somewhere on the bleak road from Imam Khomeini International Airport to the Visa Application Centre, because when he got there, there was enough grey light for Alex to count out the fare he had agreed to pay the taxi driver. The man was now pointing him towards the second or third floor of the building, shaking his head, tapping his watch and finally raising two fingers. As the taxi drove off, Alex looked up and down a wide, fairly smart street of still-closed shops and offices, decided it was marginally more interesting to the left than to the right, and began walking.

After ten minutes or so, he saw the neon light of a café blink on, twenty metres ahead. Manoeuvring his way through the dark interior, Alex sat, rubbed his eyes, and felt a dizzying kick of tiredness above his temples. He wondered if the unshaven man behind the counter, who hadn't acknowledged him yet, would notice or care if he tried to get in a half-hour kip. Probably not, but drawing attention to himself at this stage of his operation seemed unwise. There would be plenty of time for that later on when he found himself standing on a drugged dog or jemmying his way into a private villa. Instead, he ordered coffee and made his way over to the toilet where he closed the door behind him, chucked a few handfuls of cold water at his face and looked at himself in the mirror above the basin. Behind his eyes, the mist began to clear.

As he drank his coffee, however, and later resumed his walk along Orfi-Shirazi Street, the mental terrain it left behind kept slipping from the sunny uplands of rescue to a dank and dripping chasm, the latter vision staying with him as he waited his turn at the visa office, took his second taxi of the day to the heat of the station, and, after buying a SIM card and queuing again at the ticket office, managed to board the 12.35 to Esfahan with five minutes to spare.

Having wiped the station's sweat from his eyes and drunk an inch or two of bottled water, however, the ride in second class looked set to be reasonably comfortable. Opposite him, in the other window seat, an elegant middle-aged man in suit and collarless shirt put his mobile phone away and brushed a speck of dust from his trousers. He clearly belonged to the other four occupants of the compartment – a young mother in a chador and her smartly dressed kids, two boys and a girl – because they had entered and settled themselves together, but seemed too distant to be her husband. Alex took a samosa out of his rucksack and wondered if the man might be an uncle taking his niece and her children to a family celebration.

Whatever his status, he was the only one of the six not to sleep during the seven-hour journey, unless he managed to insert short naps into Alex's longer ones. The younger boy, with dark-brown eyes, a wide plump face, and a name that sounded like 'Maj-dee', jumped around a bit, particularly when the train passed over a gorge or shot out of a tunnel, and had to be pulled back by his mother several times after climbing on Alex's, not his uncle's, knees. But even he, along with his older brother and sister, slept more than Alex expected. At one time indeed, all four slept together, the mother with her arms round the brother and sister, and Majdee across their knees.

Otherwise, Alex looked outwards below the half-pulled blind onto a mostly desert landscape or, if the kids were asleep, over their heads and through the wide corridor windows at mountains and forests. Once, in the heat of the afternoon, when they had passed through Qom and Kashan, he caught sight of a small walled town on a hill, half a mile from the track. As it began to recede, two boys got up onto the top and waved at the train, allowing Alex the melancholy pleasure of imagining that he too lived there, an Englishman on the shimmering alien streets.

At Esfahan, where it was already dark, Alex decided to take a cab to the centre of town and blow some of his wad of currency on a night in the kind of posh hotel where English-speaking staff might help him negotiate the next day's trip into the Zagros mountains. He wasn't at all sure how the authorities would regard a solitary Londoner mooching around their hills so, with the help of his guide book, he had prepared the subterfuge of using the time allowed by his transit visa to check out the nearby skiing facilities for a visit he might make with his sports club in February or March.

"You can go to Chelgerd on minibus tomorrow morning. Ten o'clock," said the serious young man at reception. "Please you pay the driver."

After thanking him, Alex made his way into the half-empty tea gardens and found a small table next to a long floodlit lake, arched by jets of water. When he had wiped the film of sweat from his face, he closed his eyes and breathed in the scent of night-blooming flowers and perfumed tobacco. If the waiter came, he would order a snack, but he wasn't particularly hungry.

He reckoned that once he had arrived in Chelgerd, he'd be able to find a local taxi driver to take him on to the village of Filabad. That was when it would get risky. He couldn't ask for directions to the villa without making people suspicious. So all he had to go on was the formal address, the googling he had managed to do at his flat, and Burhan's comment, on their walk by the Thames, that you could see its flat roofs from the main street of the village, and that you could reach it on foot by a path through a forest.

Alex turned on his chair – no sign of a waiter – and stuck his hand in the illuminated water of the lake. Maybe, after this was all over, he would come back here with Carol. It was a pleasant thought to keep with him on the doubtful road ahead. He stood. Movement, after all, was the thing that mattered now. The simple act of making one thing happen after another.

Alex looked around him before committing himself to the following day's third manoeuvre. Behind him were the foothills of the Zagros Mountains; in front was the village of Filabad, where he was attracting his first inquisitive look, from a woman beating a rug against the outside wall of her house, like an extra from a movie. To his right, however, on a volcanic plug or crag high above the tree-line of the densely forested valley, stood the unmistakable tower and flat roofs of Faroukh's villa.

Alex took out his Samsung and entered the mobile number his taxi driver had written on the torn-off top of a cigarette packet. Tareef spoke no English at all, wasn't even a taxi driver in the accepted sense, just a café waiter in Chelgerd who had responded to Alex's steering-wheel gestures by pointing at a dusty Paykan Saloon on the street outside, and immediately abandoning his post.

There were missed calls and two texts from Burhan, firstly: *Are you really in Iran? Please confirm. I thought you were going to leave all that to the police?* And then: *I'm in Muscat. I've contacted Safwaan and we're making some progress on locating the cloth. Time is so short, but I'm hopeful. Please tell me how you are and where you are.*

Alex put his phone away. In the sunlight scenario he had persuaded himself to develop during the car ride, he would get Carol out without even raising the alarm, walk back with her to Filabad - thereby postponing the tricky revelation of his powers - and phone for a taxi ride back to Esfahan, where they would jump on a train to Tehran, make for the French Embassy, and contact Olmo.

Back in the present, and thinking it might look a bit odd just to cut down across open pasture towards the forest, Alex walked on into the centre of the village towards a small shop with nuts and dried fruit outside. Inside he picked up a bottle of Coke, no water available, some cheese, and a loaf of bread. The old woman sitting behind the counter smiled as Alex put out his hand and displayed a few assorted rials for her to choose from. And when she said something in the local dialect out of curiosity or friendliness, Alex pointed at himself, walking two fingers across the counter to indicate his business in the area, a hiker now rather than a potential skier. The woman looked up to where the sun would be, wiping imaginary sweat from her brow, and Alex repeated the walk, ending it early this time, showing the shopkeeper his fingers in swift retreat. She laughed and added a sweet to Alex's plastic bag.

Outside, an older man in a hat raised a walking stick at him in greeting from the shade of a doorway. Wondering if the authorities had already been alerted to his presence, Alex looked for a way out of the village, down towards the trees. The street to his right, which turned into a chalky path beyond the houses, seemed promising.

After negotiating a barbed wire fence and then fighting his way through the endless thin green branches of the lower part of the forest, he wiped the sweat from his eyes and looked at his watch. Half past one already, but he deserved a break and the going would shortly be easier anyway in the older part of the woods. Ahead of him a tree had fallen across his path. Rather than climb over it, he pulled off his rucksack and sat against its trunk. Listening for a while to the slow-motion flap of a big bird's wings and then, farther off, the sound of a stream, Alex closed his eyes, raising his head once or twice to jerk himself out of sleep, but finally letting it fall.

Soon he was making his way by candlelight along the upper hallway of a country mansion. Looking across, over the garden's moonlit statues, he saw a woman brushing her hair by lamplight in the opposite wing of the building. When he eventually entered her room, she made no movement, but a man in a navy-blue smoking jacket stood beside her now, a glass of champagne in his hand. Though older and somewhat gaunt, like Don Millman, Alex recognized him as the person who had addressed the outdoor stadium in his earlier dream.

"We're celebrating a second success," he said to Alex, raising his glass and smiling. "Toot, toot!" he added, imitating the whistle of a steam engine, but coughing afterwards, spilling his drink and putting a hand to his chest, at which point the woman finally turned and patted her skirt, inviting Alex to approach and place his head on her lap, which he did –

only it wasn't her lap any more but Carol's, the rustling red silk of the dress she had worn on the plane. As he buried his face in the material, the rustling grew louder until it seemed there was something actually moving under her skirt, pushing itself upwards, some kind of creature, clawing and snuffling.

Alex twitched his head and opened his eyes. Ten yards below him, a young boar was rootling noisily at the base of a tree. When he reached for his rucksack, it raised his snout and sharp-looking tusks towards him. Counting to three, Alex jumped up, clapping his hands and shouting, the animal sinking back onto its hind legs in fear, freezing for a moment, and then tearing its way into the trees.

Shivering in the cool of his sweat, Alex began to push on, the path soon widening and smaller tracks joining it. Maybe this was where villagers came to cut wood? But there was no evidence of human activity, no stumps or vehicle marks. The birds had gone too from this darker part of the forest. The only sound was his trudging and, when the track rose, the breath in his chest. It felt as though he had entered a cave or a tomb.

His thoughts began to wander, alighting at one point on the notion he had simply keeled over in Regent's Park, been struck by lightning perhaps, and all that had happened afterwards - the flying, the cloth and Carol - were the illusions of his last microseconds on Earth. Raising his eyes, he wondered if there might be a trio of judges up there above the trees, hemming and hawing while he tramped the endless path. But surely his offences, revealed to him in flickering images on his very first flight to Oman, were trivial? Unless, of course, it was more subtle than that. What if, though born with a very limited capacity to do evil, you stretched it to the full by a lie or minor betrayal? Maybe in the court's scrutiny that put you up there with the real players, the Hitlers and the Neros, the boys who were twisting and roasting somewhere on the other side of the forest?

That was one line of thinking, anyway, as he padded onwards. Alex was just getting into another, that Burhan, somehow, was always with him, behind a tree even now, or keeping pace on horseback, when he saw the first glimmers of sunlight at the end of his path and, as he got closer, was able to make out the grey rocks he had viewed from the village.

Soon Alex was up amongst the boulders, searching for a stopping-point on his route to the villa. The small cave ahead, once it had been checked for animal occupants, might be just what he needed. Lobbing a stone inside, he watched a pair of tiny lizards shoot out. Bending his head to enter, he arranged himself on the stony floor to tap his knee, the return journey untroublesome, and three UK hours ahead of him, he calculated, in which to rest and re-pack, before darkness would cover his final ascent to the villa.

20

On the plus side, thought Alex, as dusk became night on the Zagros mountainside, the afternoon heat had gone. It might even get quite cold when the stars came out and the climbing was over. He didn't need his torch yet, but the scrambling had turned into something closer to rock-climbing, or at least the occasional need to check the bodyweight-bearing security of a hand or foothold. The concentration and the stretching of his limbs had brought a kind of calm, however, and he would stop from time to time to watch a bird - eagle, hawk or vulture, he wasn't sure which - swing out from the crag and over the valley, scanning the ground for the twitch of a rabbit.

After edging his way up between two large rocks, he was finally able to hoist himself onto the top, a short stretch of moonlit scrubland the only thing that separated him now from the walls of the villa. He turned round. Down in the valley, the few lights of Filabad glowed beneath the black nullity of the forest, but beyond that there was no evidence at all of Chelgerd or Esfahan. Moving forward, the sweat already cold on his chest, Alex tried to attune himself to the different degrees of darkness within the night, holding his torch in reserve, hoping he wouldn't tread on a snoozing snake.

When he reached the wall, twice his height with a sloping top like a small roof, he got into its shadow, following it to the right for a time as it circled the building, and retreating onto the scrubland once or twice to watch the front of the villa grow upwards in the moonlight, a smooth cliff of brickwork with dark oblong windows, no sign of life on these upper floors. He was returning to the shelter of the wall, agreeing with Burhan that the villa and its square tower were more of a fortress than a house, when there was a scuffling sound and a piece of the darkness broke free from the shadows, propelling itself towards him, the weight of it hitting his chest like a bag of gravel, slamming him backwards to the ground.

Splayed on his rucksack, no air in his lungs but the weight gone, Alex stared up at the night sky. Whatever it was, it must surely still be close. Was it getting ready to pounce again? Drawing a first thin breath, inching his way over onto his side, Alex placed his travelling finger to his knee, stilling his trembling body the better to listen. Close by, though to his right or left he couldn't yet tell, came a quick panting sound, a rasp accompanying every fourth or fifth intake.

Alex put a hand out, feeling for his torch. Finding the bulb end a yard from his shoulders and bringing it in to his chest to minimise the light, he switched it on. With no change in the panting sound, he swung its beam first towards the area of shrub above his head, and then all the way round towards his feet, finally catching sight of the teeth, the lolling tongue, and the large black snout of what appeared to be an enormous dog.

The beast snarled, and Alex switched off his beam, fresh sweat pricking at his armpits as he got ready to tap his knee. But something odd about the position of the animal's head stayed his hand. Why was it at ground level, and why hadn't the creature moved towards him? He turned his torch on again. There was no snarl this time, just a whine and more panting. Manoeuvring his beam over the animal's body, Alex saw that the dog, like him, lay flat on its side, as if it had landed badly or was injured. Whatever the cause, it wasn't preparing to pounce. He had to inspect.

Alex got onto his knees and took off his rucksack, his back shooting an arrow of pain towards his buttocks, but no further snarls from the animal. He pushed his hand into the bag and found the muzzle of the Taser. With the gun in his right hand and the torch, directed at the dog's head, in his left, he stood up.

As if to prove it was still a threat, the creature pulled its lips back with a low growling sound, but that was all it seemed capable of. With his Taser towards its torso, Alex took a closer look. The beast was big all right, something you could saddle up for a child to ride, but it was ancient, too, and skinny, ribs protruding like a cow's in a famine. The animal must have given its half-starved all to knock him over in a last mad spurt of guard-dog zeal. Then he saw the sad broken shape of the creature's twitching hind legs. Out here, the beast was surely finished.

Alex put away his stun gun and looked for a rock, finding a large one close to the wall, almost too heavy to lift, and returning afterwards to the scene of the attack. Placing his torch on the ground with the beam on the creature's head, he knelt by its side, stroking the balding fur on its back, before raising the stone as high as he could – for the animal's sake and for his, he wanted to do this right – and bringing it down onto the dog's skull.

Collecting his things together, almost in tears, Alex walked rapidly onwards, noticing a break in the wall twenty metres ahead of him. Too soon for the main entrance, it could just be a shadow. Closer up, however, he was able to make out the ornate ironwork and heavy padlock of a small arched gate, choked in weeds. Wondering what help it might offer him, he stepped towards it, putting his left leg experimentally onto the top of the padlock and hoisting himself up by the iron bars, hoping that inspiration would follow.

Tilting his head back, he could see a groove in the brickwork a foot above the gate, where it looked as though the rendering and some of the stone had fallen out. Since there wasn't a long way to fall, he pushed his right hand upwards into the gap. Now at full stretch, he took a deep breath and flung his left arm up to join it, fingertips reaching into the groove, scrabbling legs finding new purchase on the ironwork. There he clung for a moment, sinews burning, armpits wet with sweat, his arse sticking out into the Iranian moonlight.

With nothing to lose, he attempted to repeat the manoeuvre. Steering his right hand up to the top of the wall, his body swung left, the brickwork scraping his cheek until he found a new foothold, which allowed him to free his other arm and stretch that up too, a jab of pain in his collarbone, but both hands now in position on the ridge, and his feet in the original groove. Looking up at the stars, he went to work on the final pull, shoulder muscles alive with pain, hauling his body up like a deadweight before kicking his right leg over the top until, yes, there he was, lying along the ridge, his shirt and face soaked in sweat, the apex of the mini-roof temporarily dividing one testicle from its partner.

Alex stayed in that position, a little leverage from his knees relieving the pressure on his balls, until he felt ready to kneel and then sit, precariously, on the top. As he did so, rubbing and rotating one shoulder at a time, it surprised him how much he could see of the villa's moonlit gardens: a patchwork of overgrown hedges and squares of weed-covered earth divided by a gravel drive, some sort of fountain, and a dozen steps that led up to the main entrance, shuttered windows on either side. No lights, however, or parked vehicles. Could Carol really be inside?

Alex lowered himself to the ground, making his way back along the wall and following a path to the side of the house, a blank of stonework above a railed-off basement. Taking out his torch, he checked the time. Ten o'clock. Then he let the beam fall into the darkness below, where it picked out a small window.

Straddling the railing, Alex jumped down, taking off his rucksack and pulling out the jemmy, weighing it in his hand, wondering what on earth he was up to. But it was too late to think like that. Inserting the sharp end of the bar into the tiny gap between the frames, he began to lever the right-hand pane away from the left, the catch resisting his efforts but then beginning to give. One final push and the window opened with a soft splintering sound and a faint smell of resin. Alex shone his beam in.

Below the window was a long worktop with a sink; over on the right, what seemed to be a large oven. Oblong tins – for bread? – hung from hooks on the ceiling. Alex unbolted the left-hand window, lowered himself inside, and crossed the room to the door. Since there was no light underneath and no sound beyond, he turned the handle and stepped out, finding himself at the corner of a corridor. To the left, his beam faded into limitless darkness. Straight ahead, he could make out the beginnings of a stone staircase.

Approaching the first step, he switched his torch off and began to feel his way up, his hands on the wall for support. When his right foot swung into open air, he knew he must be standing at the edge of the entrance hall. Moving forward, step by step, passing tiny shafts of moonlight that filtered through the shutters, he finally reached out, feeling for the inside of the villa's wooden door, leaning against it and listening.

Still no sound or sight of life. Wondering if he'd walked his way into an Iranian cul de sac, courtesy of the fairy, Delilah, and his own mad leaps of faith, Alex switched the torch on again, reckoning he'd search the ground floor first, seeing if he could find access to the cave-like cellar Burhan had described to him, before making his way upstairs in case Carol had been locked up to rot in a bedroom or the tower.

Half an hour later, nothing but empty rooms in the lower part of the building, and no sign of an entrance to the cellar, Alex found himself at the top of the stairs, enough moonlight there from the unshuttered windows for him to turn his beam off and, once he got going, a kind of carelessness visible in the upper part of the house – furniture covered in sheets or askew – as if a gang of kids had run riot, chasing each other and hiding. Room after room he went, one floor after another, but there was no evidence anywhere of a prisoner.

At the end of a corridor on the third floor, however, he found the small oblong entrance he was looking for. Bowing his head to pass through, he peered upwards at the darker interior, a cold smell of mud and hay about it. His torch switched on, he began to climb the spiralling stone steps of the tower. When he had passed a third set of windows, narrow as arrow-slits, the stairway came to a halt, blocked by what looked like a large manhole cover. Pushing at it with his hands achieved nothing at all, but when he added his head to the mix, cushioning it with his rucksack, he found he could squeeze the metal disc far enough open, first to smell the night air on the other side, and finally to wriggle his way out from under its giant paw and onto the roof.

Nothing here either. As he stood under the moon, surrounded by the low castellated wall of Faroukh's tower, a sick, useless feeling crept up from his stomach. Straight ahead were the forest and the foothills he had climbed; below, the gardens and the fountain; and behind him, when he had turned, a portion of the Zagros mountains, here in the form of a high flat ridge that eventually fell steeply away, climbing again to a similar level but now of crags and rocky outcrops.

Getting ready to retreat, it was a glow at the very base of the V-shape between the two masses that finally drew his attention – soft, like a low star, steady for a minute, but soon separating into two beams that soared into the sky above Alex's head, before dipping into the valley below, as a car descended from the mountain pass.

After following the lights of the vehicle as it pulled along the valley and began to climb up towards the villa, Alex descended to the first floor, slipping once on the stone steps of the tower, and took up a crouching position at the far end of the landing, where he could peer at the entrance hall through the banisters like a child at its parents' party. Removing his shoes and placing them in his bag so he could creep back along the corridor if required, he watched until the grey shafts of moonlight from the front shutters turned to gold, and the vehicle came to a stop outside, its engine remaining on until a car door had slammed shut.

As the headlights swung away from the windows, Alex waited for the turn of the key in the lock, pulling himself back into the shadows when the lights were switched on and a tall elderly man, clean-shaven and wearing a belted raincoat, entered alone. He placed a canvas bag on the floor and looked around him, his expression blank.

When the old man picked up his holdall, crossing the hall and descending the steps towards the bakery, Alex decided to follow. Rummaging in his rucksack, he pulled out the stun gun, not really wanting to Taser a senior citizen, but ready to act should the man turn on him. His bag on his back, he made his way down the stairs, trying to remember if they creaked.

The lights were on in the corridor as he edged his head round, but the man must have turned the corner. Alex crept after him, finally reaching the bakery, where he heard a door close at the far end of the passageway, followed by footsteps. When he realized they were returning in his direction, he squeezed down the door handle, slipped inside amongst the hanging tins and eased it shut again, the thumping of his heart offset by a fleeting notion that the whole thing was poised to turn into a French farce. It would just be his luck if the old bloke suddenly felt like baking himself a loaf of bread.

When the footsteps passed and the line of light under his door had been extinguished, Alex made his own way back along the passageway, climbing the steps to catch sight of the man in the distance, now without his bag, heading along a newly lit corridor to the left of the main stairs and entering one of the rooms on the right. Alex waited for a moment. Then he followed, tiptoeing forward with his Taser like a pantomime villain, crossing the hall and halting outside the room, its door ajar, pondering what to do next, given that he couldn't just barge in after the bloke, when the phone rang out from inside. After a minute or two of not being answered, it stopped. Then it started again. Why was the guy ignoring it? Was he deaf, or had he moved into an adjoining room?

Alex placed his stun gun in the waistband of his trousers, remembering to check the safety cover first. Tasering his dick with fifty thousand volts at a two-inch range would probably launch him through the floors of the villa and out into the night sky. Then he pushed gently on the door, no one to be seen through the widening gap, and silence now the phone had stopped for the second time.

The interior was lit by wall lamps, and unless he was crouching somewhere in the shadows, the old man wasn't there. Had he got the wrong room? Looking around, he could see it was the office he had briefly entered during his ground-floor search, filing cabinets against the wall, a large desk in the middle where the phone was, and a neat pile of documents next to it, held down by a glass paperweight. Leafing through them – floor plans of the house and photographs of the exterior under commercial letterheads – Alex remembered what Burhan had said about Salah consolidating his assets and, looking up from the desk, was wondering if the old bloke might be preparing to meet a prospective buyer the following morning, when his attention was caught not so much by two portraits of the same middle-aged man on the far wall, one in western and the other in Arab dress – Faroukh himself, perhaps? – but by the vertical line of shadow running up between them from the carpet to the picture rail.

As he walked round the desk, it became clear that the line was actually a crack, and that halfway up on the right, in the centre of a square that was paler than its surroundings, there was a keyhole. Pushing his fingers into the quarter-inch space next to the hole, Alex was able to lever the right-hand panel towards him and put his head round. For a moment, he didn't move.

On the other side, illuminated by beacons set at regular intervals in the ceiling, was a circular tunnel, fifteen feet or so in diameter, which descended gradually into the earth, ending fifty yards away in two lights at waist height that seemed in the dimness to suggest a second doorway or entrance. This was where the old man must have gone.

Putting his shoes on again, Alex pulled out his Taser and advanced, shivering in the damp air, making his way downwards over the gravel flooring, slowing when he came to the grey metal door and realized it was open by a foot, but giving out no light or sound. Stepping inside, he buried himself in a nook to the left and cast his eyes upwards to the weak ceiling lights that suggested the dimensions within of a small parish church. Surely, if his fleshy friend's fantastic tales were to be believed, this must have been Faroukh's chamber of treasures?

Keeping to the left-hand wall, Alex moved farther into the cavern. With its contents transferred elsewhere by Salah, as Burhan had assumed, all that remained, it seemed, was this empty space with its strange alcoved walls and something living too, from a squeak and a flutter in the rafters. But where was the old man?

Alex walked on, determined to complete a circuit of the cellar, when there was a knocking sound, of wood on rock, coming from a point opposite him. Ducking into the nearest alcove, he watched a roving beam of torchlight penetrate the dimly lit chamber, illuminating a grille in the far side of the cavern, which swung open as the old man entered with a ladder under one arm, closing the gate behind him and, from the sound of it, slamming a padlock shut.

Alex remained squashed against the left-hand wall of his tiny alcove, hoping the man's beam would bob around a bit without actually falling on him, remembering, despite the cold drop of sweat that stung his left eye, a childhood game where you would hide in a darkened room while an SS stormtrooper, implausibly required to remain in the doorway, tried to locate you with a torch. In reality, however, the old man did no more than cough a couple of times before making for the grey door, switching the lights off and locking it behind him as he left.

Alex waited for a moment or two in absolute darkness. Then he took off his rucksack and felt for his torch, turning it on and crossing towards the grille. Before he got there, though, he had to step up onto a raised platform, resembling a wooden stage. He wondered if that was where Faroukh had sat in the evening, contemplating his growing collection. When he reached the grille, Alex poked his beam through the bars. At the end of a short corridor with a wet, stony floor, there was nothing more than a small utility area with dust cloths, boxes, a mop and a bucket. "Carol!" he shouted without any hope, his voice echoing around the cavern.

Returning to the centre of the stage, he sat, arms stretched out behind him, beam directed at his feet. So what if this place was Faroukh's once, Salah's now, and soon to be sold? Carol wasn't here. Large villa with dead dog and good cellarage, he thought to himself. Tower to chuck yourself off. Woodland walks.

Gloom was settling its cold hand on Alex's chest. It would be Saturday soon. Carol had been gone for a week. Looking upwards at the roof of the cellar, he prayed: please God, he said, let her return from her fastness in Cairo, Djelfa, or wherever, even unto the iceman's arms. Picturing his bed in London, he thought of sleep, a long sleep. With the Monday rendezvous approaching, he needed rest. And surely there would be good news anyway in the morning to wake to, from his resourceful, bearded chum and his book of contacts, the photographic cloth already in his plump possession?

He picked up his torch. "Let's travel," he finally intoned, from within Faroukh's vault.

21

Unable to hold his breath any longer, Alex drew his head upwards through the water until he reached the steam-filled atmosphere of his windowless bathroom. Thirteen hours' sleep he'd had, after arriving home and texting Burhan with the blank he'd drawn in Iran. Now there were only forty-eight to go before the two of them were due to meet Salah's men at the Gare du Nord. Not that there'd been a reply from his fabulist friend, only Olmo asking him to ring back on a landline, and Jeremy saying he was in London for the weekend and would see him at Rod's.

Pulling a towel around him, Alex walked into the living-room, picked up his Samsung, and tried the detective's number again. At least if he got through this time, the dull sleep-ache in his head would have had the benefit of a pretty thorough soaking. An even electronic tone, like a patient flatlining, was disturbed once by a soft clicking sound, but otherwise Alex had plenty of time to imagine an old black handset on a wooden desk behind the frosted glass of Olmo's office.

"*Oui, allô. C'est Anne à l'appareil.*"

'Anne' was a bit relaxed for a police station, wasn't it? Alex stumbled into action. "*Bonjour. Je voudrais parler avec Monsieur Olmo, s'il vous plaît.*"

"*C'est de la part de qui?*"

Yipes. What did that mean? He'd try his name. "Alex. Alex *ici.*"

"*Bon. Ne quittez pas,*" she said, adding, in a pleasantly strong accent, "Ee is in ze garden."

Putting aside the rather breezy image of coppers in pairs, strolling a quadrangled lawn until they were buttonholed by secretaries, Alex deduced he'd been diverted to Maison Olmo, chic Anne (in pearls?) now summoning her husband from a kitchen or living-room window.

"Alex?" said Olmo soon afterwards. "Thank you for returning my call. Have you had any further news about Carol?"

"No. Nothing at all."

"Well then, I had better tell you about our investigations into the addresses. In Iran, *zéro.* We have few contacts there and no cooperation. Eventually something could be done but not quickly." Alex pushed his palm flat against the living-room window like a sucker. "Cairo is not much better," added the inspector. "My colleague in London has been looking through property records that are connected to Monsieur Salah. It isn't straightforward. There are several holding companies with different names, I'm afraid. But we will continue."

Alex tightened his towel and moved towards the sofa.

"However," concluded Olmo, "you might find North Africa to be more interesting. I asked an Algerian colleague to arrange a police visit to the address in Djelfa that you gave me. The property, as a matter of fact, is in the process of being sold. Completely empty. But ..."

"Yes?"

"Well, I made it clear that I wanted the officers to make a full search of the house and gardens and while they were doing this, they were approached by a neighbour. I say 'neighbour' but it seems her apartment is at least a hundred metres away. *De toute façon*, she said she had noticed something strange the previous evening, which she wouldn't have mentioned at all except for seeing the policemen there. Apparently, a light in a top floor window was switched rapidly on and off several times around eleven o'clock."

"A signal," said Alex.

"Well, possibly. We know your friend is resourceful. But what makes it more interesting, in my view, is the fact that the house was for sale. Do you remember when I said we might have an advantage because the kidnapping was done *par impulsion*, impulsively? You see, you wouldn't normally use a property for criminal purposes that you are in the process of selling, would you, because once a house is on the market, people automatically become curious about it."

"So they could have held her there for a night or two, before moving her on to Cairo?"

"Or Iran. Or somewhere completely different."

Now Alex had to speak. "Monsieur Olmo, I've been to Iran."

Alex wasn't surprised at the short pause that followed.

"I don't understand, Alex."

"I'm sorry but I had to do something, so I took a plane and made my way to the address."

A second pause. Alex wondered how pissed off the detective was going to be.

"*Ça se fait pas*," said Olmo quietly. "You shouldn't have done that, Mr Harrison."

"I know."

"And the villa was empty, I suppose?"

"Yes, except for an old man. A caretaker perhaps. It looked like he was there to sell it, just like the Algerian house."

"And what would you have done if your kidnappers had been there? Tried one of your citizen's arrests, perhaps?" Alex thought it best to say nothing. "Is there any other information," added Olmo, "that you would care to give me at this point?"

Alex breathed in. "Well, Burhan has been back to Oman, following leads on the cloth. He said he was making progress."

A third pause from Olmo, punctured by a bit of background saucepan handling, presumably from Anne. Alex hoped the detective wasn't busy aligning himself with one of Bill's more sceptical hypotheses on Burhan and his cousin. When he finally spoke, however, his tone was accommodating. "Okay, Alex. Don't worry. Go to the Gare du Nord on Monday, as arranged. I will ask a colleague from Paris to attend, with the utmost discretion of course. If Burhan has the cloth, hand it over. If he doesn't, say that you need another four or five days. Leave the rest to us. This is the best we can do. Do you agree?"

Alex did, and was putting the phone down when he saw the text from Burhan. "*I'm sorry you found nothing in Esfahan,*" it said. "*You did well to try. I'm working up to the last moment in Oman. I hope, by God's grace, it will bear fruit. I'll make my own way to Paris. Can you meet me at Gare du Nord? Earlier than five if I can make it. I'll text you.*"

Two and a half hours later, Alex was repeating Olmo's script, without the French accent, to an audience of Jeremy, Rod, and Max on Rod's central London corner sofa, with Constance listening or not listening in the kitchen. Through the room's other open door, a slight bulge was visible in the upper bunk of the bedroom, where Cliff, on the run again, was yet to rise.

Max, looking slightly stoned, put a large piece of paradise cake into his mouth, filling whatever space was left with a decent draught of sparkling water. Now he was ready to speak. "We need to fugging well get over there and find her," he said. "There's still time."

The other occupants of the sofa seemed to wrestle for a moment with the concept of 'there', given there was still no evidence of Carol being in Iran, Algeria, Cairo or anywhere else.

"Somewhere south or east, is that then, Max?" grinned Rod finally.

The Austrian was unfazed. "Once we're motoring, we'll pick up clues, won't we? No problem."

It was a happy notion, thought Alex, all four of them, with Cliff in the boot perhaps, speeding through North African villages, stopping to pick up one of Carol's shoes or a brooch, before haring off again on Max's latest demented instruction.

"How are you getting to Paris?" said Jeremy, leaning forward and putting his half-eaten cake back on the coffee table.

"I'm flying on Monday," replied Alex, "though not with Burhan, in the end. He's going to meet me there."

"If you've got a spare ticket, why don't I travel with you?" asked Jeremy. "I need to get back to France, anyway, and there are some chores I could take care of in Paris." He nodded in the direction of the bedroom. "Cliff'll help us to change Burhan's ticket, or I'll get a new one."

"Okay," said Alex, "and thank you. Has John been in touch with you yet?"

Jeremy raised his eyebrows. "I'm afraid so. I referred him to Olmo."

Max was working at a bit of nut stuck between his front teeth. "I reckon you'll discover they've bumped Burhan anyway."

"Bumped *off*, Max, I think you'll find," hissed Rod with a grin.

"Wouldn't that be rather counter-productive?" asked Jeremy.

Max shook his blond fringe, lit a cigarette, and put some more cake in his mouth. "He's a done a clever liddle thing on his own with the cloth, hasn't he, but they tailed him, don't you see, and bumped him to get it." He gripped Alex's shoulder with his cigarette hand. "And now they're gonna try and bump you, my friend."

Constance brought in a tray with coffee, brandy, and some tiny bottles of sparkling wine Rod had got a deal on. "They wouldn't *bump* him in the Gare du Nord," she suggested with a smile.

Max, who had a thing about small bottles, was already unscrewing a sparkler. "A big station like that is a perfect bump spot," he said to her. "With all those people shouting and shoving, no one sees a blade going into Alex's femoral. He bleeds to death in under a minute, let's say." Max sucked deeply on his cigarette. "Or they chuck him under a train."

Rod had got a hiss and grin going. "The thing about trains in stations, Max, is they're never really moving that fast. I mean, Alex would be pushed about the track a bit but not exactly flattened."

Alex discovered, as he began to form a response, that he was actually rather superstitious about contributing to a conversation around his own death. So he focused instead, while Max, continuing on the theme of railway assassinations, spat fresh bits of cake into his ear, on the hand falling out of the upper bunk, the presence of coffee being detected, Alex reckoned, through the soft skin of its palm. A leg followed soon after and the whole torso began a swivelling movement that not only allowed the ex-lawyer to slide safely to the floor, but also provided him with a robe of sheets when he got there.

"Morning, judge," beamed Rod, halfway through whatever Max was saying. Cliff nodded benignly, feeling his way along the windowsill for his glasses, and then checking the street before he sat. "How was Iran, Alex?" he said, gulping back half his cup. "Good place to hang out in?"

Rod cackled, as he drew on his latest vaping device, its tank the size of a cigarette packet. "There's a place that caffeine takes you to, isn't there, Cliff, where your ex-brain pounces on any information that may be useful to you at some point. You can't go on the run in Iran, you know."

"Fugging right, you can't," added Max. "They got a mad mullah cop network. They would have you by the balls within maybe twenty-four hours."

"Thanks for arranging the tickets," said Alex in Cliff's direction, hoping he wouldn't have to lie again about his return journey from Iran. "I made it to the villa I wanted to see."

"Good for you," said Cliff. "I'm sure it's got potential. You and Max should go over on business visas, Rod. And *you* could put some dosh in, Jeremy. Any legal advice you need, of course ..."

"A friend of Alex's has gone missing, actually, or been taken against her will," said Jeremy. "And he's trying to find out what happened."

"Oh, I see. I'm sorry," said Cliff. "And you think she's in Iran?"

Jeremy looked across at Rod and said, "Delilah did her thing with the map, apparently."

"Problem taken care of, then," grinned Cliff, as he adjusted his glasses and reached for his cup.

"Forget about Delilah," said Max, not ready to give up. "Why don't we all go to Paris? When the scumbags who took her come out of the woodwork, we jump them and we got our own hostages."

Alex guessed what was coming next.

"Wait a moment," said Cliff. "One of my clients was this explosives guy from Dundee. He could easily organise a gig like that."

The Scotsman had risen again, the bloke who didn't blow up a dam. It was time for Alex to go. "I'll be fine on Monday," he said, getting up.

Jeremy reached over, touching him on the arm. "We'll speak later."

"Keep me posted," said Rod, as he accompanied Alex to the door. "Just give me the signal, and I'll unleash Max."

22

"You seem different these days," said Céline, as she started on the nails of her right hand. "Apart from the giggling last Tuesday. That was you."

Alex, with no news from Burhan and nothing more he could do on the Carol front, had called round to collect Bill from Jessica for a Sunday-lunchtime drink, and was standing now by the window of Céline's room, where the chaise longue had been.

"Bill told me about your trip to France," she continued, "and the man from Oman and the girl who might be missing. What's her name again?"

Alex got his vocal cords into neutral. "Carol," he said, returning to plunge the coffee in Céline's mini-kitchen.

"Are you in love with her?" she asked.

Alex paused halfway across the room, somewhere between short-term comfort and the truth. "Yes," he said finally, to a hanging pan.

When he turned with the coffee, Céline gave him a look that wasn't actually one he had seen before. While he was still considering it, she stood and removed her light silk dressing gown. Underneath she had on a pink bra and a narrow skirt in one of those dark-red colours with its own name in the female lexicon.

"What does she look like?" said his ex-girlfriend, taking an ironed shirt from one of her concealed wardrobes.

"She's in her mid-twenties, I suppose, with brown hair."

Placing Céline's cup on a tissue on the glass-topped table where she had been doing her nails, Alex retreated with his to the window. Outside, it was a simple sunny day.

"You've had a close look, then," she said, and sat. "Anyway, I hope they find her."

"Thanks," said Alex, wondering if she knew from Bill about his trip to Iran or the rendezvous in Paris. "How's Mike?" he asked.

"Tom."

"Sorry?"

"It's Tom now."

"Oh. How's Tom?"

"I don't know," said Céline, who was taking a pair of black high heels out of a box. "This is our first date."

"Really? Are you going out to lunch?"

"Tom's driving me to a regimental do in Cardiff, actually."

"He's a soldier?"

Céline nodded. A rugby player and now a bloody Welsh Guard, thought Alex. Was he supposed to be getting some sort of message? "Don't they do things with swords at these events?" he said.

"No," said Céline, who was checking her eyes in one of her little round mirrors. Alex remembered sucking her eyelashes once. She didn't like it much.

"What happened about your blackout? Did you get it seen to?" asked Céline a moment later as she reached for her lipstick.

"Yes. It's okay, I think. But last time I saw Dr Patel he found a strange sort of shape above my lungs."

Céline put the mirror down. "What do you mean?"

"Well, he thinks it may actually have been a mistake on the X-ray machine. They're checking it out."

There was a knock on the door and Bill stuck his head round, saying, "Céline, you look fantastic." And then, swivelling, "Sorry, Alex. I overslept."

They both studied Bill's head. Even by regular head-round-door standards, it seemed nearer to the carpet than it ought to be. Alex got up and Céline said to him, "Let me know what happens, won't you?"

He nodded, not quite sure whether she meant in respect of his upper-lung area, or finding Carol, or simply in the rest of his post-Céline life.

Outside her room, Bill was already making his way towards the stairs in a kind of half-crouch. Alex said, "What's up, Bill? Why are you walking like that?"

"It's worse in the morning. I'll tell you in the pub," he replied.

His new gait actually seemed to speed up his descent of the stairs, possibly because he was constantly on the verge of tumbling headlong into the hall. When they were out on the street, Alex tried to ignore his friend's condition, but it wasn't easy with Bill limping along not much above the level of his waist, as if he were a tame monkey or a peculiar manservant.

After a couple of minutes, Alex said, "I didn't really achieve anything in Iran."

"You surprise me," wheezed Bill. "What's your next step?"

Alex tried to keep it light. "I thought I'd go to the rendezvous in Paris tomorrow."

"Well, at least it gets you out and about," said Bill. "Has it ever occurred to you that Carol herself might be behind this whole wind-up? She's not a distant cousin of Jessica's, is she?"

"She couldn't have set up my meeting with Burhan in the first place though, could she?" replied Alex, already positioning himself to open the pub door for his short friend.

Once inside, Alex took care of the ordering and transporting of beer, the pub welcoming its guests, it seemed, with a damp seat, a dark swirly carpet that throbbed with invertebrate life and, if their fancy took them in that direction, a plate of scampi or a ploughman's lunch of a large white roll, a brick of yellow cheese, and a pickled onion the size of a snooker ball.

"People travel miles to this place," said Bill, who looked normal now, until he sat back in his chair and his feet rose up from the carpet. "It's retro, apparently."

Alex placed his glass on a windowsill that was narrow but sticky enough to be safe. "What happened to you, then?" he said, a dull link in his brain being forged even as he spoke. "This doesn't have anything to do with me, does it?"

Bill was smiling wryly, or wincing in pain. "I tried that liquid you gave me."

Righto, thought Alex. "Did it work?" he asked, twisting his drink off the sill.

Bill leant forwards, his feet meeting the carpet again, and sucked in a quarter of his pint. "We went to Sophie's," he said, wiping his mouth, "and then to the Italian, where the waiter I had bribed was taking the night off, unfortunately. The conversation was a bit strained, but we've had a lot worse. And we did finish early enough for coffee at my place to actually mean coffee if that's how she wanted it to be."

Bill put his glass down. "I had the liquid ready in the burner, mixed with some oil, so I lit the candle under it when we got to my room. Then Jess went for a pee, and I said to myself, 'This is actually it. Probably my only chance.' We'd already had quite a lot of Valpolicella during the silent bits in the restaurant, and that was after the Randinis. Anyway, I grabbed the vial from a drawer and smeared the bulbs in both my lamps." Bill ran a hand through his hair and looked up at Alex. "Then I thought I'd give myself a bit of extra oomph by mixing a few drops in the water I was drinking. I felt a bit odd straightaway, but walked over to the window anyway and tried to relax. Jess came back a few seconds later, and when I turned round, I saw her finishing off my glass."

Jesus, thought Alex.

"To begin with, nothing happened," continued Bill. "We talked about the meal at Ricardo's and her job and stuff like that. Then Jess said I looked tense and did I want to close my eyes while she gave me a shoulder rub. I don't know what happened next. But I must have fallen asleep afterwards." He looked up. "Do you remember the time I drank that root in Brazil and ended up, according to Maisie, in a gay pride march?"

Alex nodded.

"Well, my first thought was that I'd woken in the middle of the night in that hotel room in Ipanema. My second was, why can't I move my arms and legs? It felt like I'd been placed in a tiny warm cellar and left there for weeks," said Bill, looking down at his drink. "As if I was back in the womb."

"It sounds like a false awakening," said Alex.

Bill nodded slowly. "Actually, it's not bad in there. You get fed without chewing," he said. "Most of the time you're sleeping, of course, but now and again you hear things - a thump on a drum or a kind of flowing sound like central heating pipes."

"But you're completely dependent, aren't you?" said Alex.

Bill looked at him. "Well, you can't get a pizza or take in a film."

"Don't you feel trapped?"

"No, almost the opposite. Although *you* might, Alex. I think you must have been a difficult foetus, frankly."

"How long did this go on for?"

"I've no idea. At one point, it felt like I was starting to spin round. That was quite alarming. I was bigger now, of course, so it was getting a lot tighter in there." Bill pulled his glass towards him, a look of fear altering his face. "Then, after a long peaceful period, something started to happen outside the cellar. Like an earthquake. The walls themselves began to pull inwards, but what could I do? If I kept a low profile, I thought it might all blow over. The rope was still there at my waist, after all." Bill took a gulp of his beer. "Eventually, though, I felt myself spinning again, the ceiling and the floor ganging up on me this time, pushing my head against the far end of the cellar. When the wall gave in, I think I had my first panic attack. But I was properly on the move now, squeezing my way along a narrow corridor." Bill closed his eyes. "It brought back a caving nightmare I used to have."

Alex felt he should be supportive in some way. "Christ," he said.

"That's when I came to properly," said Bill, "covered with a blanket. But I must have been dazed. All I could see were these round things, floating across the room."

"Like planets," said Alex. "Red and blue planets?"

Bill nodded. "Yes, but with a silver star in the centre. And the nearest planet throbbing, red then blue. How did you know?"

Alex shook his head.

"As my vision cleared, I saw a note from Jess on the cushion next to me, saying she'd called a cab. A *very* nice note, actually, thanking me for the evening. And I've seen her since, of course. But when I tried to stand up, I realized I'd done my back in." Bill paused, before concluding, "So when you ask me 'Did it work?', I'm not quite sure how to answer you, to be perfectly honest."

Later on, when he was back in the flat, no news from Burhan, trying to decide what to wear for a meeting with a kidnapper, Alex wondered also what would happen to Bill and Jessica - what would happen to anyone, in fact, whose relationship underwent a quadruple dose of distilled fairy aphrodisiac in its early stages. At least the tale's raw drama had had the effect of submerging his own little episode with Jessica. And Bill *had* looked better for the telling of his story, apprehensive certainly, but then a bloke would be, wouldn't he, rebirthing aside, at the start of any new liaison: the potential for happiness offset by the knowledge that your whole meaty edifice could, at a moment's notice, come clattering down in a pile of gleaming white bones.

Settling for black jeans, a polo shirt, and a suede zip-up jacket, Alex poured himself a glass of wine and got to work on a jar of pesto, separating and discarding the furry bits that had stuck their heads up out of the oil and gone off. There was a metaphor there somewhere if you could really be bothered to think about it.

When the spaghetti was bubbling, he stepped out into the garden and tried to find something small to worry about, the big thing being out of his hands for the moment. But Jeremy had already phoned to fix up their rendezvous and everything else he needed was laid out on the sofa for the morning. So while the pasta softened and thickened, Alex sat on the step outside his kitchen, allowing his mind to empty itself in the evening breeze, each new current of air taking a thought with it, out over the lawn and upwards to the sky, parachute seeds from his dandelion head.

23

Flying to France again, said Alex to himself, once they were cruising over Kent. Where Carol's scent had been light and summery, though, Jeremy's was, well, not exactly heavy but certainly complex and probably very expensive. Alex imagined monks in the first chill of a Sardinian dawn, picking, blending and simmering the subtle mix of herbs and plant oils that would find their way to his companion's perfumery in Bond Street or Park Lane.

"I'm coming with you to the Gare du Nord," said Jeremy, closing over his copy of the *Guardian*.

"But they'll spot you, won't they?" said Alex.

"No. We'll travel separately from the airport, but I'll be watching when you take up your position at the station. Don't worry," said Jeremy, putting his hand on Alex's arm, "I know how to do this without putting the whole thing at risk."

"All right, if you're sure."

Sure you want to help is what Alex meant, rather than *sure you can do it without being seen*, but it didn't matter much. He wondered whether it was Jeremy's business interests that had familiarized him with this type of encounter – picking up rare Parma hams from expatriate Sicilians, perhaps – or just the skills of discretion acquired by any gay bloke over a certain age.

"I was there at the beginning of this, after all," concluded Jeremy, his paper open again over his dark-green sweater, and staying that way until they were gliding ten feet or so above the runway of Charles de Gaulle airport.

By four thirty, Alex was perched in a café at the Gare du Nord, ordering another espresso, a text message from Burhan on his phone. *I'm on my way*, was all it said. From where he was sitting at the corner of the bar, he could survey most of the main concourse. He had been keeping an eye out for Khalid, should they send him, or for Jeremy or Olmo's man, but really, if they were all doing their jobs properly, there wasn't much point. Instead, he considered the access routes that the scholar might take to the newsagent's.

The most straightforward was to come up from the metro, below the Eurostar terminal, and walk directly through the main doors, passing Alex's café and hitting the kiosk after fifty metres or so. But you could also approach it from the taxi rank to his left or the busier street entrance on the other side of the concourse, next to the left luggage, or even from the platforms beyond, if you were to come by a mainland train.

He sipped his coffee as a young woman with long black hair took a magazine from the rack clamped to the side of Bernard's kiosk and held out a note. Something forties or fifties about her skirt and jacket reminded Alex of Carol the day she had swooshed into the London Edition hotel. While the woman waited for her change, she looked at the arrivals board but not anxiously. Was she meeting a traveller for tea in one of those little patisseries outside the station? Alex hoped so, hoped in fact, in one of those benign twitches that came upon in the oddest of moments since that evening at Kettner's, that all these people crossing the concourse – the student in the lumberjack shirt and the grey-haired man touching a handkerchief to the corners of his mouth – could be at ease for a few hours at least in their God-given skins.

Ten to five. Alex had already paid up, so he made his way to the door, tiny tremors of fear flashing now like lightning in the cavity of his chest. He'd worked out a circuit that would take him over to the ticket office, past the tourist information and drop him off at the kiosk in seven or eight minutes' time if he dawdled a little. Surely, though, he'd spot the well-made scholar somewhere along the way, a package under his arm, the miraculous cloth that would set Carol free?

Passing the ticket office, convinced that his gaze had briefly met Jeremy's through its smoked-glass window, Alex positioned himself to begin the final leg of his journey, a bit of a buzz over at Bernard's, someone getting his shoulders clapped as if he'd won the lotto. He'd thought of buying a newspaper, but decided instead to pull up a dozen feet or so from the kiosk and wait.

Five o'clock by the concourse clock. A trickle of sweat rolled down from his armpit. Scanning back in the direction of the main entrance, Alex looked up at the Eurostar terminal where a train had pulled in, its first few passengers already making their way into the arrivals area, and then down at the exit to the metro, where a surge of commuters was jostling its way into the station, a businessman in a light-grey suit in the lead, but in the close-knit pack behind him, his head bobbing up and down, the unmistakable bulk of Burhan.

His heart thudding, Alex took a step in the direction of his Omani friend, when a hand clamped itself to his forearm, a familiar voice breathing into his ear, "Let's just wait, shall we?"

Khalid, smiling.

"Where's Carol?" said Alex.

Khalid looked at him for a moment, before nodding. "In my home country, Iran, and quite safe for the moment, my friend," he replied. "Soon we will be able to release her, of course," he added, stepping forward from Alex, holding out his arms and smiling again. "Meanwhile, shall we welcome our brother from Salalah?"

Burhan finally staggered towards them, carrying a large shoulder pouch, panting so badly that he couldn't speak, ignoring Khalid and embracing Alex, one arm flung around his back, the other too close, for an Englishman, to his buttocks. Then he turned away, shouting something unpleasant in Arabic at Khalid.

The man listened without rancour, however, his hands together in front of him like a pastor's, explaining afterwards to Alex, "Our friend here needed to get some things off his chest but now that he has finished, we can proceed to business. As I stated, Carol can be released unharmed later today, when our cousin Burhan here," he said, turning towards the storyteller, "is kind enough to hand over the contents of his bag."

Alex watched his friend take the pouch off his shoulder and lower it to the concourse floor, Khalid moving forward, and then Burhan saying, almost inaudibly, "I know where it is, but I don't have it yet."

Khalid stopped. "Open the bag, please," he said.

Burhan knelt down and undid the straps. Inside were a couple of jumpers, some books and a folder. "Khalid," he said, looking up, "I only need another two days. Please..."

But the man raised his hand. "I'm not interested in anything you say, my friend. You don't have the cloth today. We can live with that." He reached into the top pocket of his navy-blue jacket and pulled out a card. "Call this number when you have it. Our business will then be resolved."

"What about Carol?" asked Alex.

Salah's man undid the middle button of his jacket. "We are serious people, Mr Harrison. Late last night your companion arrived in a place where we can carry out the first procedure. After I have made my call, she will have to begin accounting for your new friend's delay."

Alex hardly had time to react, when Burhan, head down like a bull, charged at the man, the Iranian stepping deftly aside, and a newcomer in a brown coat pushing past Alex from behind, stumbling on Burhan's bag and deflecting his second charge. Both of them fell to the ground as Khalid manoeuvred his way swiftly around the kiosk, into the crowd beyond.

Alex went after him, skidding into a woman with a child, apologizing and bundling the child to one side, before running on towards left luggage – every traveller in the station suddenly seeming to block his path – three directions ahead that Khalid could have taken, but no sight of him at all. Doubling back once, and then moving on again towards the exit, Alex was finally able to look out onto the rising, sunny street, scanning in vain for Salah's man, his phone, he imagined, already at his ear.

Trotting back towards the kiosk, Alex, who now had his own pressing agenda, heard Jeremy call out his name.

"Here," replied Alex, turning, the dark-green jumper now visible a few paces to his left.

"Are you okay?" asked Jeremy, as a smartly dressed couple with identical trolley cases cleared the path between them.

"Fine, but Salah's man has gone, and there's something I need to do. I'll explain later. Don't wait for me," said Alex, turning again and running towards the public toilets by the metro entrance, glancing once to his right, where Burhan stood dazed in a circle of onlookers, before rushing into the Gents – the cubicles occupied, two blokes at the urinals, one already at shaking stage, but what did it matter – and tapping his knee where he stood. There was no baroque journey this time, just a screeching and a flapping in his ear as if a crow had perched itself on his shoulder.

Back at the flat, grabbing what remained of his wad of Iranian currency and shoving it into his back pocket, he found the piece of paper Burhan must have slipped into his pocket during their bear-like embrace on the station platform. *My cousin Jafar*, it read in hasty blue biro, *tel. 221 0185, add. 10 Jomhuri Blvd, Kerman, Iran.* What did it mean? Putting it in his wallet, Alex picked up his rucksack, knocked back a mouthful of scotch from the bottle, spluttered, and was ready to travel again.

His second flight of the day was more complex, immediately thrusting him into a sea of freezing black water, a layer of ice above him, glowing in the rays of the moon, too thick to break, but penetrated, he saw, by a stronger shaft of undulating light twenty yards to his left, as if there were a fishing hole above. Thrashing his way towards it, lungs exploding now, muscles aching with the cold, he pushed against it with his fists, cracking its thinner surface, reaching out and hoisting his body upwards until he found himself, wet and trembling, in the shadowy far alcove of Faroukh's cellar.

The light no better than last time, it was enough to reveal the two parties seated on the wooden stage, Tarik from the Regent's Park apartment in a black suit and white shirt on the left, and facing him, three metres to the right, gagged and tied to the chair, the visitor that the old man must have been getting the place ready for, Carol.

Alex rested the back of his head against the wall, smiling despite it all. Raising his right hand to his chest, no longer confident it could contain the beating of his heart, he closed his eyes, but only for a moment, the real work yet to come. She had looked tired or drugged perhaps, but even in the dim light, it was possible to see she was unharmed, her jeans and sweatshirt in good order, her hair washed and brushed.

Had Khalid made the call? Alex turned again towards Tarik, too muscular for his suit, his legs apart, like a rugby player on a chat show, no weapon on view but a gun or knife somewhere about him, surely. Was he the one to carry out the procedure, whatever that meant, or was he waiting for company?

Alex leant forward in the shadows, easing his rucksack off and placing it carefully on the ground, feeling inside for the Taser and his penknife. He reminded himself that all he needed to do was give the guy a good stinging and, while he was down, cut Carol free and tap them both back to London. He'd have to make sure he actually hit the bloke, though.

Working the gun out of the bag and putting the knife in his pocket, Alex made up his mind. He would rise, he decided, and walk resolutely towards Tarik with his Taser out, saying 'Hands up', or anything else really to get his attention. The man was likely to comply in the first instance, standing up if Alex gestured him to do so and thus becoming an easier target. What he wouldn't expect, though, was for Alex to fire at once.

Manoeuvring himself from a sitting into a kneeling position, Alex pulled back the Taser's safety cover, a noiseless procedure he had rehearsed in London, and looked over once again at his opponent. If he didn't move now, the gap between thinking and doing would widen into a canyon.

Alex stood and started to cross the cellar, the blood pounding in his ears. "Get up!" he screamed, pointing his gun at the man on the stage.

Tarik froze for a second and then, instead of turning and standing, dived forward off his chair at superhuman speed, rolling a couple of times and, while Alex tried to fix his aim, using this momentum to begin a leap feet first through the air. Some instinct flashed through Alex's mind that the only hope of evasion lay in taking flight himself, and he made his own accelerated bound to the right.

Their bodies met in mid-air, Tarik's extended foot smashing into Alex's left knee, spinning him round and downwards to the ground, where he had the slight advantage of hitting the front of the stage while his adversary was still in flight. Flicking himself up into a sitting position, his right hand still clamped to the Taser, Alex pressed the button as Tarik reached into his jacket, the twin wires swinging out, wobbling madly through the air until they gained purchase on the guard's thigh, just below the groin.

Alex clenched his teeth, holding down the button, injecting four or five seconds of serious voltage into the man's juddering and soon motionless body.

Disconnecting the cartridge and pocketing the gun, he swung round towards Carol, already pulling at her ropes, a dozen feet behind him. As he tried to stand, his left knee turned to water, forcing him down onto all fours, where he began to crawl across the stage towards her, dragging his injured leg.

Halfway there, Carol began to moan and roll her gagged head, as if she were finally losing her senses.

"Don't worry!" he shouted, pushing on as quickly as he could, taking out his knife when he finally got his sweat-drenched head to the foot of her chair. Carol's muffled cries took on a new intensity, however, as he reached for the cords that bound her hands at the back. And instead of moving farther forward, he felt himself being held and then pulled backwards by something at his left ankle.

Alex looked round. Christ alive! No wonder Carol had been groaning. Tarik, still clearly dazed – still attached to the Taser wires, in fact – had managed to drag himself over on his belly and fasten his right hand to Alex's leg. What could he do? There was no time to reload the Taser. Should he turn, instead, and give the guy a good jabbing with his penknife? Or struggle on and try to free Carol?

Throwing himself forward with one final contortion of his chest and shoulders, Alex grasped the frame of the chair and managed to pull himself far enough round to secure her wrists with his left hand while starting to hack at the cords with his right. As he worked his blade, the sweat dripping from his chin, he could hear Tarik panting behind him and actually feel the man's arms and soon his head, pushing their way towards his thighs.

With only a few fibres of the cord left, Carol yanked her hands apart, stood up, and ripped the gag from her mouth. Immediately she was down on her knees, Alex twisting his head round to watch her hands on Tarik's shoulders, pulling and lifting, but achieving very little. Apart from being heavy, the man clearly had a plan and was making steady progress, his face already nestling in the small of Alex's back.

"I can't move him," said Carol.

"Get my rucksack," wheezed Alex.

As Carol ran over to the alcove, Tarik managed to get his left hand onto Alex's shoulder and was now beginning, so far as the immobile Alex could tell, to fiddle about inside his clothing with his right. Good God, the man wasn't about to give him a rogering, was he, in revenge for the Taser sting? But Alex saw instead the blade of the guard's knife gliding smoothly up his body towards his neck.

Carol must have seen it too, on her return, because he heard her scream "Yaaaah!" as she sprang feet first onto Tarik's right arm, sitting on him afterwards, Alex reckoned, as he gasped for breath, the man's head squashing his own sideways to the floor, and above it, Carol, who seemed, out of the corner of his eye, to be eating the bloke's ear.

To the right, however, Alex could now make out the shabby form of his rucksack. Pushing his arm into the bag, Alex thrust around until he felt the cold form of the small bottle he had packed two days before. "Put this on your sleeve and shove it in his face," he said, lifting the Forane in her direction and at the same time doing his best to distract the guard by jabbing his left elbow upwards into the guy's ribs. A dodgy couple of seconds followed, Carol, he guessed, loosening her grip to open the bottle, allowing Tarik the freedom to buck Bronco-style, until Alex saw her pull the man's head back by the hair, wrapping her soaked, sweatshirted arm around his nose and mouth.

Tarik tried a final buck or two, half-heartedly now, coughing as he did so, and it occurred to Alex, as Carol finally succeeded in pulling him up from under the man's comatose body, that her guard had really done quite well by his boss, having stayed on duty, as it were, until he had been electrocuted, chewed, and ultimately anaesthetized.

"Are you all right?" said Alex, balancing on his good leg, screwing up his eyes in pain as they both got their breath back.

She looked at him for a moment. "More or less. I mean, I didn't know you were into this sort of stuff, dungeons and ropes etc. You only needed to say."

Alex tried to smile. "I'm sorry," he said.

"They told me that you and your friend had something that belonged to them."

"I can give you an explanation," replied Alex, "but I think this guy's mates will be along in a minute."

There wasn't really time to ease Carol into the arcane world of fairies and flying, so Alex grabbed her right hand as she stood next to him on the wooden stage, pictured the sofa in his flat and said, before tapping his wounded left knee, "Let's travel."

Instead of frozen seas, however, or stars like diamonds or even cartwheels in the night sky, there was just Carol there looking at him as if to say, "Well, yes, travelling somewhere pretty quickly is definitely one of the better options."

So he tapped his knee once more, repeating the phrase, catching in Carol's eyes a note of alarm, that this might be the moment he chose to lose his marbles, but neither of them, on the saying of it, moving anywhere at all, unless the whole cellar had become a kind of space capsule. Good God, realized Alex with a lurch of his stomach, Johnny-boy's bone-crunching tackle had actually buggered up his flying knee!

"I'm sorry," he repeated, shaking his head as if to clear it. "We need to get out of here and find help."

Carol hardly had time to nod, when there was a hammering on the green door.

"Shit," said Alex.

"My guard's got the keys," replied Carol, looking round from the door to Alex. "And my passport. But how did *you* get in?"

"I sneaked in behind him and hid," lied Alex.

"Tarik, Tarik," came a cry from behind the door, with a rattling of the handle.

Their man moaned on the floor, but didn't move. Carol walked over to him, pulling her passport and the keys out of his jacket. Then she pointed at the grille. "Can you try one of these on that padlock?" she said, passing him the keys.

"Of course," said Alex. "But why?"

"It must lead *somewhere*," replied Carol. "The old man that lives here went in this morning and hasn't come back."

"Are you sure?" said Alex, remembering the utility room, but Carol had already picked up his rucksack, supporting him on her shoulder so they could hobble their way to the grille, as the first body slammed itself into the cellar door with a curse.

Fumbling with the padlock while Tarik's colleagues thumped on the door, Alex sifted his way through the keys, searching for one small enough to fit the lock. Dropping the bunch through his trembling fingers, he picked it up again as the green door resisted its second charge. Having finally found one he could insert, he turned it once and released the lock.

Carol yanked the gate open – more pounding and yelling behind them – and they stepped into the corridor on the other side. When they had got to the end, Alex took back his rucksack and pulled out the torch, aiming the beam at the boxes and bucket in front of them and afterwards to the right, past the ladder he had seen the old man retrieve, and into a tunnel beyond, rougher and smaller than the one that led down to the cavern.

24

For the first hundred metres, the two of them made reasonable three-legged progress along the winding passageway into the mountainside, at one point Carol saying cheerfully, "Bet you'll tell me what this is all about when you're ready," but after that, neither of them speaking, their spectrum of options, if they wanted to avoid whatever the door rattlers had in store for them, having reduced itself to this narrow, rough-hewn tunnel. When the beam from Alex's torch showed them their path about to divide, however, he turned to his companion. "Right or left, do you think?"

"Left?" shrugged Carol in reply, later adding, no more than a dozen paces into their new route, "Can you hear something?"

Alex listened. Silence from behind - had they gone to fetch a spare key, or a stick of dynamite? - but an echoing tapping sound in front and, when he switched off his torch, a faint glow of light. Pressing onwards, they exchanged doubtful looks as the path rose slowly upwards towards the roof of the tunnel, forcing them to crouch. But there was no doubt about the glow now. And the tapping had got louder.

Approaching a small crest of rubble a metre below the roof, they got down on their bellies, nodded at each other, and peered over the top into a full-blown cave, lit by a lamp that hung from the right-hand wall. As his eyes adapted, Carol touched Alex on the shoulder, pointing to a thin man squatting in the shadows below, his body half-hidden by a rock but his face illuminated by the light, a chisel in one hand, a hammer in the other - the old guy he had followed two days before.

"He's called Ferran," whispered Carol. "A kind of caretaker. He opened the door when we arrived in the night, and brought me some food later on. I think he might be mute." Alex looked round, voices now in the tunnel behind them. "Let's take a risk," she said.

Together they crawled forward, over the crest, the old chap turning towards them as they swung their legs round and manoeuvred their way down the rubble on their arses, Carol stopping once and opening her palms in front of her in a gesture of peace, while Alex checked the side pocket of his bag for the bump of his Taser, though he hadn't had time to reload it.

Ferran was standing now, seeming to wait for them as Alex hitched himself once more to Carol's shoulder and they crossed the floor of the cave. When they got to the rock, the old man stared at them, a shadow across his face now from the light above him. Hesitating, he looked over their heads to where the voices in the tunnel rose and fell. Then he reached up for the lamp, turning and leading them onwards towards the far side of the cavern.

Soon they were making their way along another passageway, the size of the last one before it got smaller, Ferran's tall frame partially masking the lamplight, forcing them to move at a speed they wouldn't have achieved on their own. There was comfort, too, in the fact that the man had already ignored one turning to the left and was now leading them into a new tunnel on the right, its entrance partly obscured by a boulder. Surely, with Ferran as their guide, they had a chance of losing whoever had decided to pursue them on the cave-bound fork? Unless, of course, he planned to betray them when the time was right.

The pain in Alex's knee cut into him like a knife, and under his stiff left arm, he could feel the heat and tension in Carol's shoulder. "Don't you need a rest?" he asked her. "My leg is useless." She shook her head, their path turning left to run parallel, it seemed, to the one they had just quit. "Let's get away from this place," she said, Alex wondering what had they put her through, when the old man stopped and turned, placing his lamp on the ground, gesturing them into silence with a finger to his lips.

For a moment, nothing happened. Then they heard footsteps on the gravel so close within the echo chambers of the cave that it seemed their pursuers must be passing amongst them like ghosts. Carol glanced at Alex, her arm rigid against his back until Ferran finally picked up his lamp, leading them on once more, their own path beginning to descend, gently and afterwards more steeply, eventually widening, the lamplight no longer reaching the sides or the roof, and the sense of a bigger entity ahead of them.

The old man turned again, extinguishing the lamp this time and feeling for Alex's hand, pulling them onwards into darkness, the gravel under their feet turning to pebbles; finally, a splashing sound and the chill of water. Soon they were knee-deep, a dim light beginning to suffuse the space around them. Ferran let go of Alex's hand, raising his own to pause them and afterwards moving farther ahead, into the gloom.

"Any idea what he's up to?" whispered Alex.

"Look over there," replied Carol, pointing towards the far left-hand side of the lake, where a wide arc of night sky had emerged through the darkness of the cave. They must be on their way out, thought Alex, a ripple in the water moments later indicating that their guide had returned, pulling something behind him, the prow of a dinghy.

For a while Alex watched the old man's back as he rowed steadily, catching sight of Carol each time the lean frame bent forward. Then, turning slowly around, he looked out over the front of the boat at the expanding, still distant, crescent of night, following the line of the cave against the sky, from its left-hand corner, obscured by a pile of boulders, up to its highest point, where a few stars shone through, and then downwards again towards the lake at the opposite side, where the silhouettes of two men were clearly visible, one leaning against a rock and smoking, the other training his rifle on the sky like a hunter.

Alex prodded gently at Ferran's back with his foot, pointing to the figures when their guide turned, catching Carol's eye too with his gesture. The old man stilled his oars, and then, holding the left in the water, was beginning to pull on the right to bring the dinghy side-on to the cavern entrance, when a dull knock against the rollick advertised their presence. Ferran lowered his head and froze, too late, one of the guards already pointing and shouting into the cave. So the old man grabbed his oars again and heaved instead, the first rifle shot slamming into the roof above them, a warning perhaps.

"Get down, Carol!" screamed Alex, but the echo of his voice had hardly died away before the second bullet hit the front of the dinghy with a splintering crack, Ferran immediately dropping the oars and beginning a deliberate roll to his left, Alex and Carol instinctively adding their body weights to the impetus, raising the underside of the dinghy towards the cave entrance, tipping all three of them into the water.

As the boat fell back towards the surface of the lake, a third shot thudded into its frame. On the other side, protected by the carcass of wood, Alex wiped his eyes, coughed out a mouthful of lake water, and turned to see Carol, thank God, emerge at the far end, her dripping hair flat against her scalp, and the old man in the middle, securing the centre of the vessel with his left hand, using his right to urge them onwards.

And this was how they proceeded, swimming one-handedly and pulling at the boat for all they were worth, another shot to encourage them, skimming over the dinghy. After that, however, the firing stopped. Perhaps it was too dark, the angle too acute, or the guards had formed another plan. Whichever it was, he and his companions had now entered what he hoped was the last part of their journey across the lake, when all that could be heard was the arrhythmic splashing of their strokes, the odd gasp for breath and later, the distant sound of water flowing over rock.

As they swam on, the flowing sound became more of a downward rushing and Alex discovered that their own efforts were being supported by a powerful underwater current, the moment approaching, surely, when they would lose control of the dinghy altogether. Looking back, however, he saw that Ferran had begun to swim against the side of the vessel, steering it away from the current and bringing it in towards the edge of the cavern.

By the time the dinghy finally hit rock, twenty yards from the rushing noise, they had entered a kind of eddy, where it was possible, Alex found, to touch the bottom of the lake with his feet. It was only when he caught the sound of the man's wheezing over the noise of the nearby torrent that he realized how much effort their last manoeuvre had required.

"Are you okay?" he shouted towards Carol.

"I'm fine," she replied, though she too seemed to be catching her breath.

Shivering in the near total darkness, water up to his chest, Alex could feel a fine spray from the waterfall ahead settling on his face. Tugging hard at the strap of his sodden rucksack, he pulled his bag off and got it up into the dinghy. They had lost the lamp but maybe his torch was still all right. He pulled it out and switched it on, nothing happening until he shook it, when the bulb began to glow and the glow turned into a beam.

Ahead of them was more rock and then a wide natural weir thirstily sucking in lake water at its gently grooved centre, sending it to the lower depths of the mountain with a roar. Behind him, as he swung his beam round, Ferran began to communicate something, raising his arms out of the lake, pointing at Alex, at himself and afterwards over his shoulder at Carol, finally indicating the weir, directing his fingers almost vertically downwards. Christ, thought Alex as he leant out past the old man towards Carol, resting her arms on the side of the boat, and shouted above the din of the water, "I think he wants us to go over the weir."

But Ferran was already motioning to Alex to hold the dinghy hard against the rock, while he turned to Carol, helping her to clamber up out of the water and into the back of the boat. When she was secure, he reached for Alex's waistband, hoisting him upwards as if he were a child until he was able to struggle into his old position at the prow, at which point their guide began to pull the dinghy along the side of the cave.

For a moment they glided slowly, almost peacefully. But when they reached the weir itself, the current gripped again, pushing the nose of the boat up against the pale rock, its passengers finally able to look over the edge, where the rushing water met a gentle downward slope, streaming over it in a wide arc, before dropping into a subterranean void that Alex's beam couldn't penetrate. Above it, a fine mist of water rose and swirled like smoke.

Carol turned towards him. "Fuck," she said.

Ferran, meanwhile, was working away at front of the boat, using the momentum of the current to push the prow upwards so it would gain purchase on the ledge. When the dinghy fell back a third time, Alex decided to help. Turning to his right - obliged to shift the weight of his body temporarily onto his left leg - he clenched his teeth against the pain, gripping the side of the boat as he stepped out onto the flat stone beneath the flowing water. And when the old man made to push again, Alex stuffed the torch into the waistband of his trousers and pulled, until together, Carol now a useful counterweight in the back, they had swung and lifted the front of the vessel into the groove of the weir.

Once their guide had levered himself up onto the ledge to join Alex, it was relatively easy to pull the rest of the dinghy out of the lake so that it soon lay beached on the stone, its prow suspended two feet over the downward slope, diverted water rushing past on either side. Ferran now gestured to Alex to take up his previous position in the front, holding the boat steady for him, and then reaching back to push down gently on Carol's head until she had curled herself into a foetal position in the rear of the dinghy.

Putting away the torch, Alex got his rucksack onto his back and followed suit in the prow, conscious that, a dozen yards beyond the rough layer of wood pressing into his cheek, there lay only space and darkness. A moment later, he felt the first creak of the dinghy's frame as Ferran inched the boat towards the tipping point. Alex closed his eyes, his own bones like twigs now, ready to splinter and crack, but Carol, surely, safer in the back.

The dinghy groaned forwards, dipping over the edge again but hanging there still, Alex grasping at the sides to keep his body in place. There was a clambering sound, the old man getting in, he guessed, and a slow swaying motion as Ferran began to rock the boat forwards. When the downward dip swung lower than before, Alex realized there wasn't going to be an upward response. Their journey had begun.

Alex tightened his grip as the dinghy fell first onto its side, slipping and sliding its way towards the edge of the slope. There was a moment when it seemed to stop, followed by a sharp lurch downwards when the vessel finally gave way to the black interior of the mountain, dropping silently into the void.

Clinging on as the timber-splitting smack of water jerked his body upwards, Alex shook his drenched head, gasping for breath, their vessel bouncing onwards through the wave it had created, before dipping steeply once again, sucked into the throat of a monstrous subterranean plughole. With their speed picking up and the rushing water cushioning their second descent, the dinghy was flying now, the wind whistling cold past Alex's sodden head as they twisted their way down the tunnel – a lunatic toboggan ride that left his lungs muscling for a new position somewhere down amongst his bowels.

A few seconds later, after a last half-corkscrew spin had shot them out of the side of the mountain, plunging the dinghy into the pool below, it all came to an end. The sound died, the rushing stopped, and Alex found himself free of the boat, turning and rising through a slow-motion underwater world. Pushing his breathless head upwards into the moonlit air, he looked round to see Carol and the old man breaking the surface of the pool to his right and beginning to swim, the re-surfaced dinghy ahead of them now, close to the bank.

After scrambling out of the water, bruised and shaken, recovering their breath, they found that the vessel was serviceable still, despite a hole in the prow. When their guide beckoned, they all got on board once again, paddling with their hands until the wide pool where they had surfaced led them into a modest river, its current pulling them gently onwards.

Floating downstream, out of the shadow of the mountain, dazed and exhausted, there was nothing to do but watch as a bird flapped out of a tree or a small animal, a rabbit or hare, stopped to look as they passed by in the moonlight. Carol had got herself down in the back of the boat again, Alex noticed, and might even be sleeping. Seeing she had been held prisoner for a week before their escape had even begun, it was amazing she had kept going this long. He wished he had some dry clothes for her; with several hours until dawn, she was bound to get cold.

As for their pursuers, who might well believe them dead, Alex reckoned that the boat's swift descent through the mountain had given the three of them a half-hour lead at least, though he had no idea yet what the old man was going to do with it. Why, he wondered, had their guide put himself at risk like this? Perhaps it wasn't that complicated. His employers had crossed a line by involving him in Carol's kidnapping and this was his way of making it known to them, or to himself.

Now their friend leant over the side, dipping both arms into the water and turning the boat gently towards the right-hand bank. Ahead, across a meadow, were the dark shapes of three or four small buildings in a ramshackle complex that could be a farm. Bringing the boat to the side with a soft thud, the old man put a foot out onto the bank to hold it steady, Carol rousing herself and, once they were all on dry land, Ferran pulling the empty dinghy up onto the rough grass.

"What next?" yawned Carol, looking around her and shivering.

"We follow our guide, I guess," replied Alex.

Rather than walking ahead though, the old man took hold of Alex's shoulder, presumably to give Carol a break, his grip firm to the point of minor assault, motioning them both to stay by the gate when they reached the entrance to the farm.

"Do you think that's his place?" said Carol to Alex.

"I don't know. Let's see what he does."

"Christ, I hope that's not his normal journey home from work," replied Carol.

Alex laughed. "With a bit of luck, he'll drive us to Esfahan."

"And then?"

"I don't know. Make sure we're not being followed?"

"And what'll happen to him?" asked Carol, turning her head towards the farmhouse.

"I know," said Alex. "Whichever way you look at it, he's in trouble."

Soon there was a rattling sound at the door, Ferran crossing the courtyard towards them, a plastic bag and a holdall in his left hand, a short plank under his arm, and a bike in his right. Alex and Carol exchanged a look.

Inside the bag was milk, water, cheese, bread, and a grey coat.

"For me to wear," said Carol to Alex, holding the coat up and finding a headscarf in the pocket, "once we get to town." She looked over at their guide. "Thank you, Ferran."

The old man patted his hand on the bicycle seat and pushed it towards Alex, shrugging, as if to say, 'I know it's only a bike, and you're stuck in the middle of Iran with a gang of thugs after you, but it's a sound bike.'

A clanking noise came up from the valley, probably just a farmer with his milking equipment, but it added a sense of urgency to the handover. Squeezing the contents of the plastic bag into his rucksack, Alex took the bike by its handlebars, leaning on it to support his leg while Ferran led them away from the courtyard, stopping when they got to a small road on the other side of the farm.

Alex looked along the lane and asked, "Esfahan?"

As the old man nodded, Carol put her hand out towards his arm, reaching up and kissing him on the cheek. The man didn't react at first, but then, putting down his belongings, he began to pull at one of his fingers. After a moment, he held out a ring to Carol, rubbing together the thumb and finger of his other hand to suggest they could sell it.

Refusing to begin with, but finally accepting it, she pointed at Ferran's chest, saying, "What about you?" The old man seemed to understand, making a gesture of paddling with the plank, before miming the outline of a house and, looking in the direction of the horizon, placing one hand on his heart. Finally he picked up his things and walked off towards the river.

Alex watched him leave. "Do you think he has friends out there?" he said.

Carol shook her head. "I don't know. I hope so. He seems to have a plan, anyway."

"Shall I take first shot at pedalling?" asked Alex, when Ferran was out of sight.

"What about your leg?"

"Maybe it'll loosen it up," he said, passing Carol his rucksack. "Let's cycle in the direction of Esfahan, and then hide and get some rest. If we see headlights, we can always jump off."

Carol nodded and climbed up onto the saddle behind him, though there was also a package rack she could use when he needed to sit. After a couple of passenger wobbles that took Alex straight back to childhood, and a serious twinge in his knee that would surely get easier when he found his rhythm, they set off into what remained of the moonlit night, a dynamo powering the bike's weak front light.

25

"But where on earth did you get the Taser and the anaesthetic?" concluded Carol, taking off her shoes.

After cycling for three hours, taking turns at the front, they had walked the bike as far as they could into a wood with a stream and then collapsed. And when the sun finally rose, warming them as they breakfasted on cheese and bread, they pieced their story together - minus the fairy, which Alex would keep to himself, at least until he could prove his power - from his stay in Oman to the struggle in the cellar, Carol absorbing it all, describing in turn how she had managed to toss the blue egg into the undergrowth, and the days she had spent in Djelfa, looking for ways to escape.

"Near the station in Tehran," replied Alex, having worked on this during the bike ride. "Rod, my boss, made a contact on the dark web."

"Interesting boss," said Carol, narrowing her eyes.

"I'll introduce you," said Alex, thinking he probably wouldn't.

Carol leant forward, brushed a hair from her eye, and pushed a bare foot towards the gurgling stream. Arching in the light - the tips of the toes dyed black by her wet shoes - it was probably the most beautiful thing Alex had ever seen, this pale form, catching reflections from the water, pulling at the sinews of his heart.

"You were both pretty stupid, weren't you, you and Burhan?" she said, finally.

"Yes. I'm sorry," he replied, continuing a moment later, "But they didn't hurt you, the kidnappers?"

"No, but they had to restrain me at the beginning. Tied me up and gagged me," she said, splashing her foot in the water. "I've had worse, to be honest, in some of those German spas."

Alex too had started to remove his damp shoes, deciding not to mention the threat Khalid had made in Paris, noticing again as he leant forward the faint scar on her right palm.

"It's from a motorbike accident," she said, when she saw him looking. "We went over on the side and I got dragged along the road."

"I didn't mean to stare."

"It's okay."

They both had their feet in the water now. "You said 'we'. What happened to the other person?" asked Alex.

"It was my stepdad, driving me to school," she replied. "He broke his arm. Poetic justice really, since he'd had it halfway up my thigh before we crashed."

Alex paused, struggling for something safe to say, having regularly ballsed up conversations with Céline at just this sort of moment. "And do you still see him these days?" he asked in the end.

"Sometimes he writes to me. He's a music critic when he's not depressed. When I was a child he would play me these bits from Strauss, the non-waltzing one, and at the end he'd have tears in his eyes and he'd say something like, 'Thanks to you, I now understand why the second octave change occurs six bars into Act Three.' He didn't actually start touching me until I was a teenager." Carol looked at Alex. "Anyway, now we're getting to know one another, what about *your* parents?"

"I don't have any."

"Why doesn't that surprise me?"

"I was adopted, I mean. When I found out, they also told me my biological mother had died."

"Have you tried to find your father?"

Alex stretched his right foot out into the water, the second time this summer he'd been asked the question. "No. Do you think I should?"

But Carol shrugged and looked distracted, or just tired perhaps. A moment later, she leant backwards onto the grass, stretched, and closed her eyes. Quite soon her breathing deepened. Alex looked up at the sky and then down at her sleeping face, pale against her dark brown hair. She'd be all right for a bit, before the sun rose above the trees.

Leaning towards the stream, he squeezed his swollen knee and wondered when he would be able to use it again. He decided he should wait a day or two while it healed, and then try a mini-flight over twenty yards or so. Right now, therefore, they'd have to do their best with bikes and buses. He reached behind him, where he'd left his map and phone to dry.

With Ferran gone, and no evidence of their bodies in the lake or tunnels of the mountain, what would Salah expect them to do? Get to Esfahan and head north to Tehran, presumably, for a plane back to London. Would that work, without a visa for Carol? They'd certainly be questioned. And what if Salah had done something clever, such as reporting them to the police as spies, or accusing Alex - correctly - of breaking into his villa?

Alex lay back. There was another option, but it was a bit of a long shot. Even if his phone refused to work, he still had the contact details of Burhan's cousin, didn't he? He pulled out his wallet and found the slip of paper between two damp business cards. *My cousin Jafar, tel. 221 0185, add. 10 Jomhuri Blvd, Kerman, Iran.* But where was Kerman?

He got himself onto his side to look at the map. Nothing big with that name in the north or centre, but as he turned the map over and followed the road south through Yazd and Bafq, he saw it, printed in bold, a small piece of text by its side: *Kerman, a desert city at an altitude of 1749 metres, is known for its extensive bazaar and traditional bath houses.* Well then, smiled Alex, if all else failed, at least they would be able to get a decent scrub-down and one of those tin teapots.

He reached for his phone and sat up again, switching it on and waiting. Still nothing. In the cool of the stream, Carol's foot drifted against his. He leant back to look at her. "Are you all right?" he said.

"Yes," she replied, returning his gaze through half-open eyes. Then she raised herself onto her elbows, turning her face towards him so she could touch and hold her lips against his, the sun finally pushing its way through the tops of the trees behind them and dancing on the stream.

"Thank you," said Carol, when they had finished.

"What for?" asked Alex.

Carol smiled. "For rescuing me, of course."

If Alex's reading of the map was right, their river journey with Ferran and their dawn bike ride had taken them at least twenty kilometres into the wooded hills west of Esfahan. Now, after a day of sleeping, resting his knee, planning and getting lost on forest tracks, Alex was wondering, as they freewheeled their way down a minor road, how they would appear to any local who passed them in their truck or Paykan Saloon.

But no one did, and after gliding along for another half hour, emerging from the protection of the trees, they finally got a glimpse of the traffic on the main road, pushing its way through the approaching dusk towards the city. Alex stopped the bike. "I guess you'd better put your coat and scarf on," he said.

Reaching the junction with the highway, they were able to walk the bike across the quieter southbound lane, before risking a sprint between a lorry and a van to join, on the far side, a line of assorted mopeds and motorbikes that seemed to be taking the day's farm produce into the city, not just fruit and vegetables, though, but live chickens in cages and the carcasses of ducks or rabbits, tied and stacked behind the saddles.

They had only been cycling for ten minutes, drawing curious glances in the fading light, jostled by passing traffic onto the gritty sand that bordered the highway, when Alex noticed a dark-green minibus and four white motorbikes pulled up at the side of the road a hundred yards ahead, a man in a black shirt stepping onto the tarmac and raising his hand to a moped.

"It looks like the morality police," shouted Carol above the din of a passing truck.

"The what?" said Alex, turning his head towards her.

"Don't you watch the news? They check that women are properly dressed."

"What shall I do?" cried Alex.

"Say we're tourists if they stop us," said Carol, leaning in closer to his ear. "Good that we're British rather than American."

"But what about the Taser?" shouted Alex, relaxing his pressure on the pedals.

"Keep cycling," replied Carol.

Shit, thought Alex, as a second moped was stopped fifty yards ahead, they wouldn't be too pleased to find the jemmy either if they searched them, or the half-bottle of Forane. Why the hell hadn't he chucked them in the woods?

Alex pedalled on, three serious-looking young guys in black collarless shirts apparently in charge of events, guns or radios in their belts, and an argument breaking out at the side of the minibus, a woman in a chador grabbing at a girl in jeans and a headscarf. Taking advantage of this distraction, Alex had begun to increase his pace – an overladen moped, its crate squawking, pulling up alongside him on his left, ready to overtake but wobbling in the wake of a passing lorry – when one of the young guys ran into the road and waved them both down.

"We're tourists," said Alex, smiling, after he had turned the bike off the road to face the rear of the minibus, braking but not dismounting, hoping they would be allowed to continue their journey.

"English," added his companion from the rack.

The young man, two days of stubble below a thin moustache, gestured to a colleague to take care of the moped and its rider.

"My wife," said Alex, thinking it might help, turning and taking Carol's hand.

"Come, please," said the man finally, holding the handlebars while they freed themselves from the bike, and then walking it ahead of them towards the minibus, where the argument had subsided, the girl in jeans returning towards the road, seeming to catch Carol's eye as she passed.

As the man knocked on the back of the bus, Alex tightened his grip on her hand, and thinking why not, turned his head away from her for a moment, tapping his knee and muttering the words, an image of the Abbasi Hotel in his mind, but once again, unsurprised, travelling nowhere.

The rear doors of the minibus swung open and an older, plump-looking man in uniform retreated to a bench inside, a cap on his head, a generous moustache below it, chewing on something and not looking happy to be disturbed. When two women in chadors emerged from the far side of the minibus, taking Carol and the bike aside, Alex felt the young guy's hand in the small of his back, pushing him upwards into the bus. There was a spicy smell inside.

"Papers," said the older man, spitting a crumb and holding out his hand, no expression on his face.

Alex, with his head bent under the roof of the minibus, put his rucksack on the bench opposite and reached inside, trying his best to ignore the Taser. Pulling out his passport, damp at the edges, he was aware also of how rough he must look. "We're hoping to visit Esfahan," he said with a smile, handing over the document and looking over to where Carol stood between the two women in chadors. "Beautiful city," he added, feeling like an idiot.

The man didn't respond, opening up the passport instead and turning the pages to find the visa, which Alex knew to be valid for another four or five days. The officer nodded, passing it back to him. "Bag," he said next, still no expression on his face.

As the sweat trickled down his forehead in the clammy interior of the bus, Alex's brain went into overdrive - the Taser to protect his wife, the anaesthetic some kind of medicine, the jemmy for the bike. He had just placed the rucksack on the floor in front of the man when there was a shout and a collective sigh from outside. Both of them turned round.

A small group had gathered between the bus and the road, something on the ground at its centre. The plump officer stepped down from the bus, Alex looking for Carol and then following, leaving his rucksack where it was.

When the onlookers parted in deference to the officer, Alex peered round him to where Carol lay in the dust, her head towards the road. One of the women in black knelt by her chest, fanning her face with her hand. Alex pushed his way forward and the woman shouted something in

Arabic, gesturing to the people behind her to give them more space.

As the crowd shuffled backwards into the road, there was a scream. Alex jerked his head upwards to see a speeding motorbike swerve out to avoid the group. Hitting the side of a passing truck with a whump, the bike travelled along beside it as if attached, before spinning onto the ground, spilling its rider and a thousand onions, the truck finally braking with a screech.

When the bystanders had moved off towards the motorbike - the plump officer following and shouting instructions at his juniors - Carol sat up, adjusting her headscarf. Alex got down on his haunches to her left, the woman in the chador remaining where she was on her right. "Are you okay?" he asked.

"I'm fine," replied Carol, one eye on her female companion.

As Alex helped her up, the woman was already turning away towards her superior in the cap, the new centre of attention. Face-to-face with the motorbike rider, he prodded the bloodied man's chest with his finger.

"Quick thinking," said Alex with a smile, once Carol was on her feet.

Twenty minutes later, having picked up their bike and bag from the temporarily unattended minibus, walked their way slowly past the swelling crowd and then cycled onwards again, they found themselves amongst the first of the factories at the edge of the city. A sweet chemical smell hung in the evening air.

Despite tiredness, hunger, thirst, and the throbbing pain in his knee, a kind of optimism was settling on Alex. Unless Salah had an army of spies with no other role than to sit under trees or by rivers, or in the doorways of these concrete buildings, how could he be following them into Esfahan?

Alex and Carol had already ruled out making for the train station, the likeliest transit point, they assumed, for anyone fleeing the area. So with the street map from his guidebook to hand and Carol in the saddle, Alex got ready from his position on the package rack to navigate them towards the bus stops near the Abbasi Hotel. They hadn't been much use to him on his earlier trip into the Zagros mountains, but surely there'd be transport on the major routes south to Shiraz and Kerman?

As the factories on the outskirts of town turned into blocks of flats, some of the traffic began to exit right or left off the main road, but most stayed on until they had reached Chahar Bagh-e Baia Street which, according to his map, would lead them into the centre. Halfway along, by Amadegah Avenue, Alex touched Carol's shoulder and they pulled in, abandoning their bike, as planned, amongst twenty or thirty others outside a dimly lit building that might have been a college, a ten-minute walk, Alex calculated, from the hotel and bus stops.

When they got there, dumping the jemmy and Forane in a bin but hanging on, wisely or unwisely, to the Taser, they split up. Carol took the right-hand side of the road, and Alex the left, where he met a middle-aged Canadian couple, munching rice and vegetables on plastic chairs in the second shelter: Nathan and Susan, it turned out, who had missed their connection to Shiraz, and were travelling instead to the citadel at Bam via Kerman, on a bus that was due to leave in three hours' time. Alex looked at his watch, wondering how safe it would be to return to the Abbasi, this time for something to eat. Not so risky, if they kept themselves to the relative darkness of the garden.

"Nathan reckoned it would be ten hours to Kerman," said Alex, splashing a handful of the teahouse's floodlit lake onto his face.

The familiar scents of night-blooming flowers and tobacco hovered in the air, but this time a waiter had hovered too, allowing him to order them two pork-free club sandwiches, orange juice, and water, not that they seemed to be arriving.

"Is that the final stop?" asked Carol, who had spent twenty minutes tidying herself up in the Abbasi's bathroom, accepting money from Alex to buy herself some fresh clothing from the hotel shop.

"No," said Alex. "He said they were going on to a place called Bam."

"Bam, bam," replied Carol, a coolness in her voice, "and remind me exactly what we're going to achieve in Kerman?"

"We'll ring Burhan's cousin," Alex replied, "and see if he can help us hide or get out of the country, or whatever seems best when we get there."

The waiter finally brought their sandwiches, dropping off some drinks on the way to a small group of men with hookah pipes in the corner of the garden.

"Why don't we ring him now, from the hotel?" asked Carol.

"I don't know. It seems risky to me. What if he's been got at in some way? He'd have time to contact Salah, wouldn't he?"

Carol didn't reply.

"Are you all right?" said Alex, picking up his sandwich and watching a couple of bits of tomato and not-pork drop out of the end.

"You mean, apart from being kidnapped, soaked, shot at, and bounced around on a bike rack?" This time Alex didn't reply. "Do you believe in this cloth?" continued Carol, dipping her hand in the lake.

"I don't know," replied Alex. "*Burhan* does. Why do you ask?"

"I just had this odd feeling in the bathroom," said Carol, "that perhaps we were being set up in some way."

"Set up? What do you mean?"

"The trip to France," continued Carol, rippling the water. "Finding Ferran in the caves. Following Burhan's note to Kerman. As if a road was being laid for us. Do you understand what I'm saying?"

"Should we go somewhere else instead?" he replied.

Carol looked at him and laughed, flicking drops of water at his face. "It wouldn't make any difference, don't you see?"

26

Alex looked back at the female portion of the bus, where Carol had settled herself next to Susan, wondering how she was going to explain the purpose of her trip to her new companion. Bondage, boating, and biking might be the lighthearted approach, he reckoned, squeezing himself into the empty seat between a local and the window as Nathan approached and then was obliged to pass him by.

The journey itself was eventful, but only in a public transport kind of way: a small child screaming in several registers along the road to Nā'in; half the bus making their way off at Yazd, where there was an interminable delay, and a smaller number navigating their way in, but with an even heavier load of parcels, suitcases and boxes.

Finally, after waving backwards at Carol and not getting noticed, Alex fell asleep somewhere after Bafq, half waking once or twice, unable to decide in the gloom if a small brown and white patch amongst his new neighbour's elaborate headgear was a final flourish of the textile craft or a moist living eye that never seemed to blink. When he finally awoke, wet with sweat, the sun streaming in through the window, it was to find Nathan's hand on his shoulder, and his neighbour gone. "We're almost in Kerman," said the Canadian with a smile, before wishing him a pleasant stay and retreating to his own seat.

Checking his bag was still on the rack above him, Alex turned to where Carol and Susan had begun an animated conversation with a young woman in a white hijab. Afterwards, he looked out of the window, watching as the blocks of flats became offices, car parks, hotels, and mosques, the bus finally veering left along a semicircular highway to reach the terminus.

Taking their leave of Susan and Nathan, Carol and Alex bought tea and honey-soaked sponge cake from a nearby stall, spotting a public phone by the ticket office, free for local calls, according to Nathan. "I've only got his first name. I hope he's in and friendly," said Alex to Carol through a mouthful of sticky sponge as they made their way over. "And speaks English," she added when they got there.

After he had pressed the numbers, there was a bit of a crackle and then a soft hum.

"Bar-leh," said a man's voice, pretty faintly.

"Hello," said Alex, "is that Jafar?"

There was a pause before the voice spoke again in heavily accented English. "Am I a speed king to Alex?"

"Yes," he said, raising his own voice and looking at Carol. "Has Burhan ...?"

"Where you are?" interrupted the voice.

"In Kerman. At the bus station."

Another pause. Alex wondered if the man was about to put the phone down and opt for a quiet life. But the words came again, with additional crackle. "I'm Jafar. You love my knee?"

"Sorry?" shouted Alex.

"You must take taxi. You have *money*?"

"Yes," said Alex. "And I've got your address."

"Good. We meet you soon. Don't worry."

Alex put the phone back and began to worry.

"Jafar?" said Carol.

Alex nodded. "He knew my name."

"What did he say?" asked Carol.

"He told us to take a taxi."

"Do you trust him?"

"You mean is there a guy with a gun at his side?" replied Alex.

Carol shrugged.

"I've still got the Taser, haven't I?" said Alex. "I'll reload it in the Gents."

Carol smiled. "And I'll round up the horses."

With the taxi travelling farther into the suburbs of Kerman and Carol staring out of her window, Alex found time to give his knee a bit of a rub. He couldn't claim it felt much better. At Jafar's place, if all went well, he'd give it another test. Placing the Taser in his jacket pocket – no point in not being ready – he turned to watch the houses getting posher, front lawns and sprinklers on some of the streets. For a moment, he closed his eyes, feeling the kick of fatigue behind them.

As the taxi entered an avenue of tall trees, tops brushing against one another in the breeze, their driver slowed and pulled up behind a dark-grey car, taking the money from Alex's hand and pointing them towards a large white house, set back from the road, windows on either side shuttered against the sun. When they had crossed the terrace and climbed the steps to the front door, Alex looked at Carol for a moment before raising the knocker and giving it two firm blows. Within seconds, the door swung backwards, their view inside almost entirely blocked by the blank-faced form of Burhan. "Alex," he said, reaching out an arm. "And is this ...?"

"Carol," replied Alex.

"Thank God you're safe!" said the scholar, scanning the street as he hurried them inside. "But I don't understand."

"We escaped," said Alex. "From Faroukh's villa."

"And Salah isn't with you?" said Burhan, closing the front door.

"No," said Alex. "Why?"

"We can talk later," replied Burhan, as a thin man in grey Arabic dress and a short white beard stepped into the far end of the hall. "My cousin Jafar," added Burhan, looking towards the bearded man, saying something in Arabic or Farsi, and then turning back towards Carol. "What did they do to you?"

"Nothing," smiled Carol. "Tied me up for a few days."

"I'm so sorry. It's all my fault. Did they bring you straight to Iran?"

"No. North Africa first," replied Carol.

"Djelfa," said Burhan, looking at Alex, who nodded, saying, "You gave me your cousin's address, so we made our way here on a night bus."

"It's a miracle," said Burhan, shaking his head, putting his arm round Alex's shoulder, and directing everyone to a doorway on the right, "But you must have moved fast from Paris. I haven't been here long myself."

"I managed to catch an evening flight," said Alex, easier now with his lies, as they entered a salon: three sofas around a wide low table and two arched openings that gave onto a courtyard beyond. Large prints of birds and plants hung on the walls.

"Please sit," said Jafar. "I bring tea."

With Jafar gone, they arranged themselves on the sofas, Carol and Alex opposite Burhan. "It's a beautiful house," said Carol.

Burhan smiled and nodded, explaining that Jafar, a widower with two grown-up sons in Tehran, now lived here alone. Then he leant forward. "We need to talk, I'm afraid. The good news, apart from Carol being safe, which is the most important thing of all, is that we've managed to locate the cloth."

"Really?" said Alex. "How ...?"

"There'll be time for that, my friend, and to hear your story, too, which I'm sure is more eventful than you suggest," replied Burhan, rubbing his beard. "But the bad news is that two hours ago, I rang the number Khalid gave us in Paris, told them where the cloth was, and asked them to release Carol. What else could I do?"

Burhan paused to let the implications sink in.

"Given that you were both on the bus to Kerman at the time," he continued, "they must have thought it was their lucky day."

Jafar came in with the tea. "You tell them?" he said, putting the tray on the table.

"Part of it," replied Burhan, looking over at Carol and Alex. "The other part is that Salah will be here, 'bringing the girl' in their words, by sunset."

Alex looked at Carol. "It's my fault," he said, shaking his head. "I should have rung earlier."

Jafar took a seat on the third sofa and began to pour the tea. "The cloth is at Bandar Abbas," he said.

"A warehouse in the port," added Burhan, glancing at his cousin before continuing, "The arrangement was that Salah would arrive here with Carol and two of his men. They would stay while Salah and I drove down to Bandar. When the cloth was verified and handed over, he would phone his men and they would leave. That was the plan. Now we need to think again."

Jafar nodded, waving his hand back and forth in the air as if it were obvious. "You must go there now. You take my car, you take the cloth. Go to the Oman by boat."

Burhan shook his head. "No. We won't leave you here, Jafar."

Jafar thought about this. "I come with you and I come back when it will be safe," he said.

Alex watched Jafar, wondering at his role in the retrieval of the cloth. The scholar meanwhile had closed his eyes, opening them again to nod approval at his cousin's plan. "God's hand is in this," he said. "Somewhere, God's hand is in this."

"Where is Salah coming from?" asked Alex.

"Tehran," said Burhan, removing his glasses and rubbing his eyes. "We'll allow ourselves a half hour or so. Jafar and I will get the car ready. You two will want to have a wash and something to eat. Jafar, shall I take them upstairs?"

While Carol was taking first turn in the bathroom, Burhan put his head round the door of the twin bedroom that she and Alex had been lent. "Jafar says there are some clothes in the wardrobe that once belonged to his sons. They should be fine for Carol but perhaps too small for you, in which case, let me know. I may have something in my luggage. Is there anything else you need, my friend?"

"There is one thing actually," replied Alex from the edge of one of the beds. "Do you have any kind of ointment or a bandage I could put on my knee? It got a knock from one of Salah's men."

"What?" said Burhan. "Did you really have to *fight* your way out of the villa?"

"Not exactly," replied Alex, rubbing the knee. "But it doesn't seem to be getting any better."

"Don't worry. I'll talk to Jafar. He experiments with medicinal plants and herbs when he isn't birdwatching. He may well have something." Burhan smiled. "Come downstairs when you're ready."

When his plump friend had left, Alex walked over to the chair by the window. He reckoned he had another five minutes before Carol freed up the bathroom. Closing his eyes, he visualized the bit of bed that still bore his imprint. Then he tapped his throbbing knee, making the statement one more time, and waiting.

Nothing. No movement at all. Not even a lurch in the right direction. So be it, he thought to himself. It wasn't as if Salah and his men were about to break down the front door and wave their guns around, was it? And didn't Burhan and Jafar now have a plan with a reasonable chance of success?

Returning to the bed under his own power, he stretched out, closing his eyes again for a moment, beginning to drop off despite himself, when there was a knock at the door and Carol entered, a white bath towel bound above her breasts, her wet hair straight, almost black, the vision finally embodied that he had conjured in France, while searching her bedroom for clues.

After a three-hour sleep in the back of Jafar's dark-grey Peugeot saloon, Alex and Carol - she in the washed-out sweatshirt and cotton trousers they had found in the spare room, and he in a green shirt and belted-up pair of Burhan's colossal shorts - were listening to the scholar as he began the conversation that was designed to bring them all up to date. The strange smell that lingered in the interior of the car, a mix of sour cherries and rice pudding, could be traced to the soothing ointment Jafar had applied to his knee after administering a generous injection of green fluid into the side of his leg.

"... so I flew from London to Muscat, where Safwaan was holding my father's last letters from Paris," said Burhan, his arm on the back of the passenger seat.

"The ones he wrote to an old school friend?" clarified Alex, as much for his own sake as Carol's.

"Exactly. They seem to have become a kind of diary for him. Reading through the later ones, it's clear that the cloth wasn't the first piece of merchandise Faroukh had sent via Paris to his villa in Iran. But this time, while he was still holding the package, my father received a visit at work from a stranger, a Spaniard who described himself as a lawyer. The man was relieved to hear that my father had not yet dispatched the article, explaining that it was a valuable work of art that been stolen from the monastery he represented three weeks before, and one month *after* Faroukh's associates had first approached the abbot with an offer.

"When the Spanish police showed little interest in following the lead, the lawyer made his own enquiries, discovering enough about Faroukh's methods of distribution to bring him to Paris. He told my father that he now had an opportunity not only to do the right thing in returning it, but also to earn a modest reward."

Burhan turned and rummaged in the glove compartment, pulling out a pair of binoculars in his left hand, part of Jafar's birdwatching kit, reckoned Alex, and a can of Coke in his right, which he passed to Carol. "You'll have to share this, I'm afraid. Our supplies are rather limited."

Outside, they were climbing a road between two surprisingly green hills, the sun beginning to set, the only other vehicle a battered truck they would soon be overtaking. It reminded Alex a little of a hillside pass in the Peak District that had given Bill's yellow Citroen one of its regular cardiac arrests.

"Anyway," continued Burhan, leaning over his seat again, "my father needed time to think, and besides, he was keeping the package at the flat, as instructed, waiting for the courier to call, and not in the office where the lawyer had found him. So he asked his visitor to come back at the same time the following day." The storyteller smiled at Alex. "I'm afraid the penultimate letter, which my father refers to, is missing, in the way of these things, so we can't be sure what went through his mind. Perhaps he was already uncomfortable about the business he had been doing for Faroukh. Or he didn't fully trust the lawyer and wanted to ask him some more questions. It's possible too, of course, that he opened the package, saw the cloth itself, and was inspired to act. That's what I would like to believe. Who can say? At any rate, we *do* know from the subsequent letter that he had the package with him in the office at the agreed time." Burhan took his glasses off, rubbed his eyes and looked over at Carol. "Can you tell what happens next?"

"Yes," she replied. "The lawyer doesn't show up."

Burhan laughed. "Very good. How did you know?"

"Something my dad used to say about narratives," she replied. "At any one point in a story when something needs to happen, there are only ever two things that actually *can* happen. I just took a guess."

"There we are," said Burhan. "The lawyer didn't arrive, and it may have dawned on my father, as the minutes passed, that if the Spaniard had been intercepted, someone else might call instead."

"So what did he do?" asked Carol, as Burhan turned to look at a road sign.

"He wrote a short letter to his friend in Oman," the scholar replied, "so there would be an account of his actions, and then arranged, it seems, for the cloth itself to be collected and dispatched not to Faroukh's villa but to his cousin Hasan, in Bandar, for safekeeping. Jafar's father," he explained, "the third branch of our family ..."

"The ghost-line?" said Alex. "Descendants of Sabri?"

Burhan smiled. "You remembered."

"That was the day you told me about," continued Alex, catching Carol's eye, "when your father disappeared. They must have searched your flat."

Burhan nodded in the car's darkening interior. "I can only assume that Faroukh's associates caught up with him shortly afterwards," he said, turning towards his cousin, who had just switched on his headlights, and asking, "How far to Jiroft?"

Jafar ignored this, saying instead, "My father made copy of the cloth."

"A professional job," added Burhan, "as a keepsake."

"The one we saw in London," said Alex.

Burhan nodded.

"And he give the cloth ..." continued Jafar.

"The real cloth ..." said Burhan.

"Yes, he give the real cloth to businessman in Indonesia, good man."

"A friend of the family and collector of antiquities," added Burhan.

"For to protect," concluded Jafar.

"When Hasan was in hospital in 2010 and close to death," continued Burhan, "he asked Jafar to reclaim the cloth and search for its owner, offering the businessman the copy in exchange if he wanted it. Perhaps Hasan felt guilty he had done so little himself."

"But my wife, she was very sick," said Jafar.

"My cousin had other things on his mind," said Burhan. "After the exchange, he simply stored the cloth, along with some of his father's belongings, in Bandar."

"The original was in your family all along, then," said Carol, "and the copy went to the Museum on the businessman's death."

"Exactly," said Burhan. "But I had no idea. As I explained to Alex, Jafar's side of the family and mine had lost touch. I actually spent a few months in Bandar in 2008, not knowing Hasan or Jafar were there." He looked at his cousin for a moment, and then went on, "Anyway, Safwaan and I worked together through several long nights in Muscat, trying to find a recent address for Hasan. We made phone calls. We searched documents. One of my sons even brought some files from my library in Salalah so as to save us time, but all we could discover before the appointment in Paris was the notification of his death in Bandar."

Burhan paused as Jafar swung out in the darkness, passing a man on a donkey.

"I'd booked a flight direct to France," continued the scholar, "knowing I would need all the time available before the rendezvous with Salah's men. When I arrived on Monday, after several hours of delay, I saw a text message from Safwaan, who had just managed to get hold of the lawyer who handled Hasan's will. Finally, he was able to give me Jafar's contact details in Kerman, where he moved after Hasan's death. I tried ringing him, of course, several times, but there was no response. At the Gare du Nord, as you know, Alex, I passed you Jafar's address in case anything happened to me. When I arrived in Kerman myself, I booked into a hotel, hoping my cousin would return home soon. Which he did, of course," concluded the scholar, "early this morning, from a birdwatching trip."

"Twenty minutes," said Jafar, "to Jiroft."

Burhan nodded. "Your turn now, Alex," he said.

Alex gave him a doctored version of his two trips to Iran, Carol taking over at the point of her rescue, and Burhan shaking his head in disbelief as she finished.

"But you were fortunate the old man decided to help you," he said.

"Ferran," she said. "He never spoke, but that's what they called him."

Burhan looked at her. "Are you sure?" he asked. "It's an unusual name for an Arab."

Carol nodded. "He gave me his ring when we left him," she said, reaching into her pocket and passing it to Burhan. "There's an inscription inside, which I can't read of course."

Burhan spoke a few words in Arabic to Jafar, and the car pulled over to the side of the road. Switching on the windscreen light, the scholar examined the ring, closing his eyes afterwards, bowing his head and easing his right hand under his glasses. A few moments passed.

"'One hand cannot applaud,'" he said, finally. "My father's name was Ferran, which means baker," he continued, turning to Carol and smiling, "and my mother gave him this ring when they married."

27

By the time they had finished their meal in a dimly lit restaurant on the outskirts of Jiroft, the waiter looking at his watch while Jafar spooned watery chicken stew onto their plates, Carol and Burhan had eliminated the hopeful in their speculations on Ferran's post-Paris life, and what remained was the depressing likelihood that after suffering a trauma of some kind at his cousin's hands, the scholar's father had spent the next thirty five years as a servant first to Faroukh and later to Salah, and must now be under threat once again for his second act of defiance. But at least he was alive, sheltered by friends perhaps or even, in Jafar's optimistic interpretation of Ferran's parting mime, making his way back to the family home in Salalah.

After filling the tank at the small garage opposite the restaurant, they resumed their journey, falling into silence as the headlights of Jafar's Peugeot cut through the darkness of southern Iran. Alex recalled something Jeremy, in reflective mood, had said in France about taking advantage of these quiet moments to project yourself into the minds of your companions. It had all seemed a bit of an effort to Alex at the time, something to think about when you got older, but he gave it a go now from his vantage point in the umbral rear of the car.

Jafar might be the easiest starting place. With a bit of luck, he'd be focusing mainly on the road ahead. But he'd probably also be thinking of the congenial house he'd left behind and the prospect of Salah's henchmen jemmying their way through the ornate windows of his treatment room. He might be wondering too whether his 'ghost-line' family shouldn't have remained just that, a no-man's-land between Salah and his troublesome cousin from Oman.

Burhan, of course, after the joy of discovering his father was alive, would be feeling guilty. How, in all his dealings with Salah and the cloth, had he missed the most elemental aspect of Faroukh's revenge, the transforming of Ferran into another item in his collection? The butterfly part of his friend's mind would settle elsewhere from time to time, on the fortunes of the cloth once it was back in Oman, perhaps, but it would surely return to that.

And Carol? She was the hardest to read. He glanced at her as she stared out of the window once again, the forests of the Landes now transfigured into this nightscape of mountains and villages. Irritated though she had seemed in the gardens of the Abbasi Hotel, he had recently noticed a new animation in her. Wasn't there, in fact, something more Carol than Alex-like in this whole adventure? Some opportune testing of her own resilience?

Alex yawned as the Peugeot slowed for a lean dog to complete its trot across the high street of a sleeping village. He watched the beast making its way into the shadows between two buildings, impressed by its ability to give a sense of purpose to the latest of its random manoeuvres. And when the car had pulled out once more into the dark void of the countryside, he finally allowed his eyes to close on this, the third of their nocturnal journeys since they had limped their way into the tunnel at the back of Faroukh's cellar.

When he came to, Carol was asleep beside him and they were pulling into a car park in what Alex guessed was Bandar's warehouse district. A truck passed by on the road, and there was enough daylight now to see a high dark-grey building in front of them, some of its oblong windows shuttered, others opening onto wooden gantries that supported pulleys or chains with metal hooks.

As Jafar switched the engine off, Alex reached out towards Carol's shoulder, hardly making contact before she had opened her eyes, stretching her arms and legs downwards like a cat. "This is a little off the tourist trail, isn't it?" she said, stifling a yawn and peering out of the window.

"Good morning," replied Burhan, turning as his cousin climbed out of the car. "You're right, of course. There isn't a great deal to see in this part of town, even in broad daylight." He glanced over at the warehouse entrance. "When Jafar has collected the cloth, we'll make our way to the port, and get a boat to Oman or Dubai."

Alex levered himself out of the passenger door to stretch his legs, attempting to subtract from the mix of his sensations the predictable stiffness from the night in the car; reckoning as he did so that there might actually be some improvement in the state of his knee. And by the time their driver had re-emerged with a holdall, they were all on their feet outside the Peugeot, Burhan peering at the map and Carol gazing farther along the road to the tall buildings of Bandar city, where the sun would eventually penetrate the grey sky of dawn.

Soon they were back in the car, turning left at a crossroads onto a quieter road – headlights no longer necessary – motoring along until they had their first glimpse of the green sea, the Strait of Hormuz, according to Burhan. Passing a small airport to their right, Alex looked out of the rear window at the last of the parked planes, noticing as he did so a black car that seemed to be keeping pace five hundred metres behind them in their otherwise empty lane. And, as the road swung farther south to hug a coastline littered with blocks of concrete, before veering inland again, Alex kept watch while the car passed up the several opportunities it had to turn right towards an oil refinery or the nearby towns of Isin and Anguran.

So what. Even at this hour, they couldn't be the only travellers en route to the passenger port. Despite this, he leant across and touched Burhan's shoulder. "There's a black sedan behind us. It's been there since the airport."

Keeping a hand on his map, Burhan turned round to look, muttering something to Jafar, who took the next right and then a left, navigating the Peugeot, under the scholar's directions, away from the main road and into the nearby streets of flat-roofed houses, cars parked on either side – seeing if the sedan would follow, guessed Alex, while attempting to maintain their onward progress to the port.

"I think it's gone," said Carol, turning to Burhan as they entered the longest street in their residential detour, the houses bigger now, some with front yards and plants in large pots. Alex continued to stare out of the rear window, however, watching a navy-blue car pull out of its parking space to travel in the opposite direction and monitoring the road afterwards until they got to the end, when he was able to observe the black sedan nosing its way in at the beginning. "It's behind us again," he said, adding when Burhan and Carol had both turned round, "It can't be Salah, can it?"

The scholar frowned. "He may have decided to send some of his men ahead by plane to cover the warehouse." He shook his head. "I should have thought of it. They'll have guessed by now that we're heading for the port."

"Where we go?" asked Jafar, turning left into a large square that contained a desolate park of concrete benches, threadbare hedges, and children's swings. Burhan put his hand on Jafar's shoulder and looked down at the map. In the silent moment that followed, Alex leant forward. "I've got an idea," he said. "If we have to rule out the port, why don't we drive up into the city and try to lose them there?"

When the scholar had spoken to his cousin in Arabic, Carol added, "Is there another port we could use, farther along the coast from Bandar?"

Burhan thought about this. "What about Jask?" he said to Jafar.

"Long way," replied his cousin, pulling out of the square, "but possible."

"So all we need," concluded Carol, "is to achieve a lead on the sedan, and then lose it, as Alex suggested."

As they drew up third in line at a T-junction, the city centre to their right, Alex had his second idea. "Burhan, why don't *you* take a turn at the wheel?"

The scholar considered this for a moment, before muttering something to Jafar and opening his door, the two cousins getting out and making a rapid swap around the front of the vehicle. Glancing once at the unchanging lights, their new driver wrenched the steering wheel to the right and kicked at the accelerator, forcing Jafar's Peugeot out onto the pavement with a screech of the tyres.

As Alex attempted to recover his position on the back seat, Burhan tore his way round the corner, prising the car back afterwards onto the road to join the city-bound lane inches ahead of a rapidly braking green van. Then, slamming his passengers from one side of the interior to the other, he launched the car into a mad weave between the vehicles in front and the oncoming traffic, humming something to himself, unless it was a trick of their bone-shaking speed, while Jafar covered his eyes with his hands. Quite soon, the useful complexity of the city lay within their reach. By the time they had got to the banks, restaurants, and office blocks of Bandar's commercial district, however, the gently rising dual carriageway they had joined had chosen to express its own complexity in the grandmother of all traffic jams.

A few moments after they had slowed to a stop, no sign of movement ahead, Alex opened his door and stepped out into the rising sunlight, putting his weight on his knee and surprised once more to note an improvement. To his right, beyond the second lane of static traffic, lay the shaded side streets where they might have hoped to liberate themselves from the sedan; to the left, separated by a low kerb and two metres of baked earth, the southbound traffic, crawling its way towards the port. One of the drivers caught Alex's eye, smiled and shrugged his shoulders.

Burhan and Carol joined him on the road, the scholar saying something to the driver in front, who had leant out of his window, and Carol surveying the vehicles behind them, two hundred or more, stretching down the hill, before asking, "Burhan, can I have Jafar's binoculars?" After a short gaze, she passed the glasses to Alex, saying, "Two men have just pulled their black sedan off the road, and one of them, a tall guy in blue, seems to be pointing in our direction."

Burhan turned and frowned as Alex had his go on the binoculars. A dozen or so drivers or passengers had stepped out of their cars, but the two men, one in blue sportswear and the other in a dark blazer, were easy to spot because instead of smoking, chatting or stretching their arms, they had begun an urgent trot up the hill towards them.

"They're coming our way," said Alex to his companions.

Burhan ducked back into the car, re-emerging a moment later with the holdall. "Jafar is going to stay with the car and try to make a U-turn into the southbound lane. It may divert them. Meanwhile, my friends, I fear we have to run," he said, not waiting but squeezing his way between a pick-up truck and a Jeep in the neighbouring lane, Carol already behind him and Alex grabbing his rucksack from the back seat of the car – all three of them quitting the highway for the sheltering underbelly of Bandar city.

Soon Burhan was pulling them through the side entrance to a vast indoor market. As they hustled their way past buckets of entrails and bloody hunks of meat hanging from hooks or sprawled across counters – a stray shaft of sunlight illuminating a butcher's stall like a grotesque operating theatre – it became obvious to Alex this wasn't the kind of place you brought your girlfriend to on a picturesque tour of the Middle East.

While Carol, holding onto her headscarf, jogged right towards the gutting and sluicing quarters of the fish zone, a series of memories flickered unbidden onto the cinema screen of Alex's bobbing head, from the downtown tuna market in Salalah and the sun-pierced breakfast room in Mont-de-Marsan, to the gamey delicatessen they had visited on Jeremy's bike. And when they had cleared the last of the ocean produce, Carol sending a toothy cat or dogfish flying from its stall and Alex failing to catch hold of its slippery membrane, Burhan finally brought them out of this gloomy cathedral of slaughter and into the daylight.

Flinching in the sunshine like Nosferatu's plump cousin, the speeding scholar led them across a main road, one hand up against the honking traffic, the other clutching the holdall, and into a busy interior that resembled the flight transfer desk at an overworked airport. Handing him the bag, Burhan leant forward, gasping, his hands on his knees. "I'm going to hire a car for us. We can still complete our journey to Jask, God willing."

While the scholar made his way towards the counter, Alex looked over at Carol, her eyes closed, breathing deeply through her nose in a compose-yourself kind of way. He was putting the holdall down when she opened them again and burst out laughing. "Nice market," she said, adjusting her headscarf, "but not necessarily where I'd choose to do my Saturday shopping."

Alex grinned back, rolling his shoulders to release the tension in his neck. "I don't know," he replied, "I'm sure you and Jeremy would have managed to track down the textiles section," adding, as he looked over to where Burhan, by charm or bulk, had got the attention of a thin sales assistant with a long black beard, "Shouldn't we move away from the window?"

When they had manoeuvred themselves past chatting customers to the far corner of the room, where the counter came to an end next to a door framed by black fingerprints, Carol leant against the wall, smiling again. "Does Burhan always drive like that?" she asked. As Alex tried to explain, Carol nodded, looking less than convinced. "I hope he gets us something swish, anyway," she said, "like a Buick Reatta."

"It'll probably be a Paykan Saloon," replied Alex, wondering, despite the lighthearted mood that had settled on them, whether they shouldn't be worrying about Jafar or the next stage of their escape. "Are you into cars, then?"

"Not as often as I'd like to be," said Carol. "Most of the time they're sitting in one of John's lock-ups, waiting for a new part to arrive from a dealer in Australia or the US."

Alex smiled to find a new avenue of John-baiting opening up for business. Carol, however, didn't look ready to travel there. Instead, her eyes seemed to be widening and darkening at the same time. "Get down," she said, bending her knees and lowering herself against the wall.

Alex winced as he got himself into a squat. "What is it?" he whispered, though there was still plenty of background noise in the shop.

"The tall guy in the blue tracksuit, peering in at the window."

"Shit," said Alex, turning to where Burhan's wide frame might be visible from the street, catching the scholar's eye and pointing over his shoulder at the window as if he were the front man in a SWAT team. As Burhan swung round, raised voices broke out in the doorway. Alex swivelled to see a large woman in a grey headscarf shouting at the two men who were clearly trying to muscle their way past her small family group, one in a blazer, the other in blue sports gear.

Carol leapt up, Alex grabbing the holdall, and Burhan, he saw, snatching a set of keys from the counter and diving towards the grubby door, which Carol opened inwards, letting the scholar through, and both of them following him out onto the small railed platform that overlooked the shop's subterranean garage.

Bundling the holdall to Burhan, who was already making his way down the steps to the right, Alex had no sooner pulled the handle tight behind him when there was a yank from the other side, forcing the door an inch open. As Carol joined him on his left to pull it closed, Alex twisted his neck to watch Burhan, who was staring at the dozen cars parked in the dim glow of the ceiling lights, and the daylight that filtered in through the metal exit shutters.

"I'm looking for a navy-blue Kia Pride," shouted the scholar.

Gripping the door handle with his right hand, Alex reached back with his left and grabbed the top of the railings, forming a kind of human lock. Carol followed suit, both of them scanning the cars behind – the metal shutters already beginning to rise – when a second almighty hoist on the door forced it inwards again, a black shoe ramming itself into the gap this time, and a fist emerging round the door to pound down on Carol's hand.

"Front of the garage, next to the silver car," she cried out, yelping in pain at a blow from the fist. Alex let go of the railing, surrendering a precious inward inch but able for a moment, with Carol at full stretch beside him, to drive his knuckles into the man's hand and the heel of his foot into the toes of the black shoe. Reaching back for the metal bar, he pulled once more on the door, a rivulet of sweat running into his left eye, his right shoulder burning with pain.

They both turned their heads as a car ignition sounded behind them. "Come on!" shouted Burhan from the Kia Pride's open doors, the rising shutters now drawing a carpet of daylight into the garage.

Alex shot Carol a glance. "When I say 'now', let go," he said.

As Carol nodded, Alex looked back towards the Kia, two pairs of legs now visible on the street side of the shutters. "Now!" he screamed, and they both turned, jumping from the platform and steering their way around the parked vehicles towards the Kia. As they reached the car, Carol dived in through the back door, Alex ducking to follow her, when he had the unusual sensation of being lifted backwards and upwards, like a parachutist at ripcord.

"He's got your fucking rucksack," shouted Carol, grasping for Alex's belt from the interior of the car, while he – one knee on the seat and the back of his head wedged into the curve of roof above the door – fought to free himself of his bag, finally succeeding as Burhan slipped the clutch, launching the five-foot Kia at the four feet of daylight under the shutter.

Amongst the hectic events of the next six seconds, the first Alex registered was the ear-wrecking crunch and scrape of metal against the top of the Kia's windscreen. This was followed by a jab in the eye from Carol as she grabbed at his head while he shunted his legs into the jolting car, turning, when she had let him go, to reach out for the swinging passenger door. Finally, there was the scene through the rear window as the Kia sped upwards towards the street: the man in the blazer on the right, hands still clamped to Alex's rucksack, pulling himself up from the garage floor; his colleague and the bearded shop assistant to the left, staring wildly up at them; the battered shutter hanging on at half-mast in the middle.

Alex and Carol clutched their seats as the scholar skidded the Kia rightwards onto the road, immediately cutting left in front of an oncoming car to accelerate down a narrow, dipping side street, empty except for a light-green lorry two hundred metres ahead that chose this particular moment to pull up and block the road. A moment later, the driver and his assistant descended at their leisure and began the process of unloading what appeared to be the annual towelling needs of the nearby Hormuz Hotel.

After a couple of futile jabs at the horn and a curse or a prayer in Arabic, Burhan shunted their vehicle into an even narrower street to the right, pulling it back through a maze of short alleyways. Forced at one point to reverse in a cul-de-sac, they finally re-entered the main drag on the other side of the green lorry, as the road rose upwards to a roundabout.

No sooner had they swung right, however, taking the second exit towards Jask – Alex and Carol finally able to lean back into their seats – than a silver Volkswagen Passat had drawn level on their left, staying there long enough for its passenger, the man in the blue tracksuit, to make a smile and a handgun visible to the Kia's occupants, before pulling out effortlessly in front.

For the next three kilometres, along a wide road that was almost deserted in both directions, the silver car played the game of alternately slowing and then, when the Kia came out to overtake, accelerating to prevent the manoeuvre.

Alex watched the back of Burhan's head, dipped forward like a bull's, twice meeting his glazed eyes in the rearview mirror, or he followed the movements of the Passat, impressed despite himself at Blazer's easy control; impressed too, in retrospect, at the way in which the man must have planned for their possible escape in the Kia, sending his colleague round to the front of the garage with the keys to the more powerful German car – a weapon being helpful, Alex guessed, in moving the paperwork along – before sniffing out their route to the roundabout.

Carol, meanwhile, had stopped watching the overtaking game, staring inland instead, where there were farmhouses among the low hills, and speculating, figured Alex, on the confrontation with Blazer and Tracksuit which now seemed inevitable, only the timing uncertain.

On Alex's side of the car there wasn't much to see, just dry stony fields beyond the raised road and some tiny, wooded settlements that must be close, he calculated, to the coast. He was wondering if the tall post by a roadside track half a kilometre ahead might be a sign to the next of these villages, or even to Jask, when the backseat slid away from under him, Carol crying 'Hey!' as his head slammed into her shoulder.

Pulling himself upwards, stones clanging already against the Kia's bodywork, Alex saw that Burhan had launched their car across the field in a short cut to the track. As they bounced forward in the dust, he joined Carol, scrabbling for a view through the bobbing rear window, where the Volkswagen appeared to be dipping the right side of its bonnet rather hesitantly towards the stony surface, like a bather testing the temperature of an outdoor pool. Was that the genius of Burhan's new plan, wondered Alex? To discover a hidden vein of vulnerability in Salah's rented muscle: that though they might wave their Berettas, Glocks or Lugers around, they would draw the line at scratching the hire car's paintwork or skewing its suspension?

Reaching the track and turning right, he realized that while they had certainly gained ground on the silver car, picking its way carefully across the field behind them, the road itself had begun to deteriorate from the dodgy to the downright shameful - potholes, ruts and stray bits of agricultural metalwork threatening to slice into the very fabric of their vehicle as they approached the first of the village's dwellings.

Except that there wasn't, it seemed, a great deal of dwelling going on. While Alex and Carol peered sideways, Burhan too, when he wasn't negotiating the odd pile of breeze blocks in the roadway, the Kia passed one abandoned property after another, each advertising its state by a planked-up door, see-through bedroom, or tree-sprouting roof. And after the road, improving a little, had climbed up through a small wood and then begun to descend, giving them their first full view of the grey ocean, the reason became clear. Perched to their right on a crumbling cliff top of dried red mud, the last of the village's empty houses were slowly subsiding into the sea two hundred feet below.

Burhan pulled the car in a slow circle to the left so it lay parallel to the coast, and stopped the engine. They had, after all, run out of road. Getting out of the Kia, they made their up to the edge of the cliff. Below them was a spine-breaking drop to the waves and rocks; farther out to sea, a pair of fishing vessels.

The scholar looked up at the sky, turning afterwards to his companions. "I'm sorry," he said, "but I think it's time to relinquish the cloth."

At the sound of an engine, they all looked back over the top of the Kia to see the silver Passat come out of the wood and pull up head-on, forty metres inland. And when Tracksuit stepped out on the left side of the vehicle, extending the passenger door and holding his gun above the window, Burhan moved quickly forward, reaching into their hire car and placing the holdall on the roof, before walking two paces to the right of the Kia, his empty hands raised high above him.

As Carol and Alex stood by, Blazer came into view on the driver's side, raising his head and shoulders out of the silver car. Once he had emerged, adjusting the sleeves of his jacket, he made a brief survey of the scene, catching Alex's eye for a moment, finally letting his gaze fall on Burhan. Turning to his colleague and nodding once, Blazer folded his arms while Tracksuit steadied the barrel of his gun on the rim of the passenger door, took aim at the scholar, and fired.

When their friend fell backwards, Alex and Carol ran forward, crouching behind the navy-blue bulk of the Kia. Reaching out to grasp the scholar's arms, they pulled his body towards them as a second shot slammed into the centre of the car, and a more accurate third shattered its way through the front windows, speeding over their heads to the sea.

In the period of silence that followed, pierced by the cries of gulls, Alex felt as if he had left his own body behind and was floating somewhere above the cliff, contemplating the scene below: Carol in the foreground, cradling Burhan's head, her hand on the wound below his shoulder; Alex himself, crouching between his companions and the car, edging his head upwards for a view through the shattered window; Tracksuit and Blazer on the other side, beginning their purposeful move towards the Kia.

"What's happening, Alex?" asked Carol, her voice both faint and urgent.

"They're coming," he replied.

"Fuck, fuck, fuck," said Carol. "Where's your Taser?"

"It was in the rucksack," replied Alex.

"Then throw them the cloth."

Alex reached up for the holdall on the roof, a tight, cold feeling spreading up from his stomach. He knew it wouldn't work. They'd pick up the cloth, and roll all three of them over the cliff in the Kia. He looked through the window. Tracksuit and Blazer, both armed, had separated to the left and right and were covering the distance in professional half-crouches.

He brought the bag down.

"Hold this tight and give me your other hand," he said to Carol.

"What?" she replied. "We're not going to jump over the cliff with Burhan, are we?"

Clasping the scholar's palm in his free hand, locking their fingers together and lifting his friend's limp arm towards his left knee, Alex glanced up at the sky, calculating the few absurd extra seconds he could give to Jafar's healing juices. I'm changing the agreement, he said to the pale vision inside the silvery aura, as he had first seen her in Regent's Park. I'm taking *both* of my companions with me.

And, as the black form of Blazer eased its way into his peripheral vision, Alex tightened his grip, visualizing the small square of beach where it had all started, out there across the water in Salalah, and beginning once again to activate his finger.

"Let's travel," he said, an authority in his voice that was entirely new to him.

28

I'm dead, thought Alex, as he contemplated the rather pleasant scene around him.

He was on a path by a wide brown river somewhere in the south of England, reckoning he might be seven or eight years younger than his current age, surprised by how much younger that actually felt. The slow-moving river to his right, which accompanied him like an old friend, must be in its middle years, he supposed, because the green summer fields on either side were flat for a hundred metres until they met the gentle rise of the wooded hills.

Noting that he was kitted out in a loose cotton judo suit, Alex smiled and raised a hand as he got closer to the white-canopied picnic bench set by a bend in the river. His natural father, somewhere in his forties, stood there to greet him, and, sitting at the far end of the table with a cat in her lap, was a younger sister he didn't know he had.

Instead of feeling as he often did when he was eighteen or nineteen, slightly ratty or shy or needing a fag, Alex was calm now and generous of spirit, as if at least a proper third of his being had reached out beyond its boundaries towards these people. In short, and clearly inhabiting a better version of himself, he was happy.

As he clasped his father's hand and took his place at the table, a gentle gust of wind filled the canopy, lifting the whole arrangement high up into the summer air. Soon they had followed the river past towns and villages to the sea, where they bore right and began to pick up speed. Unless Alex had got his geography wrong, they must be making their way towards the Atlantic and the east coast of America.

He looked across at his father and his sister. The impression he had formed over Salisbury or Dorchester could no longer be denied: as they smiled at him or looked at the scenery below, re-arranging their clothing against the wind, they were aging. The plumpness had left their frames and the lines on their faces grew deeper. Whatever it was, it didn't seem to be having the same effect on Alex, or the cat, and although there was a natural tug of sadness in the spectacle, there was also a strengthening and condensing of affection until, somewhere out there over the widening ocean, their fragile bones and translucent skin were no longer made of carbon and calcium, but molecule on molecule of love.

Then he was alone, and the canopy began its dive. Some instinct in Alex suggested he would be better placed for the collision with the Atlantic if he curled himself around the pole in the centre of the table, and he had just about clambered into position, screwing up his eyes, when the awful sound began – the throaty gurgling of spent bathwater, as heard not by the bather but the saturated spider, circling its way towards the plughole.

Alex's own voyage into the centre of the pelagic vortex was kinder, however, not unlike the rides you had to queue for at Water World or Aqualand. Even when it came to the ocean floor, his deep-sea twister prepared the way, burying its spinning tip into the sand and rock, carving a submarine passage not in the direction of Boston or New York, but towards the west coast of Africa, under Mali, Chad, and the Red Sea, beginning its ascent below Yemen and Oman; ending in a puddle of water on Salalah beach, an arm's length from Carol, who was sitting next to the holdall, her eyes glazed, brushing the sleeves of her jumper.

"Are you okay?" said Alex, and then, "Where's Burhan?"

Carol nodded and shook her head, in that order, and they got up unsteadily from the beach to scan the stretch of coastline, familiar to Alex, that bordered their portion of the Arabian ocean. To their right there was nothing to see, just empty sand that disappeared into a wooded headland two or three kilometres away, hazy in the afternoon sun. And to their left the only human life was a family group walking away from them towards Salalah town, their white and beige robes fluttering in the wind.

"He's not here. How did we survive the jump, Alex?" asked Carol, as a flock of gulls rose wave-like from a patch of damp sand at the water's edge, forging a path over the ocean to re-assemble above a swell in the water that revealed the target of this latest manoeuvre in their long day of seaborne activity: a scholar-shaped length of jetsam, barely floating in the brine.

Alex got into the water first, splashing his way through the waves as if he were a six-year-old, diving into the sea and swimming a lung-spluttering twenty metres until he was able to seize the sodden form and roll it face upwards. Bringing the bearded head onto his shoulder, he began to kick his legs outwards like a frog, getting nowhere very much until Carol arrived to help, securing their friend's belt with one hand, gasping for breath as she joined Alex for the shoreward pull.

When they had dragged the scholar onto the beach, Carol took charge, putting her ear to his mouth and feeling for his pulse. Alex watched as she placed her palm on his chest, four inches below the ragged bullet hole in his jumper, and began to pump, regularly and rapidly. Midway through the third series, a small stream of water pushed its way out of the corner of the tale-teller's mouth, followed by a gentle cough that proved ambassador to a mighty bellowing, as Burhan turned himself onto his unwounded side and Carol jumped backwards, grinning at Alex.

"I think you'd better get help," she said.

29

Alex looked back once at the terracotta facade of the Holiday Inn, lit up against the late-evening sky, before setting off along the boardwalk towards the beach.

The first week of their stay in Salalah had been taken up with phone calls to Jafar, Olmo, Jeremy, Rod, and John, of course; visits to Burhan – recovering in hospital from his shoulder wound and as strong as a camel, according to his doctors – and to the local police station, where, with the help of the scholar's eldest son, Hani, they had filed their report not only on Salah, the cloth (now in a bank vault), and the kidnapping, but also on Burhan's missing father. The rest of the time, Carol – at ease, but keeping her distance from Alex until she had 'resolved the situation with John' – had slept in her hotel room, or swum in the pool.

As for their miraculous escape, well, that should have been more complicated. But even before he he'd had a chance to concoct an explanation that would stop some way short of his miraculous knee, it dawned on Alex that Carol actually believed - and Salah too, perhaps - they *had* jumped off the cliff, eventually being hauled into a fishing vessel, where she had drifted in and out of consciousness for a day at least, until there was a rather aggressive argument over money, at which point they had all been thrown into the sea two hundred yards off the coast of Salalah. And Burhan, in their brief exchange on the ward, had simply seemed to accept the whole thing as a divine intervention. God's hand, as he put it, once again.

Tomorrow the scholar would be discharged from hospital, provided he promised to spend a fortnight in bed once he got home to his wife, and they would begin to make plans for Carol and Alex's return to the UK, and future arrangements for the cloth that would somehow protect them all from Salah's next moves, given that his arrest and detainment were unlikely to be imminent. Right now, therefore, all Alex wanted to do was to feel the evening breeze on his face, and the sand under his feet.

He turned to the right, away from Salalah and towards the headland at the end of the bay, enough light from the new moon, which had already laid a pathway of silver across the surface of the sea, to illuminate his solitary stroll. A pleasant scent blew in the breeze, pine perhaps, and the waves were calmer than on the morning walks he was accustomed to taking along a route, suggested by Burhan, that began on the beach but then climbed up into the hills, before descending to the port. For this evening, however, he'd go no farther than the grassy mound halfway to the headland, turning round, if he felt like it, and walking an equal distance back towards town.

Only it wasn't actually a mound, he realized, when he had covered the distance, hands in his pockets, padding close to the sea, wondering what life would be like back in London. It was a proper sandcastle, or what remained of one, a metre high, with turrets and a moat, the first he had seen in Salalah, where the kids tended to cling to their parents' arms rather than scuttle to the water's edge with buckets and spades. And as he approached, he thought he could hear a sound on the other side, of moist sand being scraped – or pawed, more likely – from the beach. Bugger, it must be one of the stray dogs he had seen hanging around the market, rabid no doubt, ready to sniff the air and leap at him, in revenge, he imagined, for the Iranian cousin he had despatched en route to Faroukh's villa. With a bit of luck, the breeze would be blowing the right way.

Halting, he took a step backwards, paused, and was about to begin his return journey to the hotel when a female voice, posh and young, asked, "Aren't you going to help me?" its owner raising her blonde head above the castle's ramparts.

Alex froze and then smiled. "It's you again," he said, as the fairy stood in jeans and a fisherman's navy-blue smock, a spade in one hand, a bucket in the other. "And you haven't changed your accent this time."

"That's all right, isn't it?" said the fairy, putting down her tools and holding her right arm out towards him across the top of her handiwork. "It's Serena, by the way."

Alex took her hand, surprised that it was warm. "Thank you," he said straightaway, "for letting me bring Carol *and* Burhan back to Salalah."

"It was a bit of a struggle, as you might have noticed," replied Serena, smiling in return. "Shall we walk on a little?"

"How long have we got?" asked Alex, refusing to move. "And how many questions?"

"Oh, there's no rush this time," laughed Serena. "Well, only a little if I'm to get in a swim. Let's head for the end of the bay."

For a moment they accompanied each other, Alex on the seaward side. The fairy's feet were bare, he noticed, beneath her rolled-up jeans.

"It *was* you behind it all, wasn't it?" he asked finally.

"Well, as I said before, not me personally," she replied. "But, yes."

"*Why*, then?"

The fairy sighed. "Look up there," she said, pointing at the stars. "How many planets do you suppose there are in the galaxy?"

"Thousands," replied Alex. "Millions."

"Well, *we* divide them into two categories," said Serena.

"Red and blue?" asked Alex.

"Exactly," replied the fairy. "You *have* been paying attention."

"And you're from the silver star," said Alex, feeling at the same time bigger than himself and smaller.

Serena nodded. "The red, we watch and support," she continued, "with the occasional, *tiniest* bit of help. And the blue, well, they're finished, really. When things get very complex," she added, "it pays to keep them simple."

"So *we're* red," said Alex, stopping in their path.

"You are for now," replied the fairy, "but it's touch and go." She smiled. "Why don't we sit down, and I'll tell you the story?"

They found drier sand, twenty metres from the shoreline. Serena sat cross-legged, facing the sea, Alex to her right, his arms circling his knees.

"Towards the end of 1940, we rather gave up on Earth," she began. "You see, if you're constantly at war with each other, there's isn't much future. The challenges go unmet. And in the *very* end, there's just wasteland, with cockroaches."

"And poisonous gases, swirling in the ether," added Alex.

"Well, I wouldn't describe it as poetically as that," said Serena. "But anyway, a motion was put to the Chamber of Visionaries..."

"The what?"

"The Chamber of Visionaries. We have a bicameral system," she explained, "like the UK or America. A Chamber of Visionaries and a Council of Apprentices." Alex nodded at the fairy's moonlit face, not entirely convinced he was having this conversation. "The motion proposed relegating your planet to the blue zone," continued Serena, "after the statutory three-month period of consultation."

"And what do they do in the three months? Take Buddha and Michelangelo into account?"

"Kind of," replied the fairy. "But it wasn't enough, I'm afraid. There's quite a lot of competition."

"Oh," said Alex.

"What saved you was an appeal. Every member of our parliament, you see, has a right to two appeals in their lifetime. On 7 January, 1941, by your calendar, with two days to spare, Franz, a young apprentice, rushed into the Chamber of Visionaries and lodged his first."

Alex uncircled his knees, stretching his arms out behind him. "It's a sort of open-air stadium, isn't it, this chamber?"

Serena smiled. "Yes, that's right. You're talking about our new building, though, which isn't really a chamber at all. The old one was getting quite stuffy."

"And what did Franz say?"

"That he'd just watched a broadcast by an American politician," replied the fairy.

"Roosevelt and the four freedoms speech?" said Alex.

"You *are* a good boy," said Serena. "Anyway, Franz, whose hobby happens to be Earth, was impressed." She picked up a handful of sand and let it fall through her fingers. "And so, after his rather moving speech, was the chamber."

"Were you there?" asked Alex. The fairy ignored this, looking out to sea. "So they gave us a second chance?" he said instead.

She nodded. "A minor *intervention* was put in place to ensure that the United Nations came into being."

"And how exactly do these interventions work?" asked Alex, conscious that the conversation might finally be getting personal.

"Well," said Serena, "we can't just *do* stuff on Earth, or any planet, come to that." She looked at Alex. "Instead, an apprentice is charged with finding and then empowering a native, so to speak, to *represent* our cause."

"Like you with me?" said Alex.

Serena smiled. "Now, yes. But not then, of course. In the 1940s it was a young chap from the European mainland, working as an interpreter in America." The fairy uncrossed and stretched her legs. "Not that it achieved much, of course, the UN."

"But how did *I* get involved?"

"Don't worry. I'll get to the point," replied the fairy, looking up for a moment at the moon as if it were a clock. "You see, a *second* motion to downgrade Earth was put to the chamber earlier this year, part of a general housekeeping bill. There's a bit of personality politics behind it, which we don't really have time for, but once again, an appeal was lodged."

"Franz's second?"

The fairy nodded.

"Good old Franz," said Alex. "Does he, by any chance, own an English-style country mansion?"

"With statues and a lake," replied Serena. "I told you Earth was his hobby. But the point is that he's now the vice-president of the Chamber of Visionaries, and a very well-respected figure. Nevertheless, it still took all the leverage he had. And also perhaps, the fact that he's dying, I'm sorry to say."

"You don't live forever, then," asked Alex, "on the silver star?"

"We *choose* not to. But that's another matter, isn't it?" said Serena. "The intervention this time is more detailed," she continued, picking up speed as she spoke. "It comes in four parts, in fact, each relating to a freedom from Roosevelt's speech. The first was freedom of worship. Hence the cloth. Hence me. Hence *you*."

"But why did you choose me?"

The fairy wrinkled her forehead. "It's complicated, but basically we flit in and out of people's minds, like a Google search, until we settle on one that seems suited to the task, though we had to *purge* you a little on the early flights."

Alex nodded without really understanding: the fairy seemed to be getting restless.

"Look," she said. "I'll tell you how it goes. We've done our bit, you see. With your help, of course. It's up to Burhan now, and whatever support he can get. He either builds a beacon, or he doesn't. Soon we'll follow up with the other three interventions, the last as far as Earth is concerned." She got up and brushed the sand from her jeans. "Then it really *is* up to you."

'You' meaning 'humanity' hoped Alex, rather than him personally. "My power's gone now, then?" he said.

"Of course," replied Serena, laughing, and then stepping lightly towards the sea. "Don't be selfish."

"And will I see you again?" he called out, getting up onto his knees as she continued on her way.

The fairy turned and raised a hand to stop him approaching. "Close your eyes, please, and count to fifty."

When he opened them again, her clothes were a pile on the sand, the sea already lapping at her waist. All he could do, therefore, was to observe her slight frame as she leant forward, slipping into the first of the waves, and afterwards, as the moments passed, swimming beyond it to meet the second and the third, along the silver pathway to the moon.

30

"I've been busy," said Burhan, half a stone lighter in his brown V-neck jumper and bandaged left shoulder, after a pot of tea and three cups had arrived for them in the lounge of the Holiday Inn, empty of guests at four in afternoon despite the elegant armchairs in black leather, and views of the pool, the palms and the beach.

"You should be at home in bed," said Carol, who sported a light tan below her knee-length shorts and above the grey jumper she wore against the hotel's air-conditioning system, on the offensive once again after a morning of restraint.

The scholar smiled. "I had a week in hospital, didn't I?"

"Even then you were making phone calls," added Alex as he began to pour their tea, two days now since he had sat on the beach with the fairy. It felt like a dream.

"Hani drove me to the police station yesterday," continued Burhan. "As far as they're concerned, you'll both be able to return to the UK at the end of the week."

"But Salah's still free, isn't he?" said Alex, looking at Carol.

"Yes, for the moment," nodded Burhan. "And while the cloth remains in our possession, whether it's in a bank vault or anywhere else, we're all at risk, including Jafar, who hasn't dared return to his house."

"Don't the police want to impound it or something?" asked Carol.

Burhan nodded. "They do, yes." He leant forward, wincing as he picked up his cup. "But I have another idea." He looked over at the reception desk, and lowered his voice. "I took the liberty, when I was in hospital, of contacting an old friend of mine who's in charge of public antiquities for the Dhofar region. She's confident, if I give her the go-ahead, that the sultanate itself will take legal possession of the cloth, at least for the foreseeable future. I think it's the best we can do."

"But what about your plans for displaying it in Cordoba?" asked Alex.

Carol leant forward before the scholar could reply. "I *will* be able to see it, won't I," she asked, "while we're here?"

From the look on his face, Burhan hadn't considered this. "Of course," replied the scholar, putting down his cup. "After they've collected it from the bank vault, we'll all go up to the Governor's House before they lock it away. I'll let you know when."

"Thank you," replied Carol, reaching for her tea.

"Well," said Burhan, casting a glance towards the beach, "I hope you'll be able to enjoy your last few days here." He smiled at Carol. "You've been swimming, I hear." She nodded. "And you've been doing my walk to the port, Alex."

"First thing in the morning," he replied.

"I might join you before the end of the week if I'm allowed to," said Burhan. "It's changed, of course, since I was a child. Just a path then, and no containers, cranes, or cruise ships at the port. But passengers would still arrive by sea from Muscat, and make their way over the hills to Salalah." He stood, adjusting his bandage. "If you're not doing anything else, why don't you both come over to my house for dinner tonight? I'm still in the doghouse, of course, as far as my wife is concerned, for the business with the cloth. But she'd be pleased to meet you in pleasanter surroundings than the hospital."

Where she hadn't looked pleased at all, thought Alex, as they agreed a time, just tired and worried and generally put upon, as you would be, he reckoned, if you were married to Burhan and his obsessions.

"Do you really think he's suited to being a father of five?" laughed Carol when they had returned from the scholar's house, Alex topping up his Coke in the lounge of the Holiday Inn, busier now at ten in the evening, a youthful Omani string quartet at the table next to them, not playing but guarding their instruments and chatting.

"I don't know. Maybe it's quite good to have a father who's distracted. Not always on your case, if you know what I mean," replied Alex, giving himself a quick mental kicking afterwards, when he recalled Carol's account of being fondled by hers.

"Perhaps you're right," she nodded, sipping her orange juice, or what she could reach of it under several wedges of lemon and half a ton of ice.

"We can fly on Friday, apparently," said Alex, not wanting to return, despite his companion's current period of reserve.

"Burhan confirmed that?" asked Carol.

Alex nodded. "While you were braiding his daughter's hair," he said. "And he thinks we'll be able to see the cloth on Thursday."

"I wonder if it was worth kidnapping me for," said Carol.

Alex smiled and looked around him, the violinist resting her hand on the top of her instrument as a small boy charged past. "What will you be doing tomorrow?" he said, an ache of pain in his chest at their diminishing time, if not together, then at least in daily contact.

"I said I'd ring John in the morning," she replied, putting down her juice.

"He told me at Jeremy's that he was going to beat me up," said Alex. Carol gave him a look he couldn't interpret. "And in the afternoon? Swimming?" he continued.

Carol smiled as she got up. "No. Why don't we go for a bike ride together?"

Stopping on his walk the following morning to wipe the sweat from his eyes, Alex turned to look back at Salalah, the real beginning – and end – of his adventure. He was in the lay-by a hundred metres from the top of the final hill, where tourists parked for the view in advance of the long decline to the ugliness (or commercial vigour) of the port.

Either he had a very serious mental health issue, he reflected as he surveyed the strand and burgeoning city, or else he had just played a small but significant part in enacting the obscure legislative requirements of an open-air parliament on a distant, silvery star. Hey-ho, he thought, remembering the sell-out revival of a hit West End play Rod had managed to scam tickets for, featuring an ex-World War Two spy whose future life had failed in all respects to live up to the excitement of her war-time experiences. Is that what would happen to him?

He took a swig from his water bottle. Perhaps he could help Burhan with his Cordoba project, if the scholar's spirits hadn't flagged? That might be dangerous enough. And there was Carol, too, wasn't there, and John? None of that was going to be straightforward. He'd also have to continue earning a living, he supposed, as he resumed his upward trudge, particularly as he'd maxed out his credit card.

There was a long, deep hoot from a container ship when he got to the top, pulling out into the Arabian sea, on its way, he guessed, to the Gulf, or Mumbai, or even Malaysia. And down below him on the path, the first fellow walker, albeit in the opposite direction, that he had seen on his morning excursions, a tall, hunched figure in a hat, somewhat burdened by a rucksack and a large plastic bag.

Alex stood, hands on his hips, and watched the traveller for a while, his progress laboured but steady. It wasn't until the man had stopped to look upwards, fifty yards from the top, that Alex found himself fumbling for his recently repaired phone, dropping it on the ground, kicking it once in his haste to retrieve it.

"It's Alex," he said, when he finally made his call, "I think you'd better get a cab and join me on my walk."

When it became clear that Burhan was coming their way from the waiting taxi, his pace fast but not hasty, holding his bandaged arm, the old man rose from the roadside rock he had been sharing with Alex and stepped away in an agitated fashion, as if the young companion who had greeted him on his journey had set a trap for him. He stayed like that, looking from left to right, but not, it appeared, finding the strength to move, until the two men, traveller and scholar, father and son, stood opposite each other, five or six yards apart.

Burhan let his right arm fall to his side, and as Alex watched from his position on the rock, began to address Ferran in softly spoken Arabic. He continued for some time, the words flowing out from him like a river, calming the old man until he had changed the expression on his father's face into something that resembled comprehension.

When the scholar had finished, Ferran raised his right hand to his chest, the gesture he had made to Carol at their leave-taking in Iran, and began to walk towards his son – half a lifetime covered in ten short paces, reckoned Alex – finally reaching out and touching Burhan's face as a blind man might: the beard, the cheeks now wet with tears, the thinning hair of a middle-aged man.

Alex was watching Carol's face as she made her third tour of the long table at the Governor's House. An armed guard stood at the door, the curtains had been drawn, and two lights at either end, like large desk lamps, assisted the weak chandelier in illuminating the cloth. Burhan and Mrs Ghobal, Dhofar's Director of Antiquities, murmured to each other at the far side of the room.

"So what do you think?" said Alex when Carol approached him on his left.

She looked at him and smiled. She had been fairly animated, in fact, since he had knocked on her door the previous day, bringing her news of Ferran – laughing once or twice on their bike ride, too, and sobbing briefly in the early evening at Burhan's house, when the old man emerged for twenty minutes from his afternoon of sleep, and she was able, at the scholar's request, to present him with his ring.

"It makes me happy," she replied.

Alex too had felt a strange kind of exhilaration rising in his chest as he examined the group in the centre of the cloth, to the left of the fountain, under the orange and lemon trees, and then cast his eyes downwards to the robed figure in the morning mist. The replica they had viewed in London now seemed crude in comparison, a dead caricature, while the original in front of them hummed with life, the conversation of the scholars and the watchful presence among the trees stilled, it seemed, only for the fraction of a second it had taken for the image to be recorded.

"And you?" asked Carol.

Alex didn't trust himself to speak. Too much had happened to him since his walk through the Regent's Park. He looked into her eyes instead and nodded.

They all came to the airport the following day: Burhan, holding his father's hand, his wife, their five children, and the young policeman who, though he wasn't in charge of the case, had taken the notes at all of their meetings.

Plans were made to keep in touch; Burhan's daughter gave Carol a scarf for her hair; and the scholar slipped Alex a small, book-shaped parcel as the travellers paused at Departures – a translation of *The Road across Africa*, Alex discovered, when he opened it in the plane, with a handwritten inscription inside from Burhan himself. *Thank you*, it said, *I'll see you in Cordoba.*

EPILOGUE

Even in the poshest parts of London, Alex reckoned, there was always a street that wasn't so posh. Strutton Row, only a five-minute walk from St James's Park, seemed to prove the point with its grey net curtains, rusty railings you wouldn't want to park your bike against, and damp basement flats where odd-looking pot plants took all the day's rain and none of its sunshine.

Number forty-three had a freshly painted door at least, plus a polished nameplate with four ivory buttons. And the brown-haired woman in her late seventies or early eighties who answered the door smiled pleasantly enough at Alex, asking after his journey in the not-quite-German accent he had already heard on the phone, while directing him along a dark corridor that led to a waiting room, empty now at six in the evening, with a leather sofa, an assortment of chairs, and a table by the window. "Martin will be with you shortly," she said, leaving the door ajar.

Alex looked out at the wet summer sky and then parked himself on the sofa, picking up a magazine that offered to extend his sketchy knowledge of Vermont in the autumn, but deciding instead to take another look at the card that had brought him here. *Dr M. S. Werner* it said on both sides, one offering the designation *Counsellor* along with the doctor's London contact details and Alex's handwritten appointment, and the other, the words *Leksikografski zavod Miroslav Krleža* followed by an address in Zagreb.

After a moment or two, there was a cough in the corridor and the door swung halfway open, allowing his underground helper, the old man in the hat, to enter the room, this time without any protection at all for his bald and rather ancient-looking skull.

"Mr Harrison, it is a pleasure to see you," he said with a smile like a dipped headlight. "I hope that your ankle has improved."

Alex half rose. "Yes, thanks," he replied.

"Shall we sit at the table?" said Martin. "My colleagues' business is finished for the day, so no one apart from my wife, Anya, whom you met at the door, will disturb us."

Alex, conscious again of the strain that underpinned the doctor's immaculate accent, took the nearest chair.

"Will you have some after-hours whisky, Mr Harrison?" asked his host, removing a key from his jacket pocket as Alex accepted, and bending to unlock the door to a sideboard. With the bottle on the table and decent measures in their glasses, Dr Werner sat back, looking equably enough at Alex, but showing no intention of speaking.

After a moment, Alex said, "I found your card with the appointment when I got back two days ago from a trip to Oman."

Martin nodded. "Well-timed, then. Business or pleasure? The trip, I mean."

Alex had already decided that if this session, or 'meeting' as the doctor's wife called it, was to serve any purpose at all, he should take a risk and stick to the truth, letting the counsellor make of it what he would. "Business, I guess," he started. "A girl I knew went missing, and I was trying to find her."

"And you succeeded?"

"Yes."

"Despite the ankle?"

Alex laughed and took a large sip of his whisky, Martin reaching for his own drink, swirling the tumbler gently on the table before lifting it to his lips. "This might be the young woman you met in the carriage that we shared?" continued the man no longer in the hat.

Alex nodded. "It's not the way I normally behave, writing messages to women."

"I'm sure it isn't," replied the doctor. He leant forward. "So why do you think you did it on that particular day?"

This was it, thought Alex. "It's all a bit complicated," he said.

Martin spread his hands to indicate that no one had a train to catch. "Why don't you start at the beginning?"

At the counsellor's expansive gesture, Alex found a sob rising to his throat, so he braced himself with a second gulp of whisky. Then, starting with the fairy, he told the doctor exactly what had happened to him before their encounter on the Tube. When he was finished, Martin, who had remained impassive throughout, said, "And how did you *feel* about the flying?"

"Good," replied Alex, wondering if the doctor had already pressed a secret button, summoning his colleagues in white coats. "I started to call myself a 'curver'," he continued, "because if it was really happening, then there had to be curves in the universe where the normal rules don't apply."

His host smiled. "And I presume that you used your gift to help this Burhan fellow in his search for the cloth?"

Alex nodded, filling the doctor in as briefly as he could, from his first meeting with Burhan in London to the display of the cloth at the Governor's House.

"Fascinating," said the doctor in the pause that followed. "*Truly* fascinating."

"But can you make any sense of it?" asked Alex.

"You saw my card, didn't you? Dr Werner, of London and Zagreb. Lexicographer, bone-fixer, and counsellor," replied Martin with a mock flourish, "brusher of my own dark-brown hair once upon a time. Of course I can." He leant back in his chair. "The fact is," he continued with a smile, "well, the fact is that I too am a 'curver'. Or I *was*."

Alex looked up, a small explosion of excitement in his chest. "*You* were the interpreter in America," he said.

"Seventy years ago," nodded the doctor. "And I got a mysterious message on my headphones, I'm afraid, rather than a visit from your fairy. But the result was similar, if in a more minor key. My gift, in brief, was the ability to read the thoughts of the participants at the Dumbarton Oaks conference, prior to the founding of the United Nations, and, at the right moments, *make them agree*."

As they continued their conversation in the darkening room, the doctor elaborating on his youthful adventure, and Anya bringing them coffee and sandwiches, Alex felt his spirits not exactly settling, but at least moving around him in a more predictable fashion. He still had some questions to ask, however. "How did you know I would be on the Tube that day?" was the first of them.

"Well," smiled Martin, "That was rather odd. One of my occasional clients, you see, arrived for our last session with a suitcase in her hand. As you can imagine, it startled me slightly. I thought she might be planning to stay. Anyway, this young woman explained that she had finally decided to leave her oppressive family and travel to Australia, hence the luggage. But after our session, as I was showing her to the door, she turned to me and said, quite out of the blue, 'By the way, I think you should keep an eye out for a young man who may need your help. What is happening to him also happened to you, many years ago.'" The doctor paused and then burst out laughing. "I'm sorry. It all sounds rather Madame Zaza, don't you think? But a week or so later," his host concluded, "I saw you in the underground carriage."

Alex smiled in return. "But after your experience in America," he asked, "were you really able just to get on with your life?"

Martin shrugged, looking tired for the first time that evening. "As the years passed, it seemed like a dream." He finished his coffee and smiled. "Which is why I'm so glad you could come this evening."

Alex nodded. "Could I ask you just *one* more question?" he said.

"Of course," replied the doctor.

"Did you tell anyone else about it?"

"Yes," said Martin. "I told Anya, soon after we were married."

"And she believed you?"

"I hope so," said Martin, laughing. "And will *you* tell your friend Carol?"

"I don't know," replied Alex, not quite ready to share the complexities of his new relationship.

"I really think you ought to," said the counsellor.

Alex sat back. "Why?"

"You said they had planned *four* interventions," replied Martin. "What if they ask you again?"

ABOUT THE AUTHOR

Ken Paterson is the author of a number of grammar practice books for students learning or improving their English, and a novel, The Story of the Cloth. He has a website at www.kenpatersonwriter.com

Ken was born in Scotland, grew up in Bath, and now lives with his wife in Bolton. He started writing grammar books while he was director of English language teaching at the University of Westminster in London.

Late one evening, as he was walking home through Regent's Park, after a long day at the office, he stopped thinking about noun phrases and relative clauses, and wondered instead what would happen if a fairy appeared in his path and offered to grant him a wish. What would he choose, and where would it lead him?

The Story of the Cloth provided the answer.